OF FLOWERS
AND
CYCLONES

Dear Sarah,
Happy Reading!

C

ALSO BY CAMILLA TRACY

Of Threads and Oceans

Of Flowers and Cyclones

https://geni.us/CamillaTracynewsletter

CAMILLA TRACY

OF
FLOWERS
AND
CYCLONES

THREADS OF MAGIC
BOOK 2

Camilla Tracy

Published by Pudel Threads Publishing

First Printing 2023

Tracy, Camilla, author

Of Flowers and Cyclones / Threads of Magic: Book Two

ISBN (paperback) 978-1-7380086-4-3

eISBN 978-1-7380086-3-6

Under a Federal Liberal government, Library and Archives Canada no longer provides Cataloguing in Publication (CIP) data for independently published books.

Technical Credits:

Cover Image: MiblArt

Editor: Bobbi Beatty of Silver Scroll Services, Calgary, Alberta

Proofreader: Lorna Stuber - Editor, Proofreader, Writer, Okotoks, Alberta

Created with Atticus

To Paul,

The sunflowers are for you.

CHAPTER ONE

"**P**ICK YOU UP IN three days?" Tariq asked.

"Thank you," Thali said. While she hadn't been able to convince her parents to let her sail alone, Tariq, her best friend, and the prince of the island of Bulstan—famed for its jewels—had convinced her parents to let her sail with him to her three-day conference.

Tariq hugged her tight, but at the same time, he patted her loose cotton shirt back and leather-vested sides before reaching for her boots with the toe of his shoe.

"Unless you want me to tell Bree that your hands have wandered all over my body, you better step away from me." Thali put her hands on her hips. She knew his intended, Bree, wouldn't be untrusting of Tariq but would scold him for having touched a lady in so many places.

"She wouldn't care. You're like my sister," Tariq retorted, though he did step away.

"And how often have you hugged Rania like that?" Thali asked. He wouldn't ever dare hug his very proper sister the way he just had her.

Tariq paled. They both knew his argument would not stand in the court of Bree. He jutted his strong chin out rebelliously anyway. "Maybe I'll start."

"Good luck," Thali said, grinning, her gray eyes shining with mirth. She'd like to see the rage on Rania's and Bree's faces if he tried. "You know, you could just ask if I have all my weapons on me. And the answer is yes. I'm not a total idiot."

"I'd still really like to go with you."

"No way," Thali replied. She tried to imagine Tariq taking on a room full of princes of thieves. "I'm a guest. We might both be killed if I let you come."

Tariq stuck out his bottom lip in a pout. "Can't I go as your servant or something?"

"You'd never in a million years pass as a servant." Thali purposely roved her gaze down Tariq's brightly-colored, gold-embroidered tunic that only served to highlight, not disguise, his athletic physique. "Besides, you have to actually go pick up what you told your father we'd pick up."

Tariq's pout deepened, quite at odds with the dark skin and eyes that usually made him look so imposing.

"If I need you, I'll send Lari," Thali said to hopefully ease his worry. Lari, Tariq's falcon, always traveled with Tariq and was now on loan to Thali for the prince-of-thieves conference she'd been invited to.

It was Tariq's turn to put his hands on his hips. "And that's the only reason I'm letting you go in there by yourself," he said.

Thali glanced upward as she tucked a long lock of dark hair behind her ear. The falcon circled above the ship and perched on top of the mast. Bree had found it laying hurt on the shores of Bulstan and raised it while Thali had been away at school. Now, she took a look at the bird's yellow thread—her mental attachment to the creature, just as she had with all living creatures—a little wary of any thread that sparkled after the events that had nearly taken her life a few weeks ago on Star Island. But this falcon had a plain old yellow thread and was very fond of Bree and Tariq. "Lari. It's a stupid name for a falcon," Thali said, coming back to the present. The sparkling threads that emanated from Star Island still tickled the back of her mind, unnerving her as usual.

"I know, but you know I can't say no to Bree," Tariq said.

"Can I go now?" Thali asked. Their ship was docked, and Thali was anxious to see Garen again. It had been weeks since she'd last seen him, or touched him, or—

"Fine," Tariq said, narrowing his eyes. "Three days. Don't do anything stupid. Actually, don't do anything exciting."

Thali nodded. Tariq whistled and Lari flew down to his arm. "Watch her closely," Tariq implored. "I know you don't understand me, but please, watch over my best friend."

Thali just rolled her eyes.

CHAPTER TWO

THALI WOULD HAVE THREE days by herself before Tariq returned. Taking a deep breath, she reached down to pet her tiger and usher her dog forward. Remembering that she'd left her tiger, dog, and even snake behind with Tariq, she took a deep breath to calm her nerves. It would have been too obvious had she strolled through this market with her animals. She reviewed Garen's instructions on how to get to their meeting. That done, she calmed her butterflies with some time in the market looking at all the wares they had to offer and taking notes on stone sculptures so she'd have something to send back to her family. Then, she steeled herself and made her way to a booth that sold spices, specifically the one with the sunflower-yellow canvas stretched above. Pulling up her mental checklist of steps, she saw she had the right place and person: the man with a sea-blue hat and shoes.

"Do you stock dragon earwax?" She pretended to look at the various spices as she spoke.

He raised a single eyebrow, surprise crossing his face before he schooled his expression. "You need to look deep in its heart to find what you're looking for." He motioned to the back of his shop with his eyes.

Thali meandered to the back of the shop, slowing her steps. After carefully checking behind her, she pulled a dirty old potato-sack curtain aside. Walking in, she found a courtyard stacked with crates. It was a pseudo-storage room with a tiny garden in one corner and a few benches. A respite from the frantic market. In the farthest corner of the courtyard, next to one of the benches, a freshly placed wooden door lay in the ground. Checking around and above her, she opened it and walked down the stairs. It was dark and she let her hand trail the rough stone wall for what felt like hours. The passageway finally flattened, and she walked further yet around various bends and turns before a stairway finally led back up.

Just as she thought maybe she should have brought water, she saw a wooden door and opened it. Her jaw dropped as she walked out into a wall of humidity. Thali had walked into a dense, lush forest. Trees and vegetation occupied every inch of space as far as she could see, and Thali turned around and around to make sure she wasn't dreaming.

A yellow leaf on a tree caught her eye, and she followed Garen's explicit instruction to head the opposite way that the leaf pointed. After, thankfully, a short walk this time, pushing branches out of her way as she went, she trekked through some more greenery until she came to a waterfall. Taking a break to drink some water and splash her face, she looked for the next yellow leaf, which ultimately pointed to a path away from the waterfall and up the hillside. She readjusted the bag on her shoulder and headed a little doubtfully in behind the waterfall. There, she saw a white marble door and turned the silver knob, only to walk into the most exquisite white marble lobby she could have imagined.

As if she had walked from the jungle right into a royal hall, the floors, ceilings, and walls were all smooth white stone. Open squares within the ceiling let the jungle peek through, softening the harsh sunlight to create a warm glow in the cavernous space. She'd never seen anything quite like it. A tall woman with brown skin and black hair wearing a dress made of ... leaves? ... bowed to Thali, catching her attention. The exotic-looking woman offered Thali a beverage in a white stone cup and guided her down the lobby before pointing her toward a third set of stairs to her right.

She didn't drink from the cup immediately but followed the woman as she ascended the stairs and found a wooden door with a familiar symbol in the middle. Garen's symbol—a J with two bars above it. Opening the door, Thali didn't believe she'd ever seen opulence to this degree before. The entire room was made of white marble laced with brown roots as if stone and tree had intertwined. Luxuriously carved tree trunks served as couches in the sitting room. She dropped her bag on one of the low tree-stump tables before continuing to explore the other rooms she could see branching off from the sitting room. In one, she found an intricately carved four-poster bed, with each post a living tree creating a canopy of real leaves, and a bathing room with an actual mini waterfall feeding into a tub and then through the latrine before disappearing.

At the other end of the room was a balcony. The doors were open, and Thali grinned at the familiar lines of the person leaning on the rail. She put her cup down and padded onto the balcony. She leaned over and gasped. Below them was not only a luscious jungle filled with exotic birds and animals but gargantuan reptilian creatures with impossibly long necks and tails that trudged through the flora.

Garen turned toward her, his face fashioned first in astonishment then annoyance, "Joren really went out of his way this time."

Before she could utter a reply, Thali was enveloped in Garen's arms as they soaked each other in. She buried her face against his chest, taking a deep breath.

"I missed you," he whispered into her hair.

"I missed you too," she said.

A falcon's cry startled them both and Thali grinned. In her mind, she showed the falcon where they were, and moments later, Lari landed on the rail.

"New friend?" Garen asked.

"Tariq's actually," Thali said, "To get here, I sailed with Tariq, but he wouldn't let me go alone. So, Garen, meet Lari."

Lari turned her head to gaze at them, but her sharp beak and black beady eyes kept Garen standing where he was. With thanks, Thali sent Lari into the forest.

Thali turned only her head to look at the incredible sight before them, as did Garen. They were unwilling to let each other go. After a few moments, Garen leaned away from Thali and raised an eyebrow that only accentuated his deep sea-blue eyes, looking again at the gargantuan reptiles and then back at her.

"Can you ...?"

Thali understood. She closed her eyes, opening the door in her mind and looking for threads. She saw some unfamiliar luminescent green threads and gently slid her mind along one until she connected to the animal. He was a simple beast, huge, slow moving, but gentle. He relaxed as she brought thoughts of soothing and safety to his mind, and she soon found he was quite happy to go back to munching on the leafy greens around him. For a moment, she explored his thoughts of what it was like to move around: He was heavy and moving took a lot of effort for such a large body.

The strangeness of the strands quietly reminded her of the sparkly strands she had encountered just a few weeks earlier on Star Island when she had been taking her final sailing exam. Thali still had no idea what she'd inadvertently done then, even though she instinctively felt it was monumental. She wondered if the person who might be responsible for sending her to Star Island, when that hadn't been hers—and her fellow students'—destination in the first place, was here.

"Garen, how much do you trust Joren?" Thali asked, turning to look into his magnificent eyes. Garen had spoken of Joren at times but always with tension in his face.

"Some, but not much. Of all the brothers, I probably trust him the most though. Why?"

Thali looked again to the monstrous reptilian roaming the jungle below and raised an eyebrow meaningfully.

"I considered it too, but this one's been living here his whole life. And as big as he is, Joren says he's no danger. Plus, Joren raised him himself."

Thali closed her eyes, slipping back along the green luminescent thread. She gently followed the thoughts, dove into his memories, and saw he had indeed grown up here.

She meandered along the threads of memories, seeing the abundant foliage and an extravagantly dressed man, who she assumed was Joren. He took remarkably good care of them, so that earned him some respect in Thali's eyes.

"So?" Garen had turned away from the great beasts and faced Thali.

"I've never met Joren, but they did grow up here, and I saw someone lavishly dressed taking care of them."

"Joren does like to dress in bright colors."

"They don't see in color, so I don't know if it was him."

Garen shook his head, "You'll meet him this evening."

"Where do you think he would have gotten these creatures?"

"That's a question only for him." Garen pulled her closer, silently telling her he'd like to stop talking.

Thali had been anxious about this weekend, but now she was intrigued by Joren. Well, that and she was excited she'd get three whole days with her beloved Garen now after all the time she'd spent away from him recovering at home.

CHAPTER THREE

G AREN

"Are you almost ready?" Garen, his hands clasped behind his back, stood in the hallway waiting for Thali before heading out to introduce her to the other princes. Nervous about how they might greet her, he began to pace. Was he blinded by his love for her? Would they see her the way he did? He had brought her to the conference as a way to proclaim his love for her and show her exactly how dedicated he was. He wanted to share his world with her, show her something she had never seen or experienced before. Thali had traveled so much as a merchant's daughter, she was rarely surprised or amazed. That's why it had been such a beautiful thing to experience those giant reptiles with her for the first time and see her awed.

"Yes, I think I'm ready. What do you think? Is this appropriate? You said like a ball but not quite as formal." When she came around the corner from the bathing room, Garen was momentarily stunned silent.

Thali stood there like a green goddess in a forest-green tunic dress. Its square neckline and full, flowing sleeves that matched the hem of her hi-low skirts made her look like a leaf gliding on the wind.

"Thali, you look beautiful."

She fidgeted with a sleeve. "Really? It's one of Mia's new dresses. I'm always her guinea pig."

"Well, you are the most breathtaking guinea pig I've ever seen." With that, Garen swept Thali up in his arms, dancing them down the hall to the entrance.

A knock interrupted them.

Thali flattened her dress with her palms as Garen answered the door.

He opened the door and revealed no one.

Garen rolled his eyes. "Joren is getting impatient." He turned back to Thali and offered her his arm. They strolled out and down the short hallway to the stairs. The *click click click* of her shoes on the marble floor had her squaring her shoulders, making him puff his chest out.

Thali

As they came to the end of the last hallway, Thali's eyes bulged as they took in the main lobby. Just as their balcony overlooked a jungle, the lobby had been transformed into an evergreen forest. Giant, hundred-year-old evergreen trees filled the room. The entire space was filled with countless shades of green pine trees. As they descended the stairs, a thick layer of moss muted her footsteps. Thali couldn't help herself, so she slipped off her shoes so her toes could feel the soft greenery. They followed the plush pathway to a round clearing. There, two other men and one woman gathered in the middle around a firepit. Except inside this firepit wasn't fire but a great column of swirling fireflies, all twisting around each other like flames might lick the air.

All present stood as Thali and Garen walked in along one of several paths leading off the main clearing.

"Always looking to make an entrance." The man Thali had seen in the reptile's memories melted out of the trees. Thali had to remind herself to keep her face as neutral as possible as she took in Joren, who wore a lime-green tunic over bright-orange puffy pants with pine-green shoes that curled over themselves at the end and a transparent robe of shimmering silver belted with a lemon-yellow sash. A scarf the color of his shoes covered his head, completing the ostentatious—but lively—outfit.

Joren had not only adorned his body with wild colors, but had also given his face the same expressive treatment. His skin was painted white, with bright-blue triangles for eyebrows, red octagons on his cheeks, and an orange heart on his lips. It was the most ridiculous outfit she ever could have imagined. So Thali did the only thing she could think of: She curtsied.

"Joren, it's good to see you." Garen grasped Joren's right wrist, as Joren did in return, and they patted each other on the shoulders. It was a warmer greeting than Thali had expected. Thali's merchant eye caught Joren's black sleeves with their red hearts, noting that the hearts were embroidered—expensive. "Joren, this is Thali."

Thali was about to dip into another curtsy when Joren grabbed her right hand.

"My dearest lady. You grace us with your beautiful fashion." Joren bowed low over her hand and kissed it. Then instead of letting go, he spun her and tucked her hand into the crook of his left elbow. "Please, allow me to introduce you to the rest of our humble party."

Thali turned to look at Garen in time to see him almost imperceptibly raise an eyebrow and cock his head before he hurried to Thali's left.

Joren said, "Ming, come meet Garen's Thali."

A fit man with jet-black hair and skin the same color as Thali's mother turned to them. He was dressed in red silk robes embroidered with swirling golden dragons. He bowed low over her hand. "It is an honor, Miss Thali." Then turning to Garen, he said, "Garen, it is good to see you again." Ming shook wrists with Garen. However, Thali noted that they did not pat each others' shoulders.

In total, Thali met one more man, Henrik, the Prince to the Frozen North, and one woman, Makena, Princess to the South and East, who represented the princes and princess of thieves from all over the world. Each introduction had been identical, and Thali could feel there was significance to the way the introductions had all been conducted. She wondered if it was a good thing or a bad thing that Joren had been the one to escort her around the room.

After they had made their rounds, Joren led her to one of the couches around the firefly fire and gestured for her to sit. Garen sat down next to her, putting an arm protectively around her shoulders. The public display made a smile creep across her face as warmth bloomed in her body, and she sat a little straighter. It felt strange but wonderful. A drink appeared in his hand then, and he gave it to Thali.

Garen had warned her that the first drink would be alcoholic. She looked up at him and gave him a quick wink. Garen smiled back at her, and she leaned into his side. Eyes flicked in their direction, but it felt right. She felt like they could take on the world together.

Thali felt how charged this first meeting was. It felt like every eye in the room was on her, even though no one was overtly watching them. Thali wasn't a stranger to symbolically intense situations, so she kept her breathing steady and sipped her drink slowly, waiting for the awkward silence that had settled on their evening to melt away.

"Time for some entertainment." Joren clapped his hands twice and dancers with bright, rainbow-colored scarves glided in through the trees. They kept their distance from each guest as they swayed, leaped, and twirled, their colorful scarves and outfits waving through the air.

At the end of the performance, the group applauded. Then Thali was surprised to see Ming approaching her from the side. He moved slowly, but his path led directly to her. "Garen." Ming nodded in his direction and spoke loud enough for Garen to hear but low enough that no one else in the room could hear. "Miss Thali, I feel I ought to tell you that I know your grandmother. She was a friend of mine in my youth, and I owe her a great deal. If there is ever anything you need, please allow me the honor."

"You know my grandmother?"

Thali's family on her mother's side was one of the most famous warrior families of Cerisa. She had three uncles and an aunt—all famed warriors. Her own mother had been renowned until she had been disinherited and disowned by her grandmother when she married Thali's father. Thali had only seen her grandmother a few times, and always under tense circumstances.

"May I?" Ming gestured to the seat next to Thali.

"Of course," Thali said.

He sat down, careful not to touch Thali but close enough for both Thali and Garen to hear. "When I was a toddler, both my parents died and I wandered the streets, looking for garbage to eat. Your grandmother found me one day when she was just a girl. I was very sick. I would have died, but she took me to her family's barns. She hid me there and snuck me food for two months before her father found me and threw me out. After that, she would always accidentally drop a coin when she saw me in the street. I never forgot her kindness. I've made it my business to watch over your family since then."

Thali was suspicious of his story. From the handful of times she'd seen her grandmother, kindness was not one of the top attributes she'd give her. And what were the chances that this prince of thieves had had a run in with her grandmother? Cerisa was a big place.

When Thali said nothing, only nodded her head in acknowledgment of his words, Ming rose, bowed, and left them. Thali sucked her lips in as she hid a chuckle, both at the unlikeliness of his story and at the possibility that her merchanting, fighting family could possibly have this link to the highest echelon of thieves.

Garen raised an eyebrow, but Thali shrugged and resumed her watchful gaze around the room. She watched as various princes walked around conversing quietly with each other before moving on to another prince.

Thali looked at the firefly fire for a moment. She concentrated on them and searched her mind. Insects were usually the smallest and thinnest strands within her ability, and she wondered how Joren was able to get them to fly in such a consistent pattern for so long. She followed the thin strands and discovered they were following a scent that had been drawn in that pattern. They followed it as it circled and dipped and dived. Shaking off the strands, she focused on the real world again, squinting into the swarm of fireflies and trying to see the source of the scent they were following. Then she saw it: a tiny flower petal swirling in figure-eight patterns within the column of fireflies.

Just as she wondered how a petal could float in such a specific way, Joren appeared behind them. "So tell me, how did you two lovebirds meet?"

Garen smiled and explained, "Over an untied boot, actually."

"Oh? How quaint," Joren said with an overly wide smile.

Thali smiled at the memory. They'd been watching each other for weeks without the other knowing—until Garen had forced a situation to meet her face-to-face. "How did you get all these trees in here?" Thali asked suddenly.

Joren raised an eyebrow, "Garen didn't tell you?"

"It's not for me to tell."

Joren's face slowly spread into an even wider grin, if that was even possible. "Oh, brother, you spoil me." Joren's grin grew so wide, a mad look appeared in his eye. "Thali, do you have a favorite flower?"

"Bird of paradise." It wasn't actually her favorite flower but was the most difficult to procure.

"Indeed." Joren pursed his lips as he watched Thali's face carefully. Garen sat grinning next to Thali.

Suddenly, in front of Thali's eyes, the moss next to her feet cracked. A sprout shot up and grew rapidly until it became an actual bird of paradise that bloomed right in front of her face, the orange petals fanning out before her eyes.

Awe and amazement shone in her eyes when she looked to Garen.

Garen

"Joren has a … talent with plants." Garen could barely contain his grin as he thought about how Thali had a talent with animals. If she chose to reveal it to Joren, he wanted to be there to see his face.

Joren wasn't shy about his talent and loved showing it off any way he could, while Thali always kept hers a secret. When Thali had told Garen about her gifts, he had thought of Joren. If he hadn't already seen an ability like that for himself, Garen would have been in disbelief, but having seen the jungles and forests Joren could command, Thali's news hadn't shocked him.

And while Joren's gift with plants was useful and dangerous, Thali's gift with animals was even more dangerous and beautiful.

As Garen continued his musing, Joren grew a bouquet of birds of paradise next to Thali's left foot. Thali opened her mouth and closed it. Garen had often wondered if she'd ever met anyone with an extraordinary gift even remotely like hers. He guessed she was likely dumbfounded that Joren would make himself so visible and show off his gift so openly. Thali had been taught to hide it, never to reveal it or even explore it. Garen personally thought it was a shame and possibly even dangerous.

Thali

"How do you ... how did you do that?" she finally stammered.

She saw the entire room with new eyes as she realized just how much Joren had been showing off: The entire room, the entire building, the jungle and evergreens were all his creation. Thali couldn't begin to imagine how much effort it must have taken. She wondered if he connected and communicated with plants like she did animals or if he could just grow them with some sort of magic.

"Dance with me?" Joren offered his hand as music started in the background.

Thali placed her hand in Joren's, and he led her to the open area in the clearing, gently leading her around the big space. He held her a little closer than she was comfortable with but whispered in her ear, "In my mind, each plant is like a light. I can fuel it to burn brighter, guide it to another place, or guide its growth in the ground."

"All this ... do you have to continually fuel the light?" She looked around the clearing.

Joren cocked his head as if looking at Thali in a new light. "No, once I've encouraged it one way or another, it resumes its natural life until I come back to it."

Thali was worried that she seemed too interested, so she changed the subject. "So, have you known Garen very long?" She knew it was an abrupt change, but Thali was too frazzled to think of a more subtle way to discourage more attention and expose her own gift, so she moved on to lighter topics.

Garen, as if sensing her concern, was at her side before Joren could answer. "May I cut in?"

"Of course, dear brother." Joren bowed, handing Thali's hand to him. "Thali, I will dream of only you until the next time we meet."

Thali couldn't help the heat that flushed up her neck as Garen rolled his eyes.

They danced a few songs, Thali calming with the steady rhythm of Garen's breathing. She had so much to think about, so much she wanted to ask, so much she wanted to talk to Garen about but knew they had to wait until tonight. And even then, she wondered if Joren could spy on them through his plants as she could eavesdrop with animals. Suddenly, a cough echoed behind her, capturing her attention.

"Miss Thali, if you would do me the honor?" Ming bowed low to Garen.

"It seems you're a hot commodity tonight, my darling." Garen sighed as he handed Thali over to Ming. He had warned her earlier that if there was dancing, she would probably be on her feet all night since there weren't many women among them.

"That dress is at its most advantageous when you're dancing," Joren piped in as he waltzed by with an imaginary partner.

Thali ended up dancing the whole night with each member of this underground court. They were all expert thieves, so they were all incredibly light on their feet, allowing Thali to truly enjoy the dancing.

Garen

When they finally made it back to their room, Garen carried a sleepy Thali up the stairs and down their little hallway, her shoes balancing on his pinky fingers.

"Why didn't you tell me about Joren?" She snuggled her head into his neck.

"It wasn't my secret to tell."

Thali scoffed into his chest after a big yawn. "It's a secret?"

"Joren might like to show off, but outside of this court, no one knows."

"Oh." Thali dozed off against Garen as he eased open their door. He knew she'd be full of questions when she woke up, so he gently placed her on the soft bed and covered her with the—of course—mossy-green comforter. He crept to the couch and pulled a blanket over himself before falling asleep.

When he woke up, he realized Thali must have woken up in the middle of the night and changed because she was now in her cozy cotton pajamas, lying snoring softly on top of him.

Garen laughed silently and rolled her gently to the side so she was wedged between him and the couch. He kissed the top of her head and sent a silent thanks to Joren for making the couches extra wide.

CHAPTER FOUR

T HALI AND GAREN WOKE to the smell of the breakfast on their table as they rolled off the couch.

Garen rose and brought the tray over. "Thali, there's coffee."

She smelled it as she pulled herself up on the couch. "This is the best coffee I've ever had."

He poured her a cup and handed it to her before pouring one for himself. "He does have a way with coffee beans."

"It must be so useful."

"It is. And it's beautiful too."

"Can he hear through them?" Suddenly, Thali was self conscious about the plants that surrounded them as she remembered last night's thought.

"I'm not sure." Garen nodded, thinking. "It had never occurred to me to consider the extent to which Joren could use his plants or if he could use them as spies."

"Can we talk about last night?" Thali asked.

"Sure. What do you want to talk about?"

"Joren introducing me, was that a good thing or a bad thing? I always thought you'd be the one to do it."

Garen sat down, crossing his legs on the couch, so he faced Thali. "It was a really good thing. I'm surprised actually. Joren was showing everyone not only that he approved of you, but also that you're *his* honored guest as much as mine."

"That's good?" Thali asked.

"I know Joren looks like a buffoon, but he's smarter than he looks, and more powerful than me, probably second only to Ming. If he likes you, it'll make everything a lot easier."

Thali nodded and let that sink in. "Do you think Ming was telling the truth? That he knows my grandmother?"

Garen tilted his head. "That caught me off guard. But I'm sure it's the truth. We may be the princes of deception, but we don't lie to each other. Redirect truth maybe, but not lie. Not here."

"So, I'm walking into this with more friends than I thought?" Thali asked.

"In a way, yes. Though I wouldn't trust anyone. They all have their own motives."

They quietly contemplated the previous evening while they ate.

"Thali, did you notice the lack of partners last night?" Garen asked.

She nodded and looked up from her pastry to see Garen's steady gaze on her. It melted her insides a little, and she had to stop herself from swooning on the couch.

"It's very rare for any of us to take a partner. We are all a prince of thieves, and when we take a partner, they become our equal. We share everything with them, and they become just as powerful as we are. In council, they even have equal power in discussion. Therefore, the entire court must approve of the partner before they are accepted."

Thali put her pastry down, knowing this was a momentous occasion that would be better without jam-covered fingers.

"Thali, some of us have a lot of fun and a lot of short relationships but will never take a partner, Joren for example. He always has a new plaything, but it's never serious. You'll never see him bring a significant half to these conferences and surely not to any event of any import. But my plan has always been to bring you here to participate, as my equal partner."

Thali swallowed the last bite in her mouth. She sometimes felt out of her depth with Garen. She didn't understand why he offered her so many grand things. What made her worthy of all this, of his depthless love?

Garen continued. There was apparently much he had wanted to say. "I know out *there*..." he waved his hand as he spoke the word before going on, "...we have our complications and we have to be careful about not being seen together because of your family. And as much as it pains me, I understand and accept that. I only want what's best for you, for your happiness. But here, if you want to become my princess, you can. If you wear the medallion I gave you to the first meeting this morning, it will state unequivocally that you would like to be my princess, to be my partner and my equal."

All Thali wanted to do was say yes. But her logical side wasn't sure. "What exactly would that mean?"

"A prince can only take one partner. Ever. Some have been renounced, but it's rare. If you agree to be mine, then I will trade a favor for a sponsor, and they will put forth your nomination. The court will demand one-on-one interviews with you, then there will be a vote. If you win a majority, then you become a permanent member of the court. Even if I were to be ... replaced, you could still come to the conferences. You would also be recognized as my princess among everyone here. Some have even held celebrations in their home countries, but it's not necessary."

Garen reached over to lay a hand gently on hers. If she had felt out of her depth before, that was nothing compared to how she felt now, like she was drowning in responsibility she wasn't sure if she was ready for yet. She gulped.

He noted her gulp but continued anyway. "You would also be sworn to secrecy. All the faces you've seen here, you are not to acknowledge them if you run into them in the real world, but all our folk would recognize you by the medallion you wear and are bound to treat you as they do us." He paused and took a breath. "I love you, Thali. I've known that since the day I met you. I want you to be part of this world, and I'll do anything to help you. Being my princess would mean you are forever protected by my people."

Thali couldn't help thinking about the plethora of sparkling threads she'd seen reaching out from Star Island. Ever since she'd unknowingly taken part in a ritual instead of performing her final exam last year, she felt like something big was about to happen and she knew she wouldn't be able to handle it alone. But would this court be able to help her?

"Do you think Joren knows anything about Star Island?" Thali asked.

"I've asked. He hasn't replied yet, so that tells me he's still gathering information." Garen said. He waited patiently for all her questions.

That gave her the courage to continue. "Do you think he would help me? Would the court help me if I needed them?"

Garen nodded. "They would be obligated to."

Thali nodded back. Given the inexplicable forces she'd faced on Star Island that had nearly killed her during her final exam, she knew she was going to need help—a lot of it. Joren was the only magical person she knew, and he would have to help her. Was it wrong of her to join because she might need them?

"What does it mean for us when we get back?" Thali asked.

"I'm not sure, Thali. I could handle the business side of it while you go to school. My people would want to know you, honor you, though. Of course, they wouldn't ever touch your family's business, meaning their ships would never be plundered again. But as far as what you want to do, it's up to you. I won't influence or judge you one way or the other. Nor will I—or they—ask you to do anything you don't want to do."

Garen reached for her hands and the warmth of them steadied her. "I love you, Thali. Whatever you want to do, I'll respect it. I'll help you. You can be as involved in my business as you want. If you wanted to skip this meeting and think about it, I'm all right with that too. I know it's a lot to take in so quickly."

Thali looked at their joined hands. She had pushed her guilt to the back of her mind yesterday, but it came roaring back now. Merchanting and her family were everything to her. It was the only future she had ever wanted until she'd met Garen. Her parents would have accepted and welcomed anyone else. Anyone but a thief. She vividly remembered once when she had been helping her papa pack up some of their textiles. He had grabbed a young boy who had tried to pick his pocket. She'd never seen her father so angry. He'd marched the boy over to the city guards and handed him over. Crab had said the boy was lucky to be a child because if he had been an adult, her father would have gutted him on the spot.

But this was Garen. Her Garen. He was the only person she could talk with until the sun rose. The only person she was excited to see, to share and trust life's little details with. He was the pillar of strength she could depend on to offer sound advice, that would catch her if she fell, that she wanted to be better for. He was the one she wanted next to her when she took over her own fleet of merchanting ships. They would work it out. They had to. "I love you too, Garen. Yes, I want to be your partner," Thali tried to say with more bravery than she felt.

Garen reached across the couch to cradle her face in his hand before pressing his lips to her face. He kissed her in the way that made her bones melt and her fingertips feel fuzzy.

Once they finally parted for air, Thali asked, "So ... do I get a ring or anything?"

Garen laughed. "Do you want one? We're a little more subtle than that. You just wear your medallion around your neck this morning when we walk into the first meeting."

He rose and pulled her upright before picking her up and swinging her around in his arms. Then, he gently placed her on her feet, gave her one last swoon-worthy kiss, and said, "Now, go get ready because if we're late, Ming won't be pleased."

CHAPTER FIVE

T HALI HAD CHOSEN HER outfit carefully when she had packed for this conference. In truth, Mia had chosen the outfit. She hadn't told Mia about the exact occasion, but she had asked about an outfit to impress in a trade setting. What Mia had come up with was a combination of a billowing navy skirt, a pale-blue long sleeved silk tunic trimmed in purple with panels draping to the floor with her skirt. On top of it all was a rich brown leather corset.

It was definitely an outfit she hadn't seen before, but she trusted Mia, and Garen had grinned his appreciation.

Now, she walked with her hand in the crook of Garen's arm as they followed a mossy path to a set of the biggest trees she'd ever seen. As they approached, Thali was stunned to see that they were actually one tree that had been split in two and acted as doors. When they pushed one open, she saw it opened onto another plush mossy floor. The walls were lined with vines abloom with small white flowers. It was a relatively simple room in comparison to the others she'd seen so far, but it too was elegant. A large, round, white stone table occupied the middle of the room, and around it was an undulating tree root, creating seats around the table.

Thali saw a flicker of surprise on a couple faces as she walked into the room with Garen's medallion prominently displayed on her chest.

Joren sashayed up to them wearing an orange-and-blue jester's hat, a purple ruffle, a green tunic, orange-and-blue pants that puffed out beyond logic, red knee-high socks, and golden pointy shoes. It looked like Joren had picked the most outrageous clothing choices of the past and put them all on at the same time.

"Where did you get that spectacular ensemble?" He took his time eyeing Thali from bottom to top.

Thali looked to Garen.

As usual, he knew exactly what she was thinking. He nodded a fraction of an inch.

"My best friend is a seamstress." Thali held her head up with pride.

"She's quite the fashion genius. Would you twirl for me?" Joren was truly studying her vest dress and its barely noticeable embroidery.

"Joren, we have more important matters at hand." Ming had entered the room and stood now at the table.

Joren's eyes flashed to the medallion on Thali's neck as he sighed overdramatically. "I guess we might as well start." Without so much as taking a breath he declared, "I name myself Thali's sponsor." Joren waved his hand lazily as he gazed at the rest of the table through half-lidded eyes.

Thali felt Garen tense for a moment. He put an arm around her and leaned in close to her ear to explain. "I'm not allowed to be your sponsor, so as I mentioned earlier, I was planning to exchange a favor for your sponsorship. This is highly unusual."

Thali nodded her understanding.

"I will support this sponsorship," Ming added.

Garen's steadiness told her he had expected as much.

Then, Makena, the only woman in the court coughed. Her dark skin was well complemented by a beautifully fabricated orange dress with the most intricate geometric designs drawn onto the fabric. She even delicately balanced a hat that was easily twice the size of her head as she glided across the room. "My brothers, we are being hasty. Please, let us each have our time with her before we come to a vote."

Now it was Thali's turn to stiffen for a moment until she heard Garen's voice in her ear. "It's customary for each of the court to have ten minutes with you to judge for themselves. It will be within my sight, but I will be out of hearing. You are not required to answer any of the questions, but do not lie," Garen whispered.

Thali nodded. Joren parted the vines opposite the doors they had entered through, exposing a wide stone balcony. He waved his hand and two tree roots blossomed from the middle of floor, where he gestured for Thali to take a seat. Then the leaves of a tree grew and extended like an umbrella so she would sit in the shade.

"Can't have the sun ruining your complexion, now," Joren said.

Garen walked Thali over and guided her to the seat on the left. "I'll be right over there." He motioned to the other side of the vine curtain, which would remain open.

Makena was the first to sit down opposite her.

Thali bowed her head in respect.

"Thali, it would be awfully nice to have another woman around. But what is it you want?"

Thali had no choice but to answer truthfully. "I'm not sure I know what I want."

"Love or money?" The princess of thieves carefully studied Thali's face, watching every twitch and muscle movement.

"Love."

"Did you have a happy childhood?"

Thali thought about it a moment before answering carefully, "Yes."

"Black or white?"

"Gray."

"Sky, land, or ocean?"

"Ocean. Always."

Makena raised an eyebrow at that.

Thali gritted her teeth before she could say more. She was quite sure elaborating wouldn't be a good idea.

"I am done." As the princess rose, she leaned over and said, "I look forward to having another woman among us."

The other mini-interview was just as strange. Henrik, who Thali recognized as someone from the frozen north of Takdinida by his thick wool tunic, had the heaviest accent of all on the council, but as with merchants, he spoke the common tongue fluently. Besides greeting her, Henrik spent the entire interview staring at her, looking deeply into her eyes.

Garen, Ming, and Joren were the only ones who did not sit with her. Finally, the curtain of vines closed on the five standing ceremoniously around the round marble table, leaving Thali outside on the balcony. It felt like a thousand years passed as she anxiously sat waiting. This would change the course of her life, and her relationship with Garen, forever. A jolt of doubt went through her before she shook it off as nerves.

Finally, the vine curtain opened once again and Garen appeared. He offered Thali his arm. Pausing a moment to look in his eyes for some clue as to the outcome of the vote, she was impressed that Garen remained stoic enough to give nothing away. She nodded then and took his arm.

Garen led her back into the room where they stood before the council. Thali took a deep breath when he turned to her and pronounced, "Lady Thali, welcome to the court of thieves."

Every council member outstretched their arms, palms up, symbolizing her welcome into their court.

Then Joren flicked his wrist and another tree root bubbled up between his seat and Garen's where once there had been an empty space. Thali's eyes narrowed as she glanced at Joren. He had known this was going to happen and had planned for it.

"Now that that is settled, Garen, I expect you and Joren to teach Thali all the ways of our court." Ming nodded and the other two men nodded back. "But for now, let us begin." He motioned for everyone to sit.

Each thief sovereign reported on their territories in turn. They reported the current economic status, its predicted economic future—whether positive or negative—and the current tension level in their territories, whether that meant war was ongoing, being prepared for or planned, or if there were simply any tensions that might grow into something bigger. It was a lot to take in, but Thali found it infinitely interesting. It struck her as oddly similar to her father's meetings with his trade partners in different lands.

Nothing the council said truly surprised her since she'd heard whisperings of unrest from her father as well. The most interesting information came from Henrik, Prince of the Frozen North. "There are murmurs in the northwest. More activity, more supplies. Not supplies for human army. More meat. Hunters being paid for extra meat they can send north," Henrik said. He was the least fluent but still more so than Thali would have expected.

"What do you think it means?" Ming asked.

Henrik scratched is head. "Maybe is nothing. Maybe more babies. Maybe more dogs. Just strange for more meat needed up north so sudden."

Ming looked around the table, but no one had any additional thoughts on that matter.

When it was Garen's turn, Thali carefully listened to the news he shared, though it was nothing she hadn't heard before.

Before Garen's turn was over, Ming asked, "Garen, how is the new school working out?"

Garen grinned and replied, "It's great for our local crews. A sizable portion of the population busy learning new things means they don't always have their best wits about them."

"The news of the school's success has spread to even my people. One of our kings is quite curious about it." Ming clasped his hands before him on the table, perhaps indicating he wished to know more.

Thali wondered if Garen would tell them about her adventure at the end of last spring. Someone—someone with authority—from her school had purposely sent Thali and the rest of her crewmates to the wrong island for their final exam, and she had nearly died after the strange encounters and obstacles she'd faced. Still, no one knew why or who was responsible for it. Thali had her suspicions that her gift with animals may have opened a portal allowing mythical, magical animals through, but she wasn't really sure of anything yet. She'd have to talk to Garen about it later.

At a lull in the conversation, Thali shook her thoughts off. Though she quite enjoyed learning about the happenings in the world, her brain hurt from all the new information.

Thankfully, Ming chose then to rise and declare, "All right, it's time for a break. Let's reconvene in fifteen minutes."

CHAPTER SIX

T HALI WAS GRATEFUL FOR the break. Though the problems each territory experienced and how the council members pooled solutions and supplies globally was interesting to consider—once she'd gotten over the strangeness of it all—she was starting to feel overloaded. A small pounding was making itself known in the back of her head as a result. She glanced over to where Garen had wandered and found him in conversation with Ming. Garen must have felt her gaze because he glanced up at her and raised his eyebrows in a gesture she knew meant he was asking if she needed him immediately. She shook her head just slightly to signify she was good. He nodded. While he continued to talk, he kept his face turned so he could always see her with one eye, so she held her chin a little higher. She was proud to be his partner.

Since they were going to be there awhile, she decided to get up and get some air. A change of scenery might ease her headache, even though earlier that morning, Garen had asked her to always stay within his eyesight. Whether that was partly because he was being his usual overprotective self or because he didn't truly trust his court, she didn't know. Still, she couldn't just sit here anymore.

Garen still had his head bent in conversation with Ming, so she walked out onto the balcony, brushing her fingertips along the trees acting as columns. Thali looked back inside. No one was looking, so she slipped her feet out of her shoes, feeling the soft mossy ground as she approached the railing, and leaned over toward the forest below. She took a deep breath, closing her eyes, and just relaxed, forgetting the conflict between her merchant self and her newly instated princess of thieves self. For a moment, she pictured herself leaning on a ship's mast at the top of the lookout, breathing in salty ocean air.

"It's convincing, isn't it?" The voice startled her out of her reverie. Thali spun around, her eyes flying open to take in the bright colors now before her.

Of course it was Joren. Of all the princes, Joren was always the most flamboyantly dressed. He reminded her of a colorful fruit stand. Even his face was painted with outrageous colors and shapes. However, most startling was the quiet seriousness in his eyes that contrasted his outward floridity. She put her defenses back up so nothing could disarm her ... though her toes continued to squirm in the soft moss.

"I know, I look like a fool, but this is a lot more fun." He pulled a passion fruit from between two vines and leaned against a tree opposite her.

Thali nodded. She didn't really know what to say to him.

"So, what do you think?" Joren raised an eyebrow. He waited patiently as if gauging her reaction. "Of this grand vegetation of course."

Was he testing her, or was he normally like this? It was too early for her to tell, so she decided to go with honesty. "It's incredible, but I wish there was an ocean nearby."

"Ahh, right, you're a sailor." He leaned in closer than she was comfortable with. "So how does a merchant feel about being at a thief convention?"

Her breath caught in her throat for half a moment before she recovered. He knew she was from a merchant family? Was he trying to pry information about them out of her, or did he suspect he knew her secret? Despite joining the court, she still felt her prejudice rise as she wondered how truly trustworthy her new brothers were.

"Don't worry, my little sailor, I won't tell anyone. They probably already know anyway." He drew his finger along her jawline before bringing her face uncomfortably close to his. Gazing at her lips, he whispered, "You know, I'm a much better kisser than he is. Shall we find out?"

Thali froze as he leaned in closer yet before pausing an inch from her face. She could feel his breath on her lips and had to remember to exhale through her nose. She wouldn't be intimidated, so she only raised an eyebrow.

Then she knew he was testing her because as close as they were, he still didn't kiss her. She worked to keep her breathing calm as she matched his stare, intensity for intensity. Clamping her teeth together, Thali instinctively knew no answer was an answer.

"You know, I have ten times the wealth he has. You could have anything you could ever possibly want. I have *many* palaces like this, all over this land in fact. We could go anywhere. We could live better than royalty," Joren whispered so quietly she had to focus to hear him.

He still had her face in his hand, but she knew he was waiting for her response. "As tempting as that may be, I prefer ships to palaces. Must be the sailor in me."

As if he was an animal picking up an enemy scent, his attention suddenly flickered, and he eased back. "Well, my love, my offer will always stand, especially for someone as interesting as you." And with that, Joren gave her his most sultry smile and glided back into the room.

She gripped the rail, digging her fingernails into the wood.

Garen slid up next to her and asked, "What did Joren say?"

Thali sighed. "This court seems desperate for a woman."

"Anything I should address?" Garen's gaze suddenly turned dark and serious. He was certainly the jealous type. That she had always known, but she was too weary right now to deal with the concern on his face.

"I handled it. I *can* fight some of my own battles, you know." Garen stiffened, and Thali's heart melted. She couldn't bear to hurt him, so she promised, "I'll tell you later."

He smiled and covered her hand with his, taking it and planting a kiss on her knuckles. "Ming gave me this for you today." He handed her a cloth pouch. Inside she could feel the weight of a many-paged letter.

"Who is it from? Do you know?"

"Your grandmother apparently."

Thali's eyebrow shot up, but she slipped the letter into her sleeve, reserving her excitement for tonight. When she looked up, she saw concern in his eyes. He was doubting again whether he really should have brought her here. She'd seen that look a hundred times in the couple days they'd been here.

Thali smiled, inching closer to him so he had to put his arm around her. "I'm glad you brought me. These are tremendously interesting people. Besides, I have to say the things you all talk about are intriguing. I'm enjoying the challenge of learning and keeping up, though I never thought five people could be so different." Her thoughts drifted to how forward Joren was and then to how quiet Ming was.

Garen sighed and said, "We're six now and we're all different, but we work toward the same goal." A gong rang behind them and they pushed off the railing. Suddenly, he sniffed Thali. "Did Joren try to kiss you?" He raised an eyebrow quizzically.

Thali laughed. "He made me an offer, but I kind of like what I already have." She smiled and slipped back into her shoes.

Garen just smiled.

Their meetings had adjourned for the day, and Garen and Thali had just finished enjoying some tea in their sitting room. Now Garen was preparing to leave on an errand he'd just said he had to run, though he'd been rather vague about it.

"Garen, do you think I should tell Joren about my ability?" Thali asked.

"That's up to you. He's clever. So I think he already suspects you aren't normal."

"He knows I'm a merchant."

Garen paused before continuing to tie up his boots. "I'm not surprised, I suppose. Information is his specialty."

"Should I be concerned?"

"No, he tends to watch and store information for a later date. And he seems to like you, so I wouldn't worry. I'll know if he's planning something."

Thali noticed Garen wasn't just getting dressed but was strapping his spare daggers to his shins.

"It's customary for one of us to visit the oracle when we have these conferences. This year it's my turn, and I have to trek to get to her. And yes, I have to go alone, but I'll be back by evening."

"You don't sound excited to go. Is it a real oracle?"

"I'm afraid so. I don't want to know the future, but it's a precaution our court takes. She's given us fair warning that's helped before." He shrugged. "So, we all take our turn."

"I wish I could go with you." Thali was intrigued by the mention of an oracle.

"Me too," Garen said. Thali let Garen encircle her in his arms, and they stood there, holding each other for a minute, soaking each other in. "Joren wants to show you around this afternoon."

"Oh?" Thali was surprised at how much interest Joren had in her. She was a little anxious at the prospect after this morning but didn't want Garen to worry.

"I think he just wants to show off for you, but it might be interesting to find out more about how his gift works. If you want to tell him about yours, he'll make sure it's kept confidential," Garen said.

"Can I trust him?" Thali asked.

"As much as you can trust the others. There's no risk of physical harm from him or the others now that you're one of us."

"Be safe." Thali smiled tightly. Garen kissed Thali's forehead and they reluctantly slid apart.

"Have a good afternoon. I'll be back as quickly as I can." Garen flashed her a brilliant smile before opening the door and slipping out.

Thali sighed and pulled out the letter from her grandmother. She had never heard from Amah. She thought of the haunted, sad look her mother always wore whenever they visited her home country. Somehow, Thali felt like reading the letter was a betrayal to her mother, so she tossed it—still in its cloth pouch—into her bag.

A knock sounded at the door.

Thali went to open the door, only to find Joren dressed head to toe in green. He wore a palm-leaf tunic, green tights, jungle-green boots, and a lime-green cloak.

"I know, calmer than my usual, but I figured we'd want to blend in today. Shall we?" he asked as he offered her his arm.

Thali grabbed her waxed cloak, glad she had already strapped her extra daggers on when Garen had.

Joren led her through a maze of mossy corridors and out through marble doors to the jungle she'd seen below.

"Garen told me you were intrigued by the reptiles," Joren said.

"I've never seen anything like them." Thali noted that Joren paced himself to match her shorter legs.

"They are unique. I raised them myself, you know," Joren said, but he puffed out his chest with pride.

Thali nodded. She noticed that this Joren was a much different version of himself. He was much calmer and more relaxed trekking through the depths of his jungle, among his plants, just as she was more relaxed in a forest of animals. As they walked, she watched his posture visibly loosen.

"How did you first realize you had a way with plants?" Thali asked.

"I was always drawn to them. My mother had this vine plant that she had carefully grown in our home. We didn't have much, but she'd bought the plant on a whim when she found out she was pregnant with me and took care of it, as she did me. When I was born, it blossomed and started growing like crazy. It circled the entirety of our small house! It's a part of every childhood memory. Anyway, one day when I was about ten, my little brother took one of my books and scribbled all over it. He was just a kid and didn't know any better, but I was so mad when I saw my book there with scribbles all over it. The next thing I knew, a vine had reached out and clasped his neck."

Thali stopped walking to look up at Joren. She well knew times like that.

Joren sighed and smiled, urging her to keep walking with a nod. "Not to worry. Bless my dear mother, she ran in and took one look at the vine. Then she just looked at me, stepped closer, and asked me calmly to put my brother down. It was her calm that snapped me out of my rage and made me realize that my feelings and a vine strangling my brother were linked."

"What happened after that?" Thali asked, thinking of the random animals that always seemed to find her or show up conveniently.

Joren shrugged. "My mother sat me down and told me that I was different from most people, but I had a responsibility to control it. So she made me practice. She asked me to look inside myself and describe what it felt like. Then she invented small exercises to help me focus my gift, be aware of it, and learn how to use it."

"Lucky." Thali thought about how her parents had always told her to hide it, to suppress it.

Joren was quiet for a moment. They were deep inside the forest now where it was quietest. The only sounds were the small movements of insects, leaves rustling, and the odd twig cracking. "You'll forgive me, but you seem to have a very different perspective from most people. Usually people shrink away in fear or hesitate. Instead, you leaned in closer when I showed you. I can't say I've ever seen that reaction."

Thali faced a big decision in that moment. She had already told Garen about her gift with animals in this last year, and after keeping it a secret for so much of her life, she felt like she was exposing herself too much lately. She stopped and looked at Joren, still undecided.

He had pulled his hood off as they'd walked, and for the first time, she saw most of his face. Though it was still covered in green paint, it was the most human she'd ever seen him look. She thought for a second about what she'd do if their roles were reversed. She was now sworn to the secrecy of the court, as was he, so if he swore not to share her secret with anyone, it'd be an honest oath. He looked younger now, this far into the forest, with his posture having melted into a much lither and more relaxed stance.

"You now, if there's something you want to share, I'm bound by the court not to repeat it or hint at it unless it has direct influence on our court." Joren summoned a couple tree roots for them to sit on. Small flowers started to pop up around them and she grinned.

Thali thought a moment, remembering that she had always wanted to know she wasn't alone. With that thought in mind, she decided to test the waters first. "Have you ever met anyone like yourself?"

"No, and certainly not with my gift with plants. Though I've heard rumors of other abilities, things like influencing the weather and such. But I've never actually met anyone else with a gift." He narrowed his eyes as he studied Thali's face.

Thali took a deep breath and dove in, haltingly. "Your talent with plants ... the reason I leaned toward you ... well, I'm so intrigued by your gift with plants because I have a ... a similar ... way with animals."

Joren's eyebrows rose and his brow crinkled in surprise. She wondered if it was manufactured or genuine surprise.

Thali closed her eyes and looked inside her mind. She found the illuminated strands of the great reptile beasts and called to them, like a beacon, and showed them her location. She opened her eyes to see Joren closing his. As the great reptiles moved, they rustled through the jungle, affecting his plants.

There was a rustle of leaves as a rounded head popped out of the foliage and bowed before them as he placed his head in Thali's hands. She scratched his chin and he let out a soft huff of air.

"Remarkable." Joren sat very still as the reptile turned his attention to him and placed his head in Joren's lap.

Thali surfaced from the green thread in her brain that now showed affection. "He loves you very much."

"How do you see that?" Joren asked.

"They appear as threads in my mind. Usually, the different species are different colors. For example, this fellow is a luminescent green. I can feel what they feel, see what they see, share images and feelings, and ask them to do things for me."

Joren's eyes narrowed. "Humans?"

Thali shook her head. "With people, it's a lot fuzzier. It's more like a general feeling than anything specific. Anger, or malice, or happiness. And I can't establish a thread with them. For example, all I can see or feel of you is the same relaxed feeling I get when I'm among my animals in a forest." Thali rubbed the head of another reptilian creature that had dipped its head onto her lap.

Joren grinned. "That explains your horde of animals."

Thali raised her eyebrows.

"Please, a beautiful young woman with a tiger, dog, and snake as companions hardly blends in." Joren grinned.

"You knew," Thali said accusingly. So, it had been manufactured surprise.

"No, I didn't know you had the ability to communicate with them, but I suspected there was something different about you." Joren raised a palm, and a reptilian creature rested its large oval head in his hand.

"Won't Garen be a little surprised to know you've been snooping on his territory?" she asked.

Joren rolled his eyes. "If my little brother has a problem, he can take it up with me."

A realization dawned on Thali then. "Wait, like the little brother you strangled as a kid?"

Joren pouted dramatically. "He didn't tell you? I wonder if he's still mad at me then. Our relationship hasn't been ... well, perfect over the years."

Then Thali realized then that under the make-up and the posturing, Joren moved like Garen. She had assumed it was because they were both princes of thieves and the best at what they did, but them being related made more sense the more she thought about it.

"That's why he wasn't really surprised when I told him," Thali muttered.

"It seems my brother's a magic magnet," Joren said.

Thali put this new information away for later. She wondered momentarily why Garen hadn't mentioned it before it occurred to her that there might be a bigger reason he didn't trust his own brother. So, she changed the subject. "So, what can you do? Do you feel the plants? Or talk with them? Or hear and see through them?"

Joren grinned and said, "There's only certain plants I can use to listen through, and it takes a lot of concentration since plants don't listen and process like animals do. And I can sense what they do process: sunlight, moisture, vibration, minerals. I can feed them all that too, but it takes a lot of energy from my being. Does your ability tire you?"

"Yes, depending on the distance. If I follow the thread of an eagle soaring, it takes a lot more of my energy than if I were to follow a little mouse nearby."

"How do you ask them to do something?" Joren asked.

"I send it in a series of images. Usually I throw in a reward at the end. For example, I use messenger bats to communicate with my family, and when they return, I show them where their family is and where they might find some extra food that day."

"How intriguing." Joren was uncharacteristically quiet then, and she noticed the plants around him also become uncharacteristically still. His face became soft and thoughtful.

Thali was glad she had decided to go on this outing with Joren—and to share her secret with him. They spoke at length for the rest of the afternoon and into the evening, with Joren growing berries for them to eat when they got hungry. She was glad to have found someone who hid similar secrets from the world. When they finally walked back, it was much later than she had realized, and Thali's heart felt lighter for having made the connection. Even if she didn't fully trust him, she felt a kinship with him.

When she returned to her rooms, she was surprised that Garen hadn't returned yet. She had stayed out later than she had meant to, yet he still wasn't back. She would worry if she didn't know him as well as she did, so she decided to prepare for bed. It had been a long day and her heart was happy and full. Thali fell fast asleep even though she had meant to wait to hear Garen come in.

CHAPTER SEVEN

G^{AREN}

It was the middle of the night before Garen returned to their rooms. Though he was exhausted, he still bathed before slipping into bed with Thali instead of heading to the couch. He circled his arms around her and held her close. Right now, he needed to feel her, hear her breathe, feel her heart beat. Garen didn't want to believe what the oracle had said. He wouldn't be sleeping tonight, but by holding her in his arms, he could hope he could delay it. He couldn't imagine his life without her; it was selfish, but he wouldn't let her go without a fight.

When his body finally needed to move as the light poured into the room, he extricated himself and stepped onto the balcony. When Thali woke, she tiptoed as quietly as she could up behind him. He had known she was there the moment she had woken up though. When he turned, he drank in the radiance shining from her eyes. Thali looked truly happy. His heart did flip flops like it always did when she looked at him like that. She wrapped her arms around his waist, resting her head on his shoulder. He appreciated her body pressed up against his and leaned into her, wrapping an arm around her to hold her closer. The zaps of electricity as warmth bloomed over his body made them press even closer together.

Garen took a deep breath, closing his dark eyes. He felt Thali smile into his shoulder; their love had come so far. She had been so unsure of herself when he had first met her. After her brother's death, she'd been lost and drifting, the life she had imagined taken away. She'd been sent away to school with a bunch of strangers instead of sailing her own ship around the world, and that had made her reserved and skeptical. Now, she was bold, voicing her thoughts with confidence. He had beamed with every comment she had added in their meetings yesterday. And just now, she had felt emboldened enough to come to him. He wanted to stay in this moment forever.

"Hey, thief," she whispered in his ear.

He took a step back in her grasp so they were face-to-face. He stared into her eyes. Taking his time, he scanned her face, memorizing every curve, shape, and color: her smooth skin, her prominent cheek bones, the stormy darkness of her eyes. His hand cupped her jaw and he smiled. His heart swelled with all the love he had for her. If there was something he would—could—never doubt, it was his love for her.

Thali cocked her head like a puppy dog as concern filled her face. "What's wrong?"

Garen smiled. "You are brilliant ..." He gently planted a kiss on her temple. "And beautiful ..." He planted another kiss on her eyelid. "... and bold." He kissed her lips, and she deepened it. Long moments later, he pulled away and took in the glow of her satisfaction at the compliments and the passion of their kiss.

Holding her close, they turned to watch the large reptiles as they glided through the giant leaves. The oracle's words pealed like a bell in his head. This damned conference. It was the reason his heart ached now. Because it was his turn to see the oracle on the council's behalf, he'd left and traveled to see an old, poor lady up in the heart of the mountain. Before he'd even sat down, the old lady's eyes had glassed over as her focus had rolled inward.

"You must let her go." Her surprisingly strong voice had filled the cave, echoing in every crevice. "She will do great things, but not for you. She will change the kingdom, but not with you. She must save the world."

He had tried to ignore the oracle's advice all the way back. Perhaps she had meant someone else. Garen was good for Thali. She'd blossomed with confidence. They were in love. She was good for his people. They were meant for each other. He knew all that to be the truth as much as he sadly knew deep within the truth of what the oracle had spoken of.

Garen shook his head to clear it as he came back to the present. Thali's hand crawled across his chest to his shoulder, and he closed his eyes as he enjoyed the moment. "I love you." Opening his eyes and looking down at her, he drank in the light in her eyes as the concern that had appeared on her face melted.

She smiled. "I love you too." Her grin filled her face as she beamed at him.

His insides melted as he held her. He was hers. No matter what happened, he would always be hers. Tragedy would have to wait until tomorrow. Maybe tomorrow he could be brave enough to break their hearts.

CHAPTER EIGHT

T HALI

True to his word, Tariq was there, waiting for her on his docked ship. It had been excruciating to tear herself away from Garen. She had even contemplated blowing Tariq off and following Garen for the next few days before returning straight to school. Alas, Lari had flown in loops above her, and she knew Tariq would have torn down half the city looking for her. And then her parents would have come. That would have been disastrous.

"What if we disguise you, and then you can come back with me?" Thali had asked Garen before they'd parted.

Garen had groaned and replied, "There's nothing I want to do more, but I still have a few private meetings with the others before I can head back. I won't be back until a week after your classes start."

Thali had deflated in his arms then. Though he'd squeezed her, she'd felt his shoulders sinking.

She came back to herself when Tariq leaped onto the dock.

"Are you hurt? Are you all right? Have you been robbed?" Tariq asked as he spun her around and inspected her with his own eyes.

Thali winced at the concern on his face. "I'm fine, Tariq. Thank you. Let's go."

"Ah ... I'm also grumpy about leaving Bree. I miss her like I'd miss half my heart," Tariq said as he led Thali back to his ship.

Thali didn't dignify his comment with a response. Tariq looked back over his shoulder at the city beyond. Thali knew he was wondering if he could see Garen. She didn't want him to even try, so she took Tariq's arm and led him back to the bow, not letting him turn back around.

They stood, in silence at first, at the ship's bow as it left the dock. Thali wanted to look for Garen, but she knew that Tariq was trying to spot him too, so she stopped herself. Somehow, it felt like sharing Garen, and she wanted to keep him for herself in her heart, her mind, for now.

"So ... was it ... good?" Tariq sounded unsure of what to say.

"It was ... interesting." Thali looked at her hands. She could feel heat bloom in her cheeks.

"You're probably not allowed to talk about it, huh?" Tariq asked, somehow seeming to shrink inside his enormous, wide-shouldered self.

"Not at all," Thali said.

They were quiet as they glided into the open ocean. It would take them no longer than a day to get back to Bulstan before she had to turn immediately around and leave with her parents to get back to Adanek in time for classes.

"I can see why you love sailing on the ocean so much," Tariq finally said.

Thali just nodded. She'd wrapped an old piece of sail she'd found belowdecks around her shoulders.

"Would you give it up for him?"

Thali looked to her best friend and smiled weakly. "He wouldn't ask me to." And she knew it in her heart to be true.

They stood together until it was too dark to see anything more before they headed belowdecks for a late dinner.

Chapter Nine

T HALI HAD BARELY ENOUGH time to say her goodbyes as she had hopped off Tariq's ship and right onto her mother and father's. They had sailed smoothly and without incident back to school, bypassing Densria, their family home, to make Lanchor in time to drop Thali off so she wouldn't be late for the start of her classes.

"Don't cause too much trouble," her father had warned as he'd hugged her.

"I won't. Sail safely." Thali had hugged her father back ferociously.

Her mother had then tucked a stack of parchments into her bag as she'd hugged her, a little longer than usual Thali noticed. "Drills for you to practice."

"Thanks, Mom!" Thali had said as she'd jumped off the ship with her dog, Ana, and her tiger, Indi. Bardo, her snake, had been huddled within her sleeve. Mia, Thali's best friend had thankfully brought Arabelle, Thali's beloved horse, back to school for her.

Now Thali walked through town as the sun sank below the horizon. She thought she saw a few shadows nod at her as she passed through some of the busier streets. When she made it to her common room, Mia greeted her with an endless hug strong enough to belie her small stature, then handed her a letter with Prince Elric's seal on it.

"There's more where that came from, but this is the latest. Oh, and you missed dinner, but I brought up a few things for you," Mia said.

"Thanks," Thali said. She grabbed the tray and started munching even though she'd just finished dinner aboard her parents' ship. "How was your journey?"

"Arabelle is the sweetest horse. She didn't even rear when we were startled by someone rounding a corner."

"Oh good, I'm glad. Did you meet up with any of your classmates for the ride back?"

"Oh, yes! We stayed at that little inn you suggested and stared at all the handsome blacksmiths there." Mia grinned then glanced at the letter still in Thali's hands. "I'll say goodnight for now though. I need my beauty sleep for the first day of classes." She stretched and yawned then ducked into her own rooms.

I am the luckiest person to have a friend who knows me so well, Thali thought as she tucked the last bit of fruit from her tray in with the other fruits on their common table before heading to her own rooms. There, she dropped her bag on the floor and flopped onto the tiny space her tiger and dog had left for her after leaping onto the bed. Looking at the letter, Thali was surprised she hadn't thought more about Elric in the last few days. She sighed and opened it.

Dear Thali,
I wonder why you haven't responded to my earlier letter this week and am just a little worried. However, I do understand you're probably traveling back to school, so you might be preoccupied. It's a rather exciting time at the palace: We have a lot of foreign guests right now, so there's always someone interesting to talk to. No one's as interesting as you though.

Prince Callum of the Northern West is especially annoying. He's younger than I am and likes to follow me around. He's been stuck inside his castle for an entire year. I guess they've had some kind of trouble with people going missing in his kingdom. So, he's been cooped up for months and now he's been unleashed on me!

I've never had siblings, but Stefan tells me this is what it's like to have a younger brother.

Anyway, I hope you're well and that you reply to my letters soon. I may send out a search party if you don't reply in ... oh, the next two weeks. Just kidding! But seriously, I'm starting to worry. I always look forward to your letters.

Yours,
Elric

Thali folded the letter and tossed it on her desk. She would reply before she went to bed to reassure Eric that she was quite all right and let him know that while she had been away, her bats had delivered her letters to Mia.

"You know, I was lucky to get one letter a week. And I usually only got one every two weeks from Aron," Mia said from Thali's doorway, startling her.

Thali looked at her, wondering what had kept Mia from her beauty sleep. She held a needle and thread, and a swathe of fabric draped down the length of her.

"How do you have homework to do? Classes don't even start until tomorrow," Thali asked.

"This is for you—Welcome Ball, remember?" Mia replied, raising the colorful fabric to show her.

Thali made a face. She'd forgotten all about her responsibilities as a founder's daughter. Before she could remark on it, a thunderous pounding on the door to their common area shook the stone walls, startling them and leaving Thali wondering how stone walls could tremble at all.

"Thali, are you back?!"

Thali put a book over the letter and the girls hurried to the common room. Thali swung the door open to reveal her friends, Daylor and Tilton. While Daylor was still a huge bulk of blacksmith's son, and had somehow gotten even larger, Tilton had grown taller and broader. Where last year he had looked like a young boy, this year, he looked like a refined gentleman.

Tilton blushed, likely from the look on her stunned face. *So he was still the same on the inside then*, Thali thought.

Daylor swept her up into a breath-squeezing hug, and Indi padded out to leap up and hug him from behind. Ana licked Tilton's face, unfazed by his physical changes.

"It's good to see you too, Daylor." Thali laughed as he finally put her back on the floor.

She then went to hug a now more solidly built Tilton.

"I think Tilton is going to make all the girls swoon this year, hey Thali?" Daylor grinned.

"Oh, I'm already swooning." Thali pretended to fall out of Tilton's arms, only to have him catch her as he turned an even darker shade of red.

"Cough it up, Tilton. What did you do this summer?" Thali backed away and raised an eyebrow to stare him down.

"Nothing. My family's famed for being late bloomers. My dad was the same way." He shrugged as the redness spread to his neck, then all the way to his hands.

Thali turned to Mia, who closed her gaping mouth at her friend's glance before rushing forward to greet their friends. Shooing the animals away, Mia hugged Daylor, then Tilton. "They're right, Tilton. You're going to be the Daylor of this year."

"Now, wait a second ..." Daylor chimed in.

They all laughed and settled into the common room and talked late into the evening, depriving Mia of her so-called beauty sleep.

Chapter Ten

T HALI WAS EXHAUSTED THE next morning and dreading class as she headed to weapons practice. Isaia, her former sparring partner, had received a position with her father after finishing school last year, so Thali was left to wonder and worry about who she'd be partnered with this year.

When she joined Daylor and Tilton in the practice area, the few girls in merchanting were whispering and giggling as they sneaked glances at Tilton.

"Lady Routhalia."

Thali turned to see a serious-looking boy in the green robes of a healer. He was as large as Daylor but had the white-blond hair and ice blue eyes of Isaia. The newcomer studied her as he advanced.

Daylor took a half step in front of her.

"Please, I mean no harm," the stranger said as he stopped where he was. "My name is Idris. I am Isaia's younger brother." Thali nodded, understanding dawning, and the boy continued. "You've done my family a great honor by saving my brother's life. My family is indebted to you and has tasked me with giving this to you." Idris bowed and presented a long dagger with a simple black leather hilt and a blue metal cross guard that coiled down the hilt to the pommel.

Thali gasped. The Quinto family was globally renowned as swordsmen and sword makers. Their products cost a fortune because it took months to make a dagger and almost a year to make a sword. "It's beautiful, but truly, this is too much." Thali swallowed, though her hands imperceptibly twitched toward the dagger.

"Please, my brother's life is worth much more to my family. This is only a small token of our appreciation. Isaia made it. He was disappointed not to be able to present it to you himself."

Thali swallowed again and nodded, then grasped the dagger reverently with both hands. "Please tell your family I thank them. It will become a prized possession in my family." Thali bowed, touching her forehead to the dagger.

Idris nodded, then turned and left, just as Isaia would have done. Thali examined the dagger a few moments longer before delicately tucking it into her belt.

Then a voice interrupted her admiration of the dagger. "Now, if we're ready to start, pick up your wooden swords and let's see what you remember from last year. First years, off to the side fer now." Master Aloysius clapped his hands to get everyone moving.

Thali ended up helping run drills with Master Aloysius rather than being assigned a new partner. She did, however, get to spar a little with a student easily two and a half times her size, but he was slow and Thali managed to outmaneuver him easily.

By the end of the day, she discovered her classes were a little more interesting than last year, but there was still nothing new to learn. She was so bored, she offered to continue teaching Daylor how to swim after classes. He gladly accepted. After he'd almost drowned last year, he jumped at every opportunity to strengthen his swimming skills. Thali had made sure Daylor could keep his head above water before their final exam on the ocean last year, but she hoped to turn him into a strong swimmer this year in case he had to swim in rough seas.

"Okay, today's our last swimming lesson in the lake. We're going to the ocean after this. You'll have to learn to coordinate all your massive limbs in moving water."

"Thanks, Thali. I really appreciate this." Daylor grinned one of his goofy grins.

She just shrugged. After showing him a few new ways to maneuver through the water and giving him some tips, they began to swim toward the other, more forested bank. The lake was just north of their school and a favorite spot for students when it was hot out. After just a ten-minute walk, the trees parted to reveal a grassy bank that sloped into a calm lake with a steep cliff on the right and forest on the left and opposite bank. It wasn't a particularly large lake, but it was deep enough that you didn't have to constantly touch the slimy bottom. No one else was in the lake today, so Thali swam at a leisurely pace to keep an eye on Daylor. She noticed him splashing more than usual, so they stopped at the halfway point to rest. He panted as he treaded water and she waited patiently, remembering that Daylor's heavy body was developing muscles he'd never used before. She was proud that her friend was doing so well in the water. It was a far cry from when she'd had to rescue him after he'd sunk like a rock after falling off a bridge into the river.

"You should float, save your energy," Thali said as she watched Daylor relax, his middle finally buoyant. It had taken him three lessons to finally relax enough to float.

"Thali, I consider myself one of your closest friends," Daylor said when his breathing started to return to normal.

"I'd agree with that."

"I know there's someone special in your life, maybe since the first ball last year?"

Thali was silent.

"Don't worry, I get that you have your secrets. Maybe you're just not ready to share or you can't. We all have our secrets," Daylor continued.

Thali relaxed a fraction of an inch so she wouldn't sink while she floated.

"But if you want someone to talk to ... well, I know what it's like to love someone and have to keep it a secret."

"How? What do you know?" Thali panicked a bit as she flailed. She thought she and Garen had always been so discreet.

"Nothing really. Just that at the beginning of last year, you were surprised, and frankly, overwhelmed whenever someone would flirt with you. Then, after the ball, the welcome one, you changed. You were still oblivious to the many gentlemen looking your way, but more carefree. You're happier now, more confident and open with the rest of us. That's what love does. You've started coming out of your shell. Most romantic relationships can't help but overflow into one's personality, even if the relationship is a secret. I'm just glad you're happy, though I'll admit I'm dying to know who it is."

Thali floated quietly, contemplating Daylor's words as she gazed at the clouds above them. She'd been so caught up in her own life—Garen, the council, the sparkling threads emanating from an island that supposedly didn't exist but that she'd discovered during her final exam voyage last year—that she had never considered her friends might have problems of their own. She considered who Daylor might love. Did he pay special attention to someone in Mia's group of friends maybe? Thali would have to pay more attention next time they were all together. She'd had such a small circle of friends for so much of her life that she hadn't realized it had grown since she had started school.

Finally, she replied as she began to tread water. "Daylor, I appreciate that, and I'll keep it in mind. And I'm a pretty decent secret keeper myself if you ever want to talk too. Now, let's get back before it gets dark and I freeze to death." Instead of continuing to the opposite bank, she turned and headed for shore. Her heart felt a little lighter as she swam back, knowing she could confide in Daylor if she needed to.

Chapter Eleven

T HE NEXT MORNING, THALI dragged her feet to weapons practice. She wanted so desperately to be challenged—maybe Master Aloysius would take her on as a private student. Maybe she should write to Crab, Master Aloysius's cousin and her family's most trusted shiphand, and ask him to plead her case.

As she got closer to the field, she noticed a clump of students surrounding someone with bright copper hair. She hurried her pace to see what was going on. But she wasn't quite fast enough.

Master Aloysius shouted, "To your places!"

At that, the students formed their lines, allowing Thali to better see the new person. He was tall, lean but broad in the shoulders, and well-muscled. Bright copper curls capped his head, and even with freckles, his grass-green eyes made him incredibly handsome. His gaze caught hers and he grinned. She felt his arrogance like a slimy coat wrapping around her and immediately didn't like him.

"Oy, who are ya, lad?" Master Aloysius asked.

"My apologies, Master Aloysius." The boy bowed. "I am the son of Lord Byron in the far Northern West. This school is unique, and I've traveled far to learn the merchanting trade. We ran into some trouble on our way here, and that's why I'm late beginning my classes."

"Aye, lad, ya may be the one from far away, but what do I call ya?" Master Aloysius asked.

"My apologies, Master." He bowed again. "Alexius, at your service."

Thali thought he looked too perfect, and that he knew it.

She knew of the people from the far Northern West, but with his fair, almost translucent complexion and contrasting bright hair, he looked like he came from the Highlands. There was something that seemed untruthful about him.

"An' yer skills with a sword, how are they?" Impatience tinted his voice. Master Aloysius clearly wanted to get class started.

"Fair," Alexius said. Thali noticed his musculature suggested he was being humble. He had the perfect swordsman's shape.

"Thali, come 'ere." Master Aloysius signaled for her to come join them.

Master Aloysius kept his sword in his hand as he handed Alexius a wooden one. Thali gripped her wooden sword and stepped forward, gulping back a groan. She had wished for a challenge, but she already didn't like this boy.

However, she maintained her decorum and they nodded to each other. Despite his irritating grin, she started by going easy on him. He matched her with the same ease. Slowly, she started to parry faster, using more complicated patterns. Still, he matched her easily. She wiped her brow before she even saw a single drop of sweat glisten on his forehead.

"Looks like we have a sparring partner for ye after all, lass," Master Aloysius declared before turning his attention to the other students.

Thali barely heard him. She grinned when she finally knocked Alexius off balance and smacked his shoulder blade with the flat of her wooden blade.

He regained his footing quickly, though his eyebrow had shot up when she had smacked him. Then he grinned and jumped back into it with unnatural grace, his sword meeting hers. They were both drenched when the bells finally interrupted them.

"Lady Routhalia, it has been an honor. I look forward to tomorrow morning." He grinned, showing pointy canines before being engulfed in a cluster of overly helpful first-year merchant girls who led him off to their next class.

"Now that was a show." Daylor had brought her bag to her.

"I don't trust him," Thali said. He was the definition of too good to be true.

"I agree. Someone that good-looking shouldn't be trusted." Tilton had come up on her other side. The trio silently watched Alexius leave the practice area with his gaggle of followers, similar looks of distrust and wariness on all three faces.

CHAPTER TWELVE

B Y THE END OF the week, Thali had sent a letter to her father and to Tariq, asking if they knew anything of a Lord Byron and his son Alexius—who had turned out to be an impressive warrior.

She was practically vibrating now as she lay in bed, waiting for Garen to both return from his business out of town and to ask him if he knew anything about this mysterious stranger who had known her name.

"How was your trip?" She rolled over the moment the window moved. Garen climbed in backward and sat on her bed. Then he scooted closer to her, and she kicked off the blankets to wrap her body around his. He was cold from being outdoors, but she welcomed his presence. He wrapped his own limbs around her, holding her close to him. She rested her head on his shoulder, breathed in his scent, and despite herself, started to drift back to sleep.

"Hey, beautiful, wake up." Her eyelids fluttered open, and she now saw how tired he was. Dark circles made his eyes look ghostly hollow, and new wrinkles had creased his beautiful face. He looked like he hadn't slept in days.

She sat up, "What's wrong?"

His forehead scrunched as if he was trying to think of something. Something that was difficult to recall.

"Do you remember the last afternoon of the conference? That day Joren showed you around the forest?"

She nodded.

"And you remember that I went to see an old lady—an oracle? We always check with her to see whether the resolutions of the conference will fare well, and we take turns doing it—this year being my turn, if you'll recall. This year, she told me something unrelated and unasked for."

He looked away and took a deep breath. Thali watched his jaw muscles work as though he had to say something he didn't want to. "She told me that we can't be together."

Thali tightened her arms around him, and he held her closer. "I've been trying to ignore her, but it's haunting me. I haven't slept since that night. I feel like I'm delirious half the time. I just … I can't … I can't call you mine knowing this." He choked up.

Thali's mind blanked from shock. This was her worst nightmare come true.

Garen

It felt like he was pushing a dagger into his own heart. How could it be that he couldn't keep the one thing he loved most? She was his whole world, his whole heart, and he felt it cracking.

"What do you mean? I don't understand. Why would an old lady care about us? I don't understand!" Tears pooled in Thali's eyes before running down her face and creating twin puddles in their interlaced hands.

He swallowed, hoping against hope that maybe he could resist, that he could disregard the oracle and hold out for them. But he was so tired. Ilya, his third, had had to carry him to the school and Thali's building. His vision swam and he saw only blurs of colors. Thali squeezed him. It was the only thing that kept his heart from shattering, but with every crack, he could feel the soft lull of sleep and rest like a balm just out of reach. "I will always love you. But this kingdom, the times to come, they need you more."

His thoughts drifted back to when he'd walked into the oracle's cave, how her eyes had rolled back as soon as he had entered. "She cannot be yours," she had pronounced. "For others, she will do more. She needs to save the world, save your world. You must leave her to save her." He wished he hadn't heard it. He wished she'd stopped there, but she'd continued, and he blocked the rest from his mind.

"I just don't understand. Why can't you be with me? I'm helping, aren't I? You said I was essential at the conference," Thali pleaded.

He finally looked into her eyes. They softened as he hoped she saw how this was breaking his heart as much as hers.

"If you stay with me, the world will fall into chaos. You're going to save the Kingdom of Adanek and thereby save the world. But you can't do it with me." He struggled through a few breaths, the soothing call of rest and sleep brushing against his mind. "I'll always protect you, and I'll always love you, but we cannot be together. I have to let you go." They lay in a tangled pile of limbs as they clung together.

"No! Don't I get a say? Forget Adanek. We'll go somewhere else. What if I don't want us to be apart? We can move to another kingdom. My mother has family in Cerisa. We can go there."

She looked into his eyes, and more tears started to flood her eyes, her beautiful eyes. He hated that he was causing her pain, that he was breaking their hearts.

Her voice came out tiny and soft. "Why don't I get a say in this?"

"You're meant for so much more than just me, more than this underground world." Garen gritted his teeth. He didn't want to say the second half of what the oracle had told him. But the oracle had been clear. Sleep would not come for him unless he told Thali of it. He struggled to keep his sob at bay. "One day, Prince Elric will ask you to marry him, and you must say yes. At his side, you'll be able to make a difference in the kingdom ... in the world." The oracle had made him promise to tell her. The dagger in his heart twisted as it broke into a million little pieces with the telling of that last bit.

She threw her balled fists against his chest and he held her tight, letting her do what she would. Her anger eventually melted away and she sobbed into his chest. He kept his arms around her, letting his own tears soak into her hair. She wrapped herself more tightly around him, and he squeezed back. Her fists clenched his clothes as if to hold him there forever. They fell asleep in each other's arms as their sobs slowly died out, leaving them drained.

Thali

When she woke up, he was gone.

Her eyes were puffy and she felt dry from all the crying, but for a moment, she thought it had all been a dream. Then, she saw the note Garen had left on her desk and grabbed it.

> *Centuries locked away,*
> *Legends await the one*
> *To bring the worlds together.*

Thali turned the paper over and saw Garen had scrawled a final line on the back.

> *I will always love you.*

She clung to the medallion he'd placed prominently on her pillow. She had promised him she'd wear it no matter what. But now it was the only piece of him she had left. Maybe one day it would bring him back to her. Clinging to the medallion, she scooped up Ana from the floor as Indi crawled in behind her, and she cried herself back to sleep.

Chapter Thirteen

M IA, DAYLOR, AND TILTON had been doing all they could to cover
for Thali, telling everyone she was sick. A healer came after two
days. Mia had faithfully brought both the animals' food and Thali's.
Her friends quietly spent time in her room or the common rooms,
whispering as they tried to figure out what had happened.

Thali barely ate. She barely spoke. She was barely responsive. Her
cheeks were streaked with tears, her eyes puffy and red. Thali didn't
want to do anything or see anyone. A sad quiet had settled on the forest
surrounding them. Thali hadn't said what had happened, but Mia knew
her well enough to guess.

After the eighth day, Thali had finally had enough of herself. Her heart
was broken in pieces, and they might not ever go back together again,
but this was not her. She was not the girl to be destroyed by a boy. So
she woke early the next morning, sneakily taking all her animals into
the forest. She went north to avoid *their* tree and started running. Her
tiger and dog were glad for the exercise, and their enthusiasm invigorated her. She came across a river, and without taking her clothes off,
ran right into it. She headed straight for the waterfall and widened her
stance, bracing herself as she stood beneath it.

Letting the pounding waters drown out the cries of her broken heart,
she sobbed and sobbed until she was empty. When her body shivered
uncontrollably from the cold, she walked back to her rooms.

When she walked in the door, Mia looked up and stepped back. She
opened her mouth, but Thali cut her off. "Mia, I'm sorry for the last
week. Thank you for being such a good friend." She hugged her, settled

her animals into her room, and changed before heading to weapons practice. Mia still stood in their common room gaping at Thali when she emerged from her room. Before Mia could ask hard questions, Thali said goodbye and left for combat practice. Ban pointed and snickered with his goonies when she showed up. After the terrible rumors Ban had spread about her last year, she tried to avoid him so she wouldn't be tempted to physically harm him. Today would be a good day to get into a fight. Alexius stepped in front of her as she turned her body toward Ban.

"And the lady resurfaces. Would you like to borrow my comb?" Alexius asked as he produced a comb from his sleeve.

"No, I meant to look like this," Thali said as she tried to comb her hair back with her fingers. Her anger flared.

"And here I was afraid your absence meant I'd intimidated you." Alexius flashed a wolfish grin in her direction.

Thali swallowed, gritted her teeth, and grabbed a wooden sword. "Never."

Alexius started sparring slowly, but Thali wanted to bury her feelings, so she increased the pace. He matched her and they were quickly lost in their footwork and the *clack, clack, clack* of their wooden swords. Thali hadn't noticed the class begin and only stopped when Alexius finally lowered his sword and bowed.

"Whatever illness you suffered from, it's really brought out the warrior in you," he remarked.

She was soaked through but happy for the reprieve from her broken heart. Thali smiled at the compliment, at the satisfaction her body felt in having moved and sweated.

Thereafter, she learned to bury her sadness by throwing herself into whatever physical work she could. In class, whenever she felt the first wave of despair, she'd go into the back of her mind and explore the threads of the animals in the forest. She monitored the world around her and pushed herself to search farther for the sparkling threads she'd seen leaving Star Island. At night though, the heartbreak was impossible to ignore. Then, she'd stare out the window in her room, letting sadness envelope her as she cried herself to sleep.

CHAPTER FOURTEEN

I T HAD BEEN WEEKS since she'd last written to Elric. She didn't know what to say to him. What could she say when she and Garen had been a secret? Thali felt like her whole world had crumbled to pieces, yet the whole world around her hadn't even noticed. And marry Elric? It was too much. So, Thali kept herself busy and ignored the letters she'd shoved to the bottom of her drawer.

One afternoon, a knock on her bedroom door startled Thali as she polished her daggers for the tenth time that day.

"Come in," she said. She expected to see Daylor or Tilton, who'd come to check on her every day.

A man in a walnut-brown leather cloak walked into her room and for a moment, her heart skipped a beat as she thought maybe it was Garen. Maybe he'd come to apologize and take her back, and maybe they would run away together to another country.

He flipped his hood back, and she was just as startled to see Prince Elric standing in her room.

"Your Highness!" Thali choked down her emotions.

"Thali, please, call me Elric." He smiled, but it was too bright, too shiny for her dreary world. Even his golden-blond hair and emerald eyes were too bright to fit in her world.

Indi and Ana nudged Elric, wanting their due affection while Thali tried to regain some composure.

"Elric, sorry. What are you doing here?" Thali brushed her dark hair out of her face and tried to pat down the nest on the back of her head, trying to shape it into some semblance of style—or at least tidiness.

"I was worried. I was in the area and figured I'd drop by. Thali, you haven't written back in three weeks! I was starting to wonder if the bats were being hunted down or something."

"I'm sorry, I've been ... busy," Thali said. She lowered her eyes to the table full of lined up blades she'd been cleaning.

"May I?" he gestured at the chair by her desk.

"Go ahead." Thali tried pulling the corner of her sheets over her bed to cover at least some of the mess.

"Thali, I know something's wrong. Won't you tell me? Please? I even wrote Mia, and she wouldn't tell me. You look like ... like your heart was—"

"I don't want to talk about it." Thali clenched her teeth. She was moments away from crying.

Elric looked at her, narrowed his eyes, then sighed. "Well then, we'll skip straight to the cheering-up part."

Thali looked at Elric. He hadn't probed her, hadn't asked her to divulge every detail like Mia had; he had just accepted that she didn't want to talk about it. "That would be nice."

"Then, m'lady, your chariot awaits! I took the liberty of getting your horse saddled for you."

Elric led her down to the horses and chattered away about his journey there before swinging himself up on his horse with one smooth motion. Arabelle, a chestnut mare with a white blaze and a white sock on her right hind leg, pressed her face into Thali, huffing a gentle sigh of comfort.

Indi and Ana danced from paw to paw with excitement.

"Ready?" Elric raised an eyebrow as Thali mounted.

"Where are we going?"

"You'll have to follow and find out, if you can catch me!" At that, Elric's horse took off with a mighty leap. Ana and Indi were in hot pursuit as Thali finally urged her mare on. Galloping through the forest invigorated her, and Thali appreciated it. They rode and rode, too fast for words, simply enjoying the scenery around them.

Thali and Elric rode until tears streamed out of their eyes from the wind and finally slowed to a walk as they made their way toward an inn.

"All right, now for event number two ..." Elric grinned. When they neared the inn, instead of riding up to it, they rode around it and into a courtyard just beyond it. There, two large wooden crates, each with a small spout sticking out of the bottom, stood on stilts.

Thali thought she'd seen these once before but couldn't remember precisely where. Her head was fuzzy from not sleeping at night. They dismounted and tied their horses to a nearby branch. Indi and Ana were all too pleased to lay in the shade resting now.

"Bardo will probably want to sit this one out, too." Elric motioned at Thali's left sleeve.

Enjoying the mystery, Thali let Bardo slip around the horn of her saddle and rest in the sun. Then, she rejoined Elric, who was removing his boots and rolling up his pant legs as high as he could get them. He motioned for her to do the same and though she thought it strange, she did.

"In the barrel you go. I think you'll know what to do once you see what's inside."

Elric cupped his hands to boost Thali into the barrel, but she deftly leaped and swung herself right into a barrel half-filled with fruit.

Grinning, Elric swung himself into the barrel and said, "I know you're sad, but trust me when I say this is fun. Just start stomping!"

They stomped and jumped, and Thali really got into it, releasing her anger and frustration and sadness and enjoying the strange feeling of the squishing fruit oozing juice all around her legs. By the end of it, they'd both fallen into their barrels twice and were completely covered in purple juice from the waist down.

Afterward, Elric motioned, and someone Thali hadn't noticed came over with bottles. Using the spout at the bottom of the barrels, he filled a bottle from each barrel.

"If you don't mind, I'll keep these, and when they're ready, we'll drink it!" Elric's beaming smile made Thali forget how sad she was and just enjoy the moment. "Now, onto event number three!"

Elric raced ahead of her, stuffed his boots into his saddlebag, and leaped onto his horse before racing down the path, leaving Thali to do the same and follow. She took an extra moment to secure Bardo in her sleeve though, leaving far behind Elric.

It wasn't long until they rode up to the edge of the river and his horse splashed in without hesitation; Thali's mare followed excitedly. Indi and Anna, getting caught up in the excitement, also jumped in before realizing it was cold and wet and paddled back to the bank to sit and watch from the safety of a sun-warmed rock. Indi even waited for Bardo to swim near and carried him the rest of the way on her head. They all rested in the sun then, those with paws licking them and letting the sun take care of the offensive dampness.

After splashing around on horseback, Thali and Elric let their horses graze on the bank and jumped back in to swim, fully clothed. It was a hot day, and after being dyed purple from the waist down, swimming was the perfect activity.

Thali dove under the water, swimming as far as her breath would take her and resurfaced with renewed energy, noticing Elric staring at her, head tilted. His turquoise eyes bore into her, making her feel uncomfortable, so she raised her hands and splashed him right in the face.

"Hey! That wasn't fair!" Elric retaliated and soon they were a sopping wet mess.

When they were finally out of breath, they climbed out of the river and onto the rock where Indi, Ana, and Bardo were stretched out, taking in the sun. Elric went to his saddlebags and tossed Thali a wrapped sandwich.

They ate in silence for a while, Thali fully enjoying the moment and awed at the effort the prince had put into their day. She could tell he was staring at her, but she didn't care. Thali finished her sandwich and stretched out, ready to take a nap in the sun as her clothes dried on her. Thankfully, Elric accommodated her.

As they rode back later that afternoon, Elric did all the talking. He talked about the things he had to do and learn and how the palace was split in their treatment of him now: Half treated him like a child and the other half treated him like their king already. He even regaled her with tales of gossip about people she didn't know. But Thali wasn't really listening. Finally, he fell into silence.

"Thank you." Thali took the opportunity his silence offered. She had been sad for so long and today was the first time she had experienced moments where she had truly forgotten her sadness.

"Anytime." Elric grinned, and Thali couldn't stop herself from smiling with him.

Chapter Fifteen

T HE DAY OF THE Welcome Ball crept up on Thali without her realizing it, consumed as she was in her despair. She had to go though because her father was a founding member of the school. The only bright side was that Daylor had asked to take her—or rather, announced it one morning as she had showed up to weapons practice.

"Thali, I'm wearing red, so please make sure you match me so we don't look foolish," Daylor had declared.

She was grateful he had taken it upon himself as she was still overwhelmed by sadness at times. Mia had snuck in two fittings, chattering away so Thali couldn't even get a word in. All she had known was that Mia was making her a scarlet gown with a train on the back. She hadn't given the whole matter any more thought.

Now, on the night of the ball, her animals paced her room anxiously as Thali fidgeted while Mia fastened the back of her dress.

"Ready! Look at the back!" The excitement oozed from Mia's voice.

Thali glanced at the mirror, then did a double take as she stared at the back of her dress. There, somehow, Mia had embroidered a black dragon whose head began between Thali's shoulder blades and wound down the back of the dress's train. The black contrasted so strongly against the red, it was impossible to look away.

Thali felt like she was wearing art. When she moved from side to side, the dragon looked like it moved, too.

"The face isn't quite right, but I don't have a clue what dragons look like."

"Mia, this is the most beautiful dress you've ever created!"

Mia grinned. "He whom we cannot name is going to be so jealous."

"He won't see it." Thali couldn't bring herself to say his name yet, and while she couldn't stop the pang of pain that lanced her heart, she was able to keep the waves of sadness at bay.

"Well, you'll be so busy dancing tonight, you won't even have time to think of anything else but the fun you're having."

Thali put her hands on her hips, a serious look on her face. "Mia, I don't understand why you dress so ordinarily while you make me this piece of art!"

"Thali, you're my best friend, and I wouldn't be here if it weren't for you. I never told you this, but I was supposed to marry Fitzy. My brother told me he was going to propose, and I had no reason to deny him. Fitzy's a good man, but I would have married, had children, and then been expected to do nothing more than cook and clean. Here ..." She spread her arms wide. "I get to learn and try and do the thing I love most." She grinned and added, "Plus, I like hearing people whisper, 'That Mia is a genius!'"

"Fitzy? Really? I guess he did always follow you around." Thali felt heat rise to her cheeks. She didn't like to think of the things that could separate her and Mia. "Are you sure you don't want to wear your own art?"

Mia shook her head. "No, Aron's wearing green anyway, so I like my dress plenty. Besides, I'm not a flashy sort of girl. You know me, I prefer subtle and understated."

"Well, thank you, Mia, truly. I'm honored." Thali made a promise to herself then to do everything in her power to make Mia's dreams come true. She didn't deserve Mia's steadfast friendship.

They hugged and left their rooms, cutting across the courtyard to the building housing the ballroom.

Garen

Garen sat on a rooftop in the dark, barely able to choke down the sob as he watched Thali, a vision in red, walk confidently by, a sight to behold in that stunning dress. His heart squeezed in a vise of his own making as he fought to stay still while the pain shot through him.

"Wow, you weren't kidding."

Garen spun around to find Joren standing nearby.

"Why Garen? You obviously love her. Why are you giving her up?"

"I can't explain. You know I can't reveal what the oracle told me personally. I'm just not right for her. She deserves better."

Joren laughed at the naked truth in that, but he saw the pain in his brother's face, so he changed the subject. "Anything I need to know?" Joren asked.

"Not that you haven't already learned." Garen swallowed his heartache and stood.

"Safe journey." Joren extended his arm, and they grasped elbows.

"Look after her. Let me know ... let me know if I can help her."

Joren thought of a clever remark but held his tongue at the torment in his brother's eyes. He nodded.

Garen slipped off the roof with Fletch, his second in command, slipped through town to the docks, and quietly boarded a ship bound for Joren's territory.

CHAPTER SIXTEEN

MIA LEFT THALI WITH the other founders' children in the hallway outside the ballroom and joined the rest of her friends at the ball.

"You look beautiful, Lady Routhalia. If there's anything I can get you, please let me know." Idris kept her company as they waited for their entrance. Thali nodded and smiled. It was kind of Isaia's brother to check in on her. She always felt alone now, even in the company of others.

The usher nodded to her, and she took a deep breath and walked through the double doors. Head high, she focused on the steps leading to the ballroom and tried not to trip as she descended. Thankfully, Mia had warned her that the stunned gasps would only come when she started to dance since she'd left the front unremarkable, so Thali wouldn't have to worry about that just yet. She was halfway down the steps before she looked for Daylor.

He stood at the bottom of the steps, clad in a red and black tunic with red trim, an encouraging smile filling his face. She smiled and continued down, counting the steps to her freedom from all the staring eyes. Suddenly, she felt everyone's gaze shift from her to the edge of the crowd. Following their gaze, she turned, and a familiar set of emerald-green eyes met hers. Prince Elric, clad completely in head-to-toe black stepped out of the crowd. He wore his usual infectious, wide smile and everyone dropped immediately into a bow or curtsy—including Thali, who forgot she was on a staircase and tripped down the last two steps.

Elric and Daylor caught each of her arms. She straightened and glanced between them. Daylor bowed his head and grinned as he melted back into the crowd. Elric nodded his thanks before Daylor turned to go and placed Thali's hand securely in the crook of his arm.

"What are you doing here?" Thali asked in a low whisper.

"I was in the area." Elric led her around the ballroom as gasps erupted from the crowd when everyone saw the back of her dress. "You are more breathtaking than I could have imagined, Lady Routhalia," Elric said.

Thali looked down at the floor as her cheeks flushed. "It's the dragon on the back. Mia really outdid herself." *Elric certainly had a strange knack for always 'being in the area,'* she thought.

"Oh?" Elric raised an eyebrow and moved away to twirl Thali so he could see the back of the dress.

When she faced him again, Elric had a glint in his eyes and a lopsided grin on his face. He scanned her expression.

"So, on a scale of one to ten, ten being happy as a child in a sweets shop, how have you been?"

Thali scrunched up her face, thinking. "Overall? Four. Right now? Seven."

He nodded. "Good enough."

Two dances came and went before Elric and Thali went to find refreshment. When they did, they joined Mia, Daylor, and Tilton. They all looked a little pale and nervous. Elric nodded to them and left in search of water.

"Mia, did you know he'd be here?" Thali asked.

"No! I swear!" She pulled Thali off to the side, away from Daylor and Tilton, who blocked them from most of the rest of the crowd.

"Thali, Tilton just told me something, but you can't be mad," Mia said, wringing her hands.

"What?" Thali noticed while Daylor and Tilton were within earshot, they were purposely looking elsewhere as they made their wall so she and Mia wouldn't be disturbed.

"The queen's crest before marriage was a dragon. It doesn't look quite like the one on the back of your dress, but ..." Mia started. She bit her lip.

"But what?!" Thali asked. She could see Elric returning with water.

"You didn't see the back of his coat, did you?"

Thali felt her stomach sink as she shook her head.

"It's a lion. A lion and a dragon—that's the royal crest. The two of you dancing looked like the royal crest floating around the ballroom," Mia finished quickly.

Thali stopped breathing for a second as Daylor and Tilton turned back to them. The last words of the oracle rang in her head.

"Well, whatever it looks like, I'm a little mad that he stole my date tonight!" Daylor piped in.

"My greatest apologies, Master Daylor. I hope you'll be able to forgive me?" Elric had chosen this moment to return and was right behind them.

Daylor blushed and mumbled as he bowed. "Of course, Your Highness."

"Miss Mia, you've really outdone yourself. This dress is beyond stunning." Elric grinned. "What a happy accident we match so well."

"Thank you, Your Highness." Mia curtsied.

"May I have the honor of this dance with a fashion genius?" Elric asked with a glance at Mia, who gently put her hand in his and curtsied.

"Thali, may I?" Daylor, recovered from his embarrassment, jumped in.

As Daylor led her through the crowd to the dance floor, Thali caught sight of Ban staring at her, a sneer on his face. He glanced quickly at Elric. She shoved his unpleasantness out of her mind. She was going to enjoy her night with friends.

Daylor and Tilton had taken her around the ballroom three times each before Thali escaped to the side with them to catch her breath.

"Masters Daylor, Tilton. Lady Routhalia." Alexius came out of nowhere and bowed. "These are strange dances and I've been watching to learn, but would you be so kind as to take pity on me and complete my education?" He offered his arm to Thali.

Alexius's red hair, bright against his dark-navy shirt and jacket—the latter with white piping—along with his navy and white tartan kilt made his green eyes stand out like a grassy island on the ocean.

"Of course," Thali curtsied, then accepted his arm out of politeness.

She didn't have to do much teaching as Alexius seemed to know all the steps. Of course, she knew he'd be a good dancer; he was, after all, her sparring partner. They moved fluidly together, and after all the hours spent together with weapons in their hands, their movements were more in sync than any other couple. While she still didn't trust that Alexius was who he said he was, she couldn't argue that he was the perfect dance partner for her. While she and Elric moved majestically together, she and Alexius moved like the waves in the ocean.

"I fear I'm not teaching you much of anything. You already know all the steps," Thali finally said.

"Steps, yes, but we're sparring partners. Our bodies know how to move around each other, and because yours knows this pattern so well, yours is teaching mine the subtleties. I'm forever grateful," Alexius replied.

At that, Thali focused for a while on Alexius's arms and body like she did in combat class. Then she turned off her brain and let the movement take over. Surely there was nothing to fear from him right now.

Elric

Elric stood to the side of the dance floor with Daylor for a time before he had to resume his duty of dancing with each young woman. He wanted a chance to get to know Thali's friends.

"They look like they know each other," Elric pointed out, raising an eyebrow as he watched the pair float gracefully around the dance floor as in sync as two dolphins skimming over the ocean waves.

Daylor snorted and said, "That's Alexius. They're sparring partners. If you think this is good, you should see them with swords."

After the music stopped, Alexius murmured something to Thali, bowed, and proceeded to ask another girl to dance. Thali made eye contact with Elric and made her way over.

"You've never mentioned Alexius in your letters before," Elric mentioned as he guided Thali back out to the ballroom floor.

"There's nothing to mention about him. He's my sparring partner. We're not even friends," Thali said.

"Really?" Elric eased back to look at her face.

"Really." The earnestness in Thali's face seemed to be enough for Elric. Surely he couldn't be jealous anyway? Of Alexius? Hardly.

Thali and her friends danced the rest of the evening away, Elric's eyes always following her as she moved about the room. In fact, everyone's gaze seemed to be on her, on them, all night. She had to admit they worked well together, though she didn't know how she felt about how they embodied the royal crest as they floated around the room. Somehow, she wasn't sure how—or why—things felt different between them.

To stop from delving too deep into that thought, she dove instead into enjoying the wonderful evening with her friends.

CHAPTER SEVENTEEN

G LOBAL CULTURE CLASS HAD moved into a turret this year. Thali thought it was appropriate since she always felt like she was trapped in a dungeon as she counted down the minutes to the end of this class. As everyone left the circular classroom today, Thali was the last to pack up her bag and walk through the tunnel that led to the next building. It had been raining all day, and she didn't want to get wet if she could avoid it. Suddenly, in the dark of the tunnel, a hand gently took hold of her elbow, and a second warm hand grasped her shoulder blade as if leading her onto a dance floor. A dagger was in her hands as she turned her head, ready to gut whoever had been bold enough to grab her. She was taken aback when she looked up into Joren's face. He wore a plain gray cloak, but she could still see his blindingly colorful outfit underneath, even in the weak light of the tunnel. Those familiar blue eyes from another face she so dearly loved made her falter.

"I need to talk to you," was all he murmured in her ear. Remembering that she wasn't in any danger and curious as to why this particular prince was not in his own kingdom, she let him guide her down a hidden hall she hadn't known about behind what she had thought was just a large pillar. She supposed she could have resisted, but Joren had never hinted at any ill-intention toward Thali. If anything, she was intrigued to find out more about a fellow magic wielder.

Joren finally stopped in a corner and sat Thali down on what she thought was probably an antique bench not meant to be sat on. He took an equally valuable seat across from her and stared hard at her, as if he was searching for something in Thali's expression. She had never seen him look so serious, and she started feeling uncomfortable despite his silly appearance.

"You know, I've been trying to figure out what's really going on between you and Garen. You obviously didn't have a falling out, but I don't understand why you are no longer his lover." He still had that intense stare, as if any twitch in her face would give him all the answers he was looking for.

"I don't really see how that's any of your business," Thali began carefully. She didn't want to relive the pain; she'd only just begun to learn to live with it.

His usual sardonic mask reappeared, replacing his seriousness, and his mouth quirked into a smirk. "I have ten times the riches Garen has and could have ten times the power …" Then, his smirk faltered for a moment, telling her this was some kind of test.

Her defenses went up; now it was Thali's turn to smirk. "I thought you were smarter than that Joren. I never wanted the riches before, so what makes you think I'd want them now?"

His face became serious once again as the seconds dragged on. "Did you know I saw you first?" The corner of his lips turned upward. "Years before Garen met you, I spotted you with your family. You were at the night market, and I followed you all the way to the fortune teller. The old man has mostly lost his touch, but after he sat with you, he told me you could be a very important person for our particular community."

Thali was now exceedingly uncomfortable. She didn't know where this conversation was going, and it sounded a lot like what the oracle had said. Joren was usually filled with fun, light-hearted, ridiculous flirtations. "Figures that he was part of the thieving community. I really should reconsider all the things I've done in the past."

Joren continued as if she hadn't said anything. "I tailed you, personally, for the rest of your trip, but I was called away the night you left, so I didn't have the chance to meet you. When Garen showed up with you, it took all I had to keep a straight face. Of all the people that I've ever met, watched, or heard of, I've never been so intrigued by anyone else."

Thali's smile faltered.

"When Garen renounced your romantic status, I tried to figure out why. He's not allowed to tell me what the oracle said, so I summoned the old man who read your fortune and asked if he could tell me anything else about you. Strangely, I only had to give him your handkerchief. He read from the handkerchief what the oracle had told Garen."

Thali's blood raced in her veins. Was anything a secret anymore? Thinking of Garen flooded her heart and burst every crack and fracture their break-up had caused. Her body slumped and Joren caught her arm as the pain refreshed. She fought just to breathe as the tears began.

"He surprises me. I didn't know he would be so affected by you. At the same time, it's his loss. I, on the other hand, don't want to be humiliated again at missing an opportunity. Would you do me the honor of being *my* partner?" He raised a challenging eyebrow, daring her to say yes.

"You should already know my answer," Thali choked out, swallowing back the tears in her eyes before they could fall.

"Well, let me propose the conditions. You see, the thieving world is my whole world, so I don't care if you have greater things to achieve in the rest of the world. I want you to affect mine. I'm willing to offer you absolutely anything for your hand in marriage, for a partnership with you."

"There's nothing you have that I want." Thali clenched her jaw. She was trying to keep the sadness in, and it was crashing against the walls of her composure.

"Are you sure about that?" Joren stood, pulling her up too.

Suddenly he wrapped his arm around Thali's waist, whispering in her ear as they swayed gently to silence. "I can offer you adventure, beautiful silks, teas, spices. I can offer you freedom. You can do whatever you want, anywhere in the world. Open a restaurant, own a building, build a wonder of the world. Only I have the resources for all that. You can even continue school, learn another trade, learn ten more trades. All I ask for is your sole dedication to my court. If you marry me, you can't marry Elric, so the prophecy might be null and void. You'll be free to make your own life."

"What makes you think Garen doesn't offer the same?" A lump appeared in Thali's throat as she struggled to hold her emotions at bay. "If I was going to take anyone's hand in marriage, it would be his. As much fun as it is to flirt with you, when have you ever seriously considered me? So stop mocking me and my pain." Thali turned her sadness into anger as she hurled the last words at Joren. She pushed away from him, but he held firm.

"I'm no fool. He released you to let you pursue other things because he recognized that you could—had to—do more for the rest of the world, and consequently ours. I'm offering you a way out of what will become something between a rock and a hard place." He held her in place with little space between them.

"You're lying. Garen loves me, and I love him. He has my best intentions at heart. I know it. That's the only reason he would have left me." Thali was about to crumble. She wanted to believe what she said, but she didn't sound convincing to her own ears.

"He may love you, but don't doubt that Garen still has his own ambitions. Just ask yourself this: what *can't* you do as his princess? He could have given you the opportunity to change the world from right here, at his side. But maybe he's sending you out as a scout for his own purposes. Maybe I've loved you since I first saw you, and out of respect for my brother, I never said anything. But now I can't stand by while he leads you into an impossible position when I have the opportunity to offer you a better one. Just think of how powerful we'd be together. Animals and plants at our command. We could do anything in this world."

"No, Joren. Just no." Thali's voice cracked as she turned away. Then silence fell. Thali closed her eyes to focus on her breathing.

"He's gone, you know. We traded territories," Joren said.

But after a brief hesitation, she only nodded. She backed up into the cool stone wall, using it to brace herself. It was a full minute before she opened her eyes and saw that Joren had melted into the shadows and disappeared.

Thali slid down the wall and sat on the ground in disbelief. She had always figured that Joren's ridiculous flirtations were part of some game he played, that his close relationship with Garen was what made him think kindly of her. But even as she thought out his proposition, the weight of what he had said about Garen started to sink in. She didn't know what to think anymore and slumped to the floor, laying prone and hiding in the dark corner, letting the tears roll down her cheeks.

Daylor

Daylor had been the one to find her hours later. He hadn't said anything, just wrapped his cloak around her, picked her up, and carried her quietly through the dimly lit hallways back to her room.

Tilton had run into Mia, who had told him about Thali, and now the four hunkered down in Thali's rooms to eat their supper. Mia and Daylor chattered on for a while, letting Thali be whatever she wanted to be while Tilton handed her his dessert.

Thali smiled weakly. Despite everything that had happened, she still had her friends. They didn't question her. They just accepted her. She never would have experienced this if she hadn't come to this school she hadn't even wanted to come to after her brother's death.

Later, Tilton and Mia went to inspect some new textiles in Mia's room, leaving Daylor and Thali to clean off their little wooden table after supper.

"Thali, I know we're not supposed to talk about it, but I want you to know we're all here for you. If you want to talk, we're here. I just wish I knew who the worm was. I'd pummel him into the ground for hurting you like he did."

Imagining Daylor meeting Garen made her smile. They seemed like two pieces of different puzzles on the same table.

"It's good to see that again." Daylor's bright smile made hers grow bigger.

"Thank you, Daylor. It ... it wasn't his fault," Thali said. This seemed to confuse him, but he kept his lips pressed together. Tilton walked back into the room and read it immediately.

"Thali, how does one brush a tiger?" He picked up a brush with remnants of orange fur in it on her table. Thali was glad for Tilton's tact at changing the subject. Indi jumped up onto the table as if ready for the attention, and Thali was happy to focus on something else as she explained how she went about it. Mia continued a sewing project while Thali, Tilton, and Daylor brushed out Indi and Ana until Tilton and Daylor decided it was time to head back to their own rooms. Thali went to bed thinking she was eternally grateful for supportive friends and their endless ability to distract her.

Chapter Eighteen

The next afternoon, Thali took Indi, Ana, and Bardo with her to the forest. Halfway through her run, she realized the forest was no longer safe. With Joren nearby, prince of this thieving territory now, she might as well have invited him along. She had just decided to turn around when a rustle in the bushes caught her attention. She hadn't sensed any threads leading from there and was surprised when Alexius walked out, bits of leaves and twigs in his hair and sticking to his navy tartan cloak.

"Forgive me, Lady Routhalia." He bowed.

"Forgive you for what?"

"For startling you. I was walking in the forest when your hound startled me, and I fell into the bush. I didn't mean to startle you in turn," he said.

Thali's eyes narrowed. Her animals hadn't warned her there was someone else here. They usually pinged their connected thread in her mind in warning.

Indi and Ana eyed Alexius suspiciously. Even Bardo poked his head out to see the red-haired stranger. They had been just as startled as she had. Indi stayed alert in front of her, on guard, while Ana slunk behind her.

"May I accompany you on your return?" Alexius asked.

Thali shook her head to clear it. "Yes, of course. Are you injured?"

"No, thankfully. I'll be in tip-top shape for tomorrow morning, don't you worry."

He grinned, again showing sharper than normal canines.

They started back up the path, and Thali remarked, "You're quite the warrior. Where did you train?" She tried to think of exactly why she didn't like Alexius. She just couldn't put her finger on why he made her suspicious.

"My family believes in the ways of a warrior. Where I come from, our people are few and far between, with great rivers or mountains and cliffs between. Everyone must know how to fight if only to defend their own home. I had a wooden staff in my hands as soon as I could hold one."

"Where exactly *are* you from?"

"They call it the Highlands here, but it's in the Northern West lands, more north than west." He matched her stride and replied calmly and openly.

"And why did you want to come here?"

"I have two brothers and a sister. I'm the youngest. If I'm lucky, I might end up as head of the guard in our lands, endlessly patrolling the territory. Coming here, learning this trade, is my opportunity to do something with my life. It's the freedom to see the world."

Thali laughed outright.

Surprise lit Alexius's face. "Did I say something funny?"

"Everyone has such fancy notions of being a merchant—and yes it's fun to see other lands—but you all forget the fortnight spent on a ship staring at nothing but the ocean to get to those lands."

Alexius bowed his head. "Of course." Then he looked at her, one eyebrow raised. "But is it worth it?"

"Absolutely," Thali said, smiling.

"Then that settles it. We're on the same side, Thali. Friends?"

Thali eyed him sideways. "Sure." She wasn't sure about Alexius at all yet but didn't want to insult him. Besides, maybe he'd feel comfortable enough to divulge more of who he really was if she kept up the guise of friendship.

"Now, would you tell me how a girl comes to keep company with a tiger, a hound, and a snake?"

Thali was surprised he'd seen Bardo, who was usually small enough to be missed. But this was a story she'd practiced often enough, and it rolled off her tongue smoothly. By the time she'd finished, they'd returned to her building. Surprisingly, Alexius took it all in stride; in fact, he didn't even question her further—which was odd in itself.

Thali still didn't know if she trusted Alexius; in some ways, he behaved as someone foreign to Adanek, but in other ways, he seemed to know more than he should. She couldn't put her finger on what it was that triggered her suspicion, but she kept it at the back of her mind. Both her father and Tariq had given her little information about him except to confirm that the Highlands were indeed filled with great warriors as the small families often went to war against each other. Her father had heard of a Lord Byron but didn't know much of his family beyond that they lived far inland. Tariq had no additional information at all. She wished with all her might that she still had Garen to talk to.

CHAPTER NINETEEN

E VER SINCE JOREN HAD taken over Garen's territory, Thali felt eyes and ears on her whenever she was near a plant. Now, she didn't feel as comfortable in the forest as she used to, and she'd even moved her tiny money tree to the common room.

Tonight, Mia was trying out a new clothing dye, and it had stunk up their rooms. Thali decided she didn't want to be around other people, so she climbed out her bedroom window onto the roof, leaving her animals to sleep in bed. It was late, the same time she usually used to meet Garen on the rooftop. Though her head told her he wouldn't be there, her heart held its breath as she pulled herself onto the roof and instinctively looked to where he used to wait for her, bread and cheese on a cloth laid out.

Thali's heart sank seeing it was empty. She sat down, chastising herself for hoping. She let a few tears roll down her cheeks as she stared up at the sky. Her heart was still shattered to pieces, but time was like the ocean, sometimes bringing waves of sadness, sometimes washing away the sharp edges. The pain didn't sting as badly anymore, and the waves of sadness were less frequent. She was grateful for Mia—she at least had known about Garen. Thali was amazed at how lucky she'd been to gain friends like Daylor, Tilton, and Elric, friends who accepted her without explanation. She'd finally even written Tariq to tell him that Garen was no longer in her life. She couldn't bring herself to explain more beyond that it wasn't meant to be, that Garen wanted better for her, no matter what she thought.

Oh Tariq, how I wish we lived nearer to each other, she couldn't help but think. At that moment, a bat entered her mind-thread's range, and she recognized it as the one she had sent to Tariq. She waited impatiently for its arrival.

Dear Lili,

Bree said there's no worse feeling than a broken heart, and if Rania's episode last year was any example, I hope his love for you was much greater than yours for him. As much as it may anger you, I am glad and grateful. It will cause you much less grief with your family if you love someone else.

Don't be mad at me, I'm just pointing out fact. You know deep down it rings true.

I'm also glad I don't have to set off on a bone-breaking quest for your honor. You can at least be comforted by the fact that he did love you enough to want more for you than he could give. He's now given you the world, after all.

As for this Alexius of the Highlands, son of Lord Byron, your father definitely knows more than island-bound me. Doesn't he have family in that area? I haven't unearthed anything more about him or his family, I'm sorry to say. But you must have gone soft since I saw you last to be challenged by someone so easily! I've sent along a page of drills I've newly developed for you. Make sure you master them with staff, sword, and scythe.

Yours, Tari

By the way, Bree is sending along some goodies she says will make you feel better, but they'll be arriving a little later. Poor bat who has to carry them.

Thali didn't know if it made her feel better or worse to hear Tariq's council. Her hand fell to her waist pocket as she thought, her fingers running circles around the medallion Garen had given her, her thumbnail tracing the engraved symbol.

She absentmindedly searched the threads around her, trying to reach a bat carrying something heavy. As she stretched her mind to the east, a brief glimmer to the north caught her attention. She tried to sort through the threads and pick out the one that had shimmered, but it disappeared. It had been no more than a flash of sparkly lightning in her brain.

Thali closed her eyes, picturing the shimmery thread, hoping to call it forward or toward her. She could feel her strength leaking away, but she pushed on, trying to follow any sparkle she could find. She could almost see a rainbow of translucent threads before a sharp pain in her arm snapped her back to her body.

Thali shook her head to clear it, blinking her eyes to focus on Joren, dressed as a dirty beggar, kneeling next to her.

"You really need to hone your skills." He panted in between breaths at the energy he'd exerted climbing to the roof and connecting with the vine's thread.

She looked down to see her arm wrapped in a thorny vine, blood seeping from the sleeve of her forearm. As she watched, the vine unraveled and melted back down the building into the shadows. "Was that really necessary?" Thali wiped at the blood and took deep breaths to calm her racing heart.

"You're going to kill yourself. You need to practice," Joren said more firmly now that his breathing had eased.

Thali pulled her sleeve up to inspect the damage, then rolled it back down. "Sure, I'll just enroll in a magical communication with animals class tomorrow morning." She was in no mood for company, let alone a lecture.

"You're still a member of our court. It'd be a real hassle if you died. Garen would be in hot water and suspect number one."

The pang hit her unprotected heart. Thali swallowed hard, nausea from overextending herself threatening to make an appearance.

"You and I will practice. In the forest, this time, every week. Understood?" Joren ordered.

"Why are you helping me?" Thali asked. After days of contemplation, she had finally realized that Joren's last proposal had been contrived. He'd been getting information in the most subtle yet indelicate way he could, and while she could understand his desire to protect his family, she was still mad at how he'd gone about it. It had nearly shattered what was left of her strength.

"You're family now. You could be more powerful than me. I don't like to be interrupted while I work. Take your pick." Joren sat down on the roof. It was simultaneously eerily similar yet so different to when Garen had occupied the same spot.

"So you do have plants watching me."

"They don't have eyes," Joren said.

"Keeping track of me then," she said.

"Something you could do even more easily than I with animals, if you practiced," Joren countered.

"Fine. Where in the forest?"

"Anywhere. I'll find you."

Thali rolled her eyes. She was done with this conversation. She tried to stand only to have her legs give out. Thankfully, Joren jumped up and caught her before she could fall off the roof. "I know, I know. I need to practice." Thali sat then—but only because she didn't have the strength to get up.

Joren reached down and wrapped his arm around her middle, and she smacked his shoulder as she ducked out of his grasp.

"Fine, sleep on the roof if you prefer." Joren crossed his arms as he stood back. The universe obviously sided with him because just then, it started to rain.

Thali barely had the energy to pull her knees up. "I'm sorry. Will you please help me back to my room?" She sighed.

Joren narrowed his eyes at her as if deciding whether it was worth leaving her out in the cold. Thali waited quietly, her hair and clothes already soaking wet. Then, he shook his head and picked her up like she was a child's doll, at the same time grabbing a tiny parcel that a bat had dropped next to her as he stepped off the roof onto a tree root that descended slowly to her bedroom window.

"If you need me, hang something on this vine." He nodded to the corner of her window where a tendril of a plant crept up the window frame.

Thali countered. She at least had enough strength to call a nearby bat. "I can send a message with a bat. See?" She nodded at the bat on the windowsill.

Joren placed her in her bed, much to Indi and Ana's annoyance. They growled in both welcome and warning as they crouched in the corner. Thali pacified them, then held Joren's hand open. The bat came and sat on his hand and licked his palm before taking off.

"As intriguing as this is, have you ever recruited ants?" Joren asked.

"Why? They'd take forever to get anywhere."

"And what if they're telepathic within their colony? What if you could send a message anywhere there's an ant, which is virtually anywhere?"

"What? Really?" Thali asked, excitement filling her eyes.

"You really need to practice. Pay more attention to each species. The more you know about them, and the limits of your own abilities with each, the more you'll have control of your gift, and the more you'll be able to do with subtlety." Joren dusted his hands off, though more dirt came off his beggar's disguise than his hands.

"Thank you, Joren." Thali stretched out, and to her surprise, fell asleep. Joren let himself out.

Joren

The root deposited him back down on the ground, and Joren took the long way back to his hovel. He'd been watching the darker alleys as a beggar when the vibrations on Thali's line—through the energy of the trees and plants around her—had gone dead. Garen would kill him slowly and painfully if anything happened to her. So, he'd had to interrupt his work to wake her.

Thali intrigued him. Though she was annoyingly naive, he wanted to hone her skills so he knew exactly what he was dealing with. She'd be a powerful weapon. And he wanted her on his side. It would take more coddling than he liked, but he sensed a shift in the world and wanted to prepare himself. An army of animals and plants could be useful, very useful indeed.

Chapter Twenty

T HALI WOKE THE NEXT morning feeling like she'd been run over by a herd of horses. The smell hit her nose before she opened her eyes.

Mia stood over her with the wretched energy-restoring tea her mother had sent. It made her stomach turn, but given the effort it took for Thali to sit up—Indi had to push to help—she knew she'd have to drink it.

"How did you know?" Thali croaked.

Putting the cup in her hands, Mia, her brassy-brown hair still mussed, answered sleepily, "Bardo woke me by landing on my face, then he rolled the tin to me. So I guessed."

"Thank you." Thali pinched her nose and chugged the black tea without letting it touch her tongue.

Breathing slowly, she let it settle in her stomach. Mia's eyes narrowed as she handed Thali another cup from a tray on Thali's desk. "How did you get home in that condition?"

Thali chugged the second cup like the first, popping a sugar cube on her tongue that Mia had proffered to help keep it all down. She didn't know what she could tell Mia, what might put her in danger.

"I don't remember," Thali lied.

Mia narrowed her eyes even further as she crossed her arms. It was clear she knew it was a lie, but she didn't push Thali. She never did. "Well, I'm just grateful you have other friends," she said.

Thali tried to keep her face unreadable. She really wanted to tell Mia everything, but she couldn't. Not yet anyway.

"You have an hour before combat class," Mia said curtly as she picked up the empty teacups and turned to the door.

"Thank you, Mia. I'm sorry to worry you. And I'm sorry I can't tell you everything."

Over her shoulder Mia sighed and said, "I'm here for you, Thali. Just tell me, was it Garen?"

Thali shook her head, unable to say his name. "He left the kingdom."

"Probably for the better." Mia left the room then, leaving Thali alone. As she looked over at the tray, she noticed the sadness that usually paralyzed her in the morning was a little less sharp. She grabbed a piece of bread and ate it slowly, concentrating on settling the contents of her stomach instead of what her heart was feeling. The wrapped package from Bree on her bedside table called to her and she opened it. After discovering its contents, she squealed and popped a squishy, sugary candy she found within into her mouth and hid the box in her drawer under some tunics.

After splashing cold water on her face, Thali dragged herself to combat class. What she wouldn't do for a cup of coffee at this moment. Just the thought of it perked her up a little bit.

"Good morning, Thali," Alexius said, far too energetically for her liking, as he joined her as she sluggishly walked down the hill to the practice area.

"Morning, Alexius," Thali managed as politely as she could.

"I was wondering if you'd like some coffee?" Alexius reached into his bag and presented her with a small warm flask.

Thali stopped dead. "Is that real?" Without thinking, she grabbed it from Alexius, opening it and breathing in the aroma of delicious coffee. She took a sip from the flask, closing her eyes and enjoying the feel of it sliding down her throat before she opened her eyes to see a surprised but inquisitive Alexius staring at her.

Thali gave him a weak smile. "You are officially my favorite person this moment. How do you have coffee?"

"My sister knows someone who grows it. She sends me some occasionally. I love the taste."

"Oh! Cheers to your sister." Thali took another longer sip of the warm liquid and shivered as it slid down her throat and warmed her body.

"I assumed you'd have as much coffee as you wanted," Alexius said. "With your family and all."

Thali shook her head. "My father insulted a coffee farmer in the south when he was young, so his relationship with them isn't all that friendly. But it's one of my favorite beverages. My parents don't care for it much, so they never cared to mend their relations with the coffee farmers in those lands."

"Oh. Well, I can probably get you some."

Thali closed her eyes again as she took another sip of liquid heaven. After a moment's appreciation, she said, "Alexius, I'm very glad we're friends." She still had questions, but in this moment, she didn't care. She took one more sip before she handed the flask back to him as they continued walking to combat class.

Alexius waved his hand. "Please, you look like you need it more. I wouldn't dare separate you and coffee right now."

Thali smiled and clutched the flask with both hands as she took another sip. By the time they arrived at the combat field, she felt a little more herself. Enough to get through sparring with Alexius.

"Mornin' merchants!" Master Aloysius called out. "Today, we'll be workin' with some different weapons."

Thali perked up even more, curious about the change of events. Master Aloysius brought out a scythe, and Thali was excited but surprised that he would start them off with a scythe right away.

"This 'ere's a scythe. It's used quite commonly in many parts of the world and was originally used as a tool for farmin'. We'll be buildin' up to them, but fer now we're changin' our swords to staffs. Staffs are much more commonplace in the world than swords anyway. The strength in a staff comes from its versatility."

Master Aloysius passed Thali and Alexius each a staff.

"Isn't the staff your weapon of choice?" Thali asked Alexius.

"First thing in my hands before I could walk," Alexius said.

She'd never sparred with a staff against Alexius and looked forward to seeing how his moves differed from the ones she'd learned. She held her staff at the ready. Alexius stalked around her as they began. They started slowly, probing each other, watching each other's movements. Alexius always seemed to move slower than he probably could even though Thali sometimes struggled to keep up.

Thali matched Alexius's grin right before his staff swept up from the ground toward her knees. She planted her own staff to block its movement while stepping back, following through, and bringing the other end of her staff toward Alexius's head. He in turn swept his all the way up to block Thali's downward stroke. While he had both hands on the staff above his head, Thali quickly changed course to sweep the staff up between his legs. He moved his staff quickly to block, then swung it to one side to sweep Thali off her feet. She jumped lightly to avoid being hit in the shins. They grinned as they picked up the pace and forgot all about the other students now getting basic instructions from Master Aloysius.

Combat class flew by in a whir of steps and sticks. By the end of it, Alexius and Thali were drenched in sweat as they said their goodbyes before heading to their different classes. Thali felt almost normal again as she joined Daylor and Tilton on their walk to the turret room for

Global Culture. This was exactly what she had needed—this and the coffee, of course.

CHAPTER TWENTY-ONE

T HIS AFTERNOON, ALL THE merchant students were on The Deck learning all the ways to swing the sails depending on what the wind was doing and what direction they wanted to go in. The only problem was since The Deck was a ship built into the ground from the deck up for training purposes, the wind moved around it instead of moving the ship into the wind as it should have.

"We'll be moving a lot faster when we're actually on the ocean," Thali grumbled. She ran her fingers along the wooden rails. Even two years in, she still couldn't reconcile their smooth feeling with the weather-worn rails of real ships. It was painful to watch her classmates struggle with the ropes and swinging sails. Kesla and Meelo, the new first years joining their ship with Alexius, would have been decapitated on the open sea from moving so slowly already, Ban would have been launched overboard from the wind, and even one of the third years, Seth, would have lost the sail and flown away like a bird.

Master Caspar yelled instructions this way and that as Thali fulfilled her job of keeping watch in the fake crow's nest. At least she could watch from a safe spot, she supposed.

From her vantage point, she could see the fields around the school, the different buildings, and even the combat field with its little dots doing practice drills. The Deck was a model version of a real merchanting ship from the deck up located at the edge of the school grounds. Behind it, a forest led to more forest. To the northwest was the lake where students like to swim and where she taught Daylor whenever they had free time. And to the southeast were her rooms and the part of the forest she liked to run in with Indi and Ana.

Thali thought she saw something approaching from the forest in the north then, like a shadow behind them. She only saw flapping wings and then a shimmer at the treeline before the shadow disappeared. Quickly searching her threads, she found nothing unusual, only the usual birds and animals. Her threads only connected to those normal animal ones. She looked to the edge of the forest where she'd seen the shimmer, squinting, trying to see it again. Thali was so caught up in trying to figure out where that shimmer had come from, she startled when Alexius popped his head up to the crow's nest.

"Hey Thali, time to switch. You're on mast ties."

"Oh, thanks, Alexius." She pointed and squinted again. "Did you see anything odd over there in the forest?"

Alexius squinted and looked where she pointed. "No, I didn't. Maybe you should drink more water? Coffee dehydrates you, you know."

Thali started to climb down from the crow's nest with ease. "Right."

Taking one last look at the forest's edge as she climbed down, she shook her head when she saw nothing and turned her attention to the task at hand. As she neared the ground, she had to concentrate on not being hit in the face with a rope while her classmates struggled with their tasks.

At the end of the day, Thali was still wondering about that shimmer at the edge of the forest when she saw a leaf sticking out of the crack between the window and the windowsill.

Roof tonight. Not forest. Don't go in the forest.

It was strange for Joren to prefer meeting on the roof. Their first training session together hadn't been very exciting; it had mainly consisted of Thali trying to reach further and further out and noting the actual distances before the prick of a thorn brought her back.

This would be their second training session, and she hoped Joren had something better planned. She didn't like being a pincushion for roses. Climbing up onto the roof, she discovered Joren was waiting in the shadows in a cloak, looking unusually stealthy in all dark clothing in place of his usual colorful outfits.

"People have been going missing in the forest," he said without preamble.

"What?" Thali asked.

"At first, I thought it was bandits getting out of control. But today is the second time someone's gone missing, and I haven't heard anything from my people. I've put pressure on them, and no one is moving without my knowledge. But something is out there. All I know right now is that it's not human and it's making people disappear."

"You think it's an animal?"

"I was hoping you could tell me that." He raised an eyebrow.

Thali sighed. She sat down cross-legged and closed her eyes to reach out into the forest. She tried to see all the threads she could and scan them for any kind of fear. Eventually, she found a handful of fearful animals just beyond The Deck.

"This afternoon, I was on The Deck, in the crow's nest, and I thought I saw something shimmering. But it disappeared. And now, all I can see is that the animals are fearful. Even the nocturnal ones are hiding tonight."

Joren sat down beside her. "Let me see what I can find."

Thali opened her eyes to watch Joren work his own gifts. He didn't even have to close his eyes as he looked in the direction of The Deck and the forests beyond it.

"Something large is moving around in there. There are lots of branches and vines being pushed away. Can you see what it is?"

"What kind of large? Like a bear?"

"No. Bigger. It's being quite gentle. Gentler than most animals. It hasn't broken any twigs or branches as it moves."

Thali closed her eyes, searching for any thread that was different from the others. She even looked through the eyes of flying birds nearby. With their help, she saw something immense moving through, about the size of an elephant, rustling the trees and bushes. She asked a small squirrel to climb nearby and watch the path Thali assumed this large creature would take. But when she tried to see through the squirrel's eyes, all she saw was blank space. She stared for a few minutes when she suddenly saw a shimmer in the forest as branches bent gently out of the unseen creature's way.

"What are you doing now?" Joren asked.

"Watching through a squirrel's eyes. It—the thing—shimmered. Just like this afternoon. I swear, there's something we're not seeing. It moved the branches aside like it was a big animal pushing through the trees, but all I saw was the shimmer in the forest, right where the branches were being pushed aside. I can't find a thread either. So, I'm asking a bat to help. They don't see like we do. They use sound bouncing back to them to see shapes and distances."

Joren trailed the creature's path by feeling the plants moving aside while Thali joined a bat's thread as he flew over that area of the forest. It sent out his sound waves to try and see the creature as he got closer, but still, all she and the bat could see was that the creature was enormous. The bat was still too far away to see its outlines clearly. Then, all of a sudden, the creature disappeared.

"It's gone. Joren, do you feel it still?"

"No, it ... I think it shrank, and now I can't tell where it went," Joren said. They faced each other. "What do you think it was?"

"I don't know. It didn't have a unique thread like animals usually do. All I know is that it's big. I'm trying to think of all the animals I know of that are that size." Thali mentally scrolled through all the animals she'd ever seen.

"That's not what's been making people disappear," Joren muttered under his breath.

"Why do you think that?"

"Because it didn't break a single branch." Joren tilted his chin as if he was listening to something else.

"So you think because it was gentle enough not to break branches, it wouldn't have eaten people?" Thali asked.

Joren nodded. His expression changed and Thali could see that was the end of the conversation. She had a million questions, but she knew Joren well enough to know he would not answer. So, she withheld her questions for another time—for now. Instead, she moved on. "So, what are we learning today?"

"We tested your distance last time. Now I want to test your strength with multiple animals."

"So ..."

"Does it affect your energy whether you follow a small or large creature?"

"No, it's pretty much the same. Each creature uses about the same amount."

"And what about more than one of the same animal? Do they take more energy?"

Thali shrugged. "Not really. Social ones like ants or bees look generally like a clump of the same color. It takes a little more effort to separate them, but I can also see them as a whole."

"Find an ant colony then. I want you to observe as many as you can."

Thali found she could keep track of about twenty at one time. Then, Joren asked her to try and keep track of different animals simultaneously, again as many as she could. With that, too, she found she was limited to about twenty depending on how far apart they were. Ones that would fly further and further away from her and each other took more energy than a cluster in the same area.

"Now, how many can you influence at the same time? Ask as many as you can to step on a root or leaf on that hill." Joren pointed to a small rise in the distance to the east.

Doing as he bid, Thali bid farewell to the twenty or so airborne animals she was connected to and switched to the land animals on the hill to the east. She sent them an image of a leaf or root and the desire to step on it.

"Interesting. That was thirty of them," Joren said.

She sent them on their way with thanks then, retreating from the threads and panting as she opened her eyes and turned to look at Joren.

"What is the most you've ever asked of one?" he asked.

Thali looked down at her hands, suddenly finding her fingers very interesting. "When I was six, my brother and I went fishing. He got frustrated that he couldn't catch anything, so he asked me to get one to swim into his net. I could feel the fear in the fish as he swam toward something he knew he shouldn't. I told my brother that it didn't want to, but he convinced me that if we didn't get this fish, we would go hungry that night because it was up to us to bring a fish home for supper. So, I went through that thread and made the fish swim into the net. He told me to put my wall up before he killed it, but I never forgot the fear the fish felt when I took over. I promised myself I'd never force them to do anything anymore. I ask. But I don't force." Thali shuddered at the memory.

"Did he ever ask again?" Joren's voice had softened.

Thali grinned. "No. I got Indi shortly after that. He couldn't force me to do anything with Indi around."

Joren chuckled and rose. "Work on how many you can observe at one time this week. And stay out of the deep forests until we figure out what's going on." He turned to leave.

"Joren?" Thali asked. Joren paused but didn't turn around.

"How's ... your brother?" Thali asked carefully.

Joren grinned. "Which one?"

Thali narrowed her eyes. "You know which one."

"He's well." With that, Joren disappeared into the shadows as he slid down a root he'd called up.

Thali stayed on the rooftop for a long time, wrapping her arms around her knees and gazing up at the stars around her. She wondered whether Garen could see the same stars where he was. A little piece of her noticed the ache in her heart was a little more bearable when she thought of him now.

Chapter Twenty-Two

T HE NEXT MORNING, THALI woke to a giant tiger sneeze. As she wiped her face of tiger snot and shoved Indi to the side, a fresh, earthy smell wafted into her nostrils.

She stretched off the night's sleep as it dawned on her that the smell of flowers wasn't just from her dreams. She swung her legs out of bed and changed into simple black pants, a loose linen shirt, and a matching vest before opening her common room door, only to be blinded by a field of sunflowers. There were sunflowers in vases on every available surface of their common room.

"MIA!"

A couple thumps later, Mia's door, across from Thali's, opened, and her best friend's eyes grew wide before she rubbed them and looked at Thali. "Happy birthday?"

They stared at the field of sunflowers, formerly known as their common room. Mia started to shift some around to try to clear a path, but it was hopeless. A sound at the window caught Thali's attention as a bat flew through the open window straight to Thali's arm. She took the roll of parchment from him before sending him off and thanking him.

HAPPY BIRTHDAY!

She recognized the handwriting as Elric's and felt her cheeks burn at the realization that he'd remembered their conversation in the palace garden when she'd last visited. He had been showing her the garden and all the fancy flowers—most of which she'd seen before—that had been gifts from many visiting diplomats. She'd stopped to smile at the sunflowers because to her they just looked so happy and sunny like they had a big smile on their face. They had reminded her of Elric himself. He was always so happy to see her and always had a big smile for her.

"Thali, you're blushing." Mia pointed out the obvious as Thali bit her bottom lip to stop herself from smiling.

Behind her, Ana whined, looking between Thali's legs at the impassable common room and doing a little dance that meant she had to relieve herself. It took Mia and Thali almost twenty minutes to clear enough of a path that they could get out the door. After guiding her animals outside and waiting for them to relieve themselves, Thali stopped by the kitchens to pick up her animals' meat allowance and returned to her rooms. Then she got Indi and Ana fed and settled in her room—she'd let Bardo hunt later—before she packed up her books, fabric swatches for Goods class, and a charted course to Densria for her Sailing class carefully into her bag. Just as she was almost ready to head to class, she heard a knock at the door.

"Come in!" Thali yelled.

"Happy birthday, Thali!" chorused Daylor and Tilton as they swung the door open, only to exclaim, "Holy rat turds!"

Stifling a laugh, she shoved the last book in her bag and patted Indi, Ana, and Bardo before tiptoeing her way back to the door.

"Elric?" Daylor asked.

Thali nodded as she took one more look at the field of sunflowers and closed the door, smiling like a fool. Daylor and Tilton escorted her to Combat class, chattering about who was coming to celebrate her birthday when they turned the corner outside the building and stopped dead. Except for a small rectangle of dirt, the entire field was filled with yellow sunflowers.

"Wow," was all Thali could say as her grin grew wider. She felt the heat rise to her cheeks and then all the way to the top of her ears. She didn't like being the center of attention, but to think someone had gone to all this effort for her ...

"I sure hope he didn't get your favorite flower wrong," Daylor said.

Thankfully, there was a clear pathway to the practice field. News of who the flowers were for and why spread quickly among her classmates. Master Aloysius stomped his way through the flowers and yelled at them all to start practicing. He sneezed with every other step. Apparently, sunflowers were not Master Aloysius's favorite flower.

Alexius grinned. "Just because it's your birthday, don't think I'll go easy on you today."

"I'd be insulted if you did," Thali replied. Somehow, being surrounded by all these sunny flowers gave her extra enthusiasm, and it showed in the extra vigor she put into her sparring.

When she and Alexius heard the bells, they dropped their staffs, and Alexius ran over to his bag. He hurried back with a wrapped package for Thali.

"Happy birthday." He smiled as he handed her the oiled canvas bag. As soon as it was in her hands, she could smell the coffee.

"Oh, thank you!" She threw out her arms to hug him, as sweaty as they both were.

"You're very welcome, Lady Routhalia."

"Hey, Thali! Would you believe we don't have any classes for the rest of the day?!" Daylor shouted from the edge of the field.

All the students gathered as Seth, a third-year student, explained. "Masters Brown, Caspar, and Kelcian are all sick. Master Brown is at the healers with food poisoning, and Masters Caspar and Kelcian got itching powder mixed in with their clothes and are completely covered in a rash."

All the merchant students burst into laughter. Thali couldn't help but smile even wider. She had a feeling this was a special gift for her from someone especially good at disguise.

"Anyone want to go swimming?" she asked.

They all cheered and headed up the hill to the lake. As they jumped in—Daylor finally being competent enough for Thali not to have to worry—Thali couldn't imagine a better way to spend her birthday. She had been sad to hear her parents would be at sea today, but that had been the way since she was little.

As she lay on the grassy bank later, drying in the sun, she enjoyed listening to all her friends splashing about the lake, the laughter and the taunting. It was the first time she had been in the same place for two birthdays.

She absentmindedly checked in on all the threads, noticing they were a lot quieter than usual for a sunny afternoon. She didn't have time to think about it though as she was interrupted by someone plunking down next to her. She opened her eyes to see her new red-headed friend sitting down next to her.

"Having a good birthday, Lady Routhalia?" Alexius asked.

"This is definitely better than sitting inside in class," Thali said.

"I can agree with that wholeheartedly. Though I do appreciate the education being handed to me instead of having to learn it through experience." Alexius leaned back on his elbows and watched the others in the lake.

"I suppose that's very true," Thali said.

"Thali, Alexius, get back in here! You're on my team!" Daylor shouted at them as the students started to separate into two teams.

They shrugged and launched themselves into the water to join the others. Half the students climbed on the others' shoulders, and they tossed a ball made of woven grasses back and forth, trying to get it to one of two blankets to the right and left of the lake as they played close to shore.

Late in the afternoon, they headed back to their buildings. While Thali had been gone, Mia had managed to stuff some of the sunflowers into the same pots, consolidating them and making a wider pathway through the room to each of their bedrooms. Once in her own room, Thali found a box from Mia and a leaf waiting for her on her desk. Text made yellow from its dying cells almost glowed on the rich green leaf.

I thought I told you NOT to go into the forest!

Thali looked at the leaf more carefully. Joren had so much control, he could make only certain parts of the leaf yellow to write a sentence! *Incredible*, she thought.

She scoffed before remembering how quiet the forest animals had seemed when she had looked for them. Maybe she should mention it to Joren.

Unsettled, she decided to take a look in the box on her bed to distract herself. Inside, Thali found Mia had made her a corset vest, intricately stitched silver animal shapes delicately swirling all over the leather and silver thread decorating the hems. It was the most beautiful thing Thali had ever seen.

She immediately tried it on, knowing full well that Mia would have intended it to be worn on top of a dress but too excited not to see what it looked like on.

"Mia! Can you come give me a hand?"

Mia appeared in the doorway seconds later. Giving Thali a big hug, she said, "Happy birthday again! You were so quiet when you came in! I didn't even hear you."

"You wouldn't hear an elephant over that machine you've been working with!"

Mia chuckled. "True. You know, this is supposed to go over a dress, right?" she pointed out as she started lacing up the back.

"I know, but it's so beautiful! I just couldn't wait to try it on. Thank you! I can't imagine how much work it took!"

Mia grinned, finished tying up the back, and walked around Thali to judge the look from the front. "You know, I think I like it better like this." She nodded her head at the fit.

"Me too."

Thali and Mia jumped at the words. Elric stood in the doorway, grinning. Thali glanced over her shoulder and glared at Indi and Ana on the bed for not having warned her but quickly turned her attention back to the prince standing in her doorway. "Elric! What are you doing here?"

"You know, I told them to fill the room to overflowing, but I think they could have fit more sunflowers in here." He glanced back at their common room.

"No!" Thali and Mia shouted together.

"I'm sorry, Your Highness, but it took us forever just to clear a path out of the room!" Mia gave Elric a quick curtsy before leaving the room.

"Ah, I never thought about that. My apologies," Elric said as Mia hurried from the room. Taking Mia's place, he was quick to grab Thali's hand and bow low over it, brushing his lips over the top of her hand. "Lady Routhalia, I would be honored if you would allow me to escort you to your birthday party."

Playing along, Thali curtsied and replied, "Of course, Your Highness."

They smiled at the playacting before Elric swept Thali up in a hug. "You look more beautiful today than I remember from my dreams," he said.

Thali giggled in response. His princely charm was just too much sometimes.

"So, did you like the flowers?" Elric offered his elbow.

"I did, but I'm pretty sure Master Aloysius wasn't pleased. Did you know he's allergic?"

"Oh? I will have to send my apologies. Shall we?"

"We shall." Thali paused as she waved to Indi, Ana, and Bardo. Her classmates were finally approaching her outside when she was with them, but they plastered themselves to the wall in the halls or ran away if they encountered the tiger, dog and snake inside. She wished her animals could come, but for her classmates sake, she left them in her room. She would be back soon. Thali hooked her arm through Elric's, and they started down the pathway through the sunflowers in the common room. Thali stopped and knocked on Mia's door.

"I'll be there in a bit!" Mia shouted from her room as the loud clacking of her machine started up again.

CHAPTER TWENTY-THREE

D AYLOR AND TILTON HAD gotten lucky and shared the most spacious common room among second-year students. Because of that, they had managed to convince Thali to let them host her birthday party weeks ago—just their small group of friends though, so they had said. But when Thali showed up with Elric and they weren't surprised to see him, Thali knew he must have warned them. That was Elric, always thinking about others.

When Elric and Thali walked in, all her friends shouted, "Happy birthday!" Thali had to let go of Elric's arm to hug every single person in the room as they rushed over to her. Amid all the bright gauzy pinks, yellows, and oranges draped around the room, turning the cold stone walls into a warm and intimate setting for their little soiree, she was surprised to see most of her merchant classmates, and even a few from the year above and a couple first-years. She even spotted Alexius by the window chatting up another first-year.

Daylor grasped her elbow then and steered her toward a cushioned chair set up before a space that had been cleared of people and furniture. After seeing Thali seated, he backed up into the open space and cleared his throat so everyone would quiet down. When they did, he asked, "Ladies and gentlemen, what does one offer the princess of merchanting herself? We have no wares that we could have possibly scraped together to pass her scrutiny, so we decided to offer instead a night of unforgettable memories!"

Elric sat on the floor, arms draped around a knee, next to Thali's chair, and Thali raised an eyebrow at the mischievous smile on Daylor's face as he said, "So, let the show begin!"

Daylor ran behind a curtained-off area she hadn't noticed earlier, while Tilton came out and produced three balls from his pocket.

To her astonishment, he started juggling them, and a moment later, he took another ball out of his pocket while the other hand continued to juggle the three balls. Before Thali could blink, he had eight balls soaring rhythmically in an arc that almost brushed the ceiling. Then, he caught all eight to rousing applause before putting all but two in his pockets. As he restarted with the two, he outstretched his left arm, palm up, and the recently arrived Mia handed him a bolt of cloth, which he added to his rotation. A few seconds later, he stuck his left hand out again, and Mia handed him a wooden ship figurine Thali recognized from Master Brown's class. Thali smiled in awe as he added a horseshoe to the mix and managed to juggle these objects with the two balls as if they all weighed the same.

When he finally caught all the objects, the audience broke out into applause, with plenty of hoots and hollers of appreciation. Suddenly, Thali could barely contain a gasp as a colorful costume caught her eye. She thought Joren had crashed the party before she realized the person dressed as a colorful jester was much too wide to be Joren. Relief and glee filled her instead as she realized it was Daylor who had returned in the colorful costume to introduce the next act. Ari, another close merchanting friend who'd been with Thali on that fateful day on Star Island last summer, showed off her knife-throwing skills, while Seth displayed his skill in sleight of hand and made small things disappear and reappear. Then Mia and Aron scared Thali half to death with an ax-throwing bit. And before she knew it, Elric even joined the fun and jumped on stage to show off a few card tricks himself, ending by pulling a bunch of sunflowers from his back to present to Thali. The whole crowd groaned at the addition of even more sunflowers.

At the end of the show, Mia came out of Daylor's bedroom with a platter full of sweets, which upon closer inspection, Thali realized must be from her parents. The whole platter was filled with tiny treats from different countries: all the ones her parents had been to in the last few months.

Thali picked a few of her favorites before the platter was passed around. She was excited to see her classmates trying the various sweets and going back for seconds.

As people started to leave, Thali went around to her friends and thanked them profusely. "This has been the most fun birthday I think I've ever had."

When everyone else had gone, Mia stayed behind to help Daylor and Tilton clean, swiftly shooing Thali out of the room so she couldn't help.

Elric walked her back to her room, but when they got to her door, he paused.

"You've been in here before, you know," Thali said.

Strangely, Thali thought, Elric blushed as they walked into the common room. But he paused again as they moved to her bedroom.

"I'm just going to let them out." Thali opened the door to her bedroom to let out a bounding tiger and dog. They knocked Elric back into a chair with their excitement, Ana covering his face with kisses while Indi pushed her head under his hands for a head massage.

Thali laughed as she sat in the chair beside him. "Thank you for all the sunflowers, Elric," she said once the animals had settled down enough for them to converse.

"It makes me happy to know that I was responsible for that smile," Elric said.

"Well then, know that I've been grinning like a fool all day."

He flashed her one of his wide grins and she felt a tug in her chest.

Rising and hurrying to the tray of food and drink on the side table against the opposite wall to distract herself, she asked, "Can I offer you anything to drink?"

"No, I'm all right, thank you."

"Oh, okay then." Not sure why she was suddenly feeling so uncomfortable, she put down the pitcher and glass she had grabbed. Then she turned back around to sit once again, only to find that Elric had come up behind her. She bumped right into him, glad she hadn't been holding anything.

Elric grasped her elbows to hold her steady. "Always bumping into me," he said quietly.

Before Thali could utter a retort, Elric's fingers were under her chin, lifting her face to his. He pressed his lips ever so gently to hers. The tugging in her chest blossomed into sunshine as warmth flooded her body. She reached for Elric's arms, needing to brace herself as he kissed her again, and she let her arms slide up to wrap around his neck.

The door creaking broke them apart and they jumped away from each other, knocking over vases of sunflowers. Mia walked in with Aron carrying a box of fabrics. Mia couldn't hide her grin as she and Aron went straight to her room. "Carry on. We won't interrupt again," she said.

Thali's cheeks turned to fire as she swallowed uncomfortably.

"I should get going." Elric coughed and he touched his lips with his fingertips.

"All right," Thali squeezed out past the lump in her throat.

"But first, happy birthday, Thali." He slipped a long velvet box out of his pocket, holding it squarely between them as he stepped closer to her again.

Taking the box, Thali ran her fingers over the top as she opened it, her heart picking up its pace again.

Inside lay a bracelet of alternating blue and white heart-shaped gems. Thali immediately recognized them as diamonds and sapphires.

"Elric, this ... this is too much!" Her merchant knowledge told her the bracelet would easily purchase her a ship.

Elric laughed. "I had it especially made for you, so there's no taking it back."

Thali leaned back against the side table. "We ... you ... this ..."

"Thali." Elric took one of her hands in his own. "I've made no secret of my intentions. I know you need time, and I'm willing to go as slowly as you want, but I'm confident in how I feel about you. I love you. And I'll wait as long as necessary for you to catch up."

Thali stood stunned still, staring at the bracelet.

Elric leaned over and kissed her forehead. "I have to go, but I'll write you when I get home." He held her hands with his, swiping his thumb over the back of her hand one last time before seeing himself out.

Mia and Aron rushed out of Mia's room then. "What did he give you?" Mia asked, hurrying to Thali's side as she tried to blink her way back to consciousness. "Holy rat turds. Those are the most jewels I've ever seen!" Mia exclaimed.

Aron quietly said goodnight to Mia and Thali and left, tiptoeing around the tiger and dog.

Ana got up and licked Thali's hand gently. Thali looked down at her sweet Ana's face and the bracelet that was now the most expensive thing she owned. She was having difficulties processing her feelings and her thoughts.

"Well, try it on!" Mia said.

Thali draped the bracelet around her wrist, clasping the ends together easily. Then, they put their heads together, admiring the way the jewels caught the dim light in the room as Thali turned her wrist this way and that.

"Ohh, it's so pretty!" Mia squealed.

"It's beautiful," was all Thali could murmur. She tried to calm the swirling thoughts in her mind. She'd convinced herself that Elric was just a friend, that his actions and flowery words were just what princes did. Could she love someone else so soon after Garen? Could she love someone else ever again? And was it hope, fear, or anxiety that fluttered in her now?

CHAPTER TWENTY-FOUR

NIGHT HAD LONG SINCE fallen and Thali had long since been dreaming when she felt something wrapping around her ankle. As she wondered if she was just dreaming it, Ana's low warning growl finally pulled Thali from her sleep. When she woke enough to realize something really was wrapped around her leg, she grabbed the dagger under her pillow and threw her blankets off, only to find a vine wrapped around her ankle. She kicked the plant off, then eased out of bed and opened her window to see what Joren wanted. Outside, she saw a thick tree branch waiting for her. She looked at the dagger and placed it along her windowsill. She sent reassurances to her animals before grabbing her cloak and wrapping it around herself as she stepped onto the branch.

The tree branch slid smoothly up to the roof, where she saw a cloaked Joren crouched in the shadows.

As she approached him, still rubbing the sleep from her eyes, she saw that his face was paler than usual. She moved into the shadows with him. As her eyes adjusted, she was taken aback by how tired and ragged he looked. He even had bags under his eyes, which was something completely new.

"Joren, what's wrong?" Thali asked.

"I need you to look into that forest and tell me what you see." Joren pointed behind the building.

Thali nodded and closed her eyes. She searched and examined the threads she could see, looking for anything amiss or different. "Is there anything in particular I should be looking for?"

"Something that did this," he said.

She opened her eyes a moment, focusing on Joren. He moved his cloak aside and she gasped. He was slumped over not in disguise but because he had three shallow claw marks gashed into his side. The size of the gashes meant the offending paw was wider than her thigh.

"Joren, you need help," Thali said.

"Look for it first. It should be close," Joren said, wrapping his cloak back around him.

She started scanning the threads of the larger beasts she could sense, but she found nothing out of the ordinary. "I can't find anything."

"Do you have to have seen the creature before you can connect with it?" Joren asked.

"No," Thali said.

"You're sure?" Joren asked.

"Yes," Thali said.

At that, Joren faltered, and Thali caught him. She eased him to the roof's surface and sent a message to Indi to ask her to bring up the little medical kit. The tiger lithely hopped up to the roof moments later, bag in her mouth.

"Lay down, Joren. It's not going to do any of us any good if you die of blood loss or infection."

Joren finally let her pull his shirt up gently, carefully peeling the cloth away from the open wounds. Indi put the bag down next to Thali and sat next to her, staring at Joren.

Thali opened the bag and pulled out a bottle of clear liquid. "This is going to hurt. Should I get my tiger to hold you down?" Thali asked.

"No, I can stay still," Joren said. He was having a staring contest with Indi.

She pulled the stopper from the bottle and splashed its contents on the wounds, watching for any foaming. Foaming would mean poison. No foaming. Joren was lucky. He twitched at the sting but kept his body still.

After pulling out a tin of salve and spreading it on some lengths of clean cloth, she covered each wound before wrapping Joren's middle. She pretended not to notice the other scars that crisscrossed his body.

"You learn all this in your travels?" Joren asked.

Tying the last knot extra snug, Thali sent Indi back inside and said, "As a little kid, my parents would always leave me with the healers in whatever land we were in when they had to work."

"If you ever need to replenish your plant supply, let me know," Joren said through gritted teeth.

"Thanks," she said.

After pulling his shirt back down, he sat up. "Why do you think you can't see these creatures?"

"Have they been around much?" Thali asked. She hadn't noticed anything out of the ordinary except for that time she'd noticed the forest animals were quiet—and she'd forgotten to tell him. She gulped guiltily.

Joren's eyes widened a fraction. "I'm surprised you haven't heard. They've taken seven people from town in the last few months. I even contacted my brothers, and they're all reporting giant feathers on the ground, tufts of fur in high places, and livestock and people going missing."

A small pang lanced Thali's heart at the mention of his other brothers, and she momentarily wondered how Garen was doing. It seemed strange that she had been so out of the loop to the news around the world. She'd certainly been preoccupied.

"What did it look like?" Thali glanced at Joren's bandaged side.

"Truly, I'm not completely sure. And the townspeople are afraid. They refuse to talk about it like they're superstitious, as if talking about it would make it appear or something. So, I went into the woods to find clues. The plants didn't even give me warning. It was as if it didn't have weight or didn't touch anything. I only felt its breath before I leaped aside instinctively. The little bit I saw out of the corner of my eye looked like a lion, but with the beak and head of a bird."

Thali thought back to all the murals of mythical creatures she'd seen while traveling. She'd always been obsessed with learning as much as she could about animals, mythical or real. She hazarded a guess. "A griffin?"

"Is that what it's called?" Joren asked.

"I think so." She closed her eyes again and this time searched for glittering threads, anything like she'd seen as she'd been sailing away from Star Island.

"What are you not telling me?" Joren's eyes narrowed.

Thali opened her eyes again. "I've never said anything because it'd reveal too much of my ... talents."

Joren raised an eyebrow, waiting.

"The merchants' final exam each year requires sailing to a specific island and accomplishing certain tasks. Except last year, my ship was given the wrong instructions and we ended up at the fabled Star Island. Our task was to move some rocks—which turned into magical gems that almost made us kill each other—from inside this crumbling tower to a table outside. As we were leaving, I thought I saw sparkling threads coming from the island, though it might have been the concussion I'd gotten trying to complete that task, which of course involved much more than just moving rocks."

"Why is this the first time I've heard of this?" Joren's lips pressed together in a thin line.

"Why is this the first time I'm hearing of what's happening in the rest of the world?" Thali was getting annoyed.

Ignoring her, Joren asked, "Have you seen anything like that since?"

"Glimpses of glittering threads. But only one ever pops up before it's gone just as fast. I've not seen tracks in the forest. I've looked. Where could they come from, and why don't we see them?"

"Maybe they can fly," Joren suggested.

She couldn't believe he'd said that out loud. She should be able to see them or their threads even if they could fly, though it did explain the lack of prints. "I didn't mention anything before because I wasn't sure if I was actually seeing those threads. What if it was just my imagination?"

"Well, I've seen the creature now, and it wasn't my imagination," Joren said. A muscle twitched in his jaw.

"You can't think all these disappearances are because these mythical animals have decided to invisibly wreak havoc on the world." Thali sat back and put everything away in her kit.

"That's exactly what I think. You've seen the same threads before. We need to figure out why you can't see them now, except for the odd glimpse. Maybe they've learned to mask themselves in their environment. Maybe that includes masking their threads." Joren was silent for a moment. Then, he took a deep breath that hitched a bit and asked, "What do you know of magical beasts?"

"Not much," Thali said.

"Well, from what I've heard from you and my brother, I think someone is purposely keeping you in the dark. And that someone manipulated you into opening some kind of portal or gate on that island that unleashed all these magical creatures. Now they've perhaps taught these creatures to hide themselves and their threads so you can't warn anyone. And knowing you'd also want to keep your talent hidden, they figured you wouldn't tell anyone even if you did happen to glimpse something. Who knows about your abilities?" Joren's forehead crinkled as he thought.

"You, my parents, some lifelong friends," Thali said.

Joren snorted. "That's what you might think. But anyone who's watched you carefully would suspect."

"That's not fair." Thali crossed her arms. She'd guarded this secret so carefully, until recently anyway.

"Yes, it is." Joren was getting snippier with every comment. "If whoever is doing this believes in magical creatures, it's not a big leap for them to assume that someone who has a tiger, a dog, and a snake as companions has some kind of magic."

Even though anger roiled inside her, she knew Joren would shut her out if she met flame with fire, so she took a deep breath to calm herself. "I'm sorry I didn't tell you about the glittering threads sooner. But you should have kept me abreast of the news, too," Thali said.

Joren's face visibly relaxed then, perhaps realizing he'd need her help as much as she'd need his. "There's no use whining about the past. What's done is done. We need to figure out what's going on." He winced as he tried to stand, pressing a hand to his side.

"Let me help you home," Thali said. She sent Indi back inside first with the bag.

Joren quirked an eyebrow. "Inviting yourself into my bed, are you?"

Thali rolled her eyes. "I don't want to be responsible if you die."

"Aww, she does care about me," Joren pouted.

"Fine, fall off the roof, die. Whatever," Thali said. She started to turn.

He hissed again with his first step, and she spun around, watching him.

"Fine, help me get to the edge," Joren said.

Thali waited.

"Please?" Joren added. Thali went over then and let him lean on her as he hobbled along the roof. A branch reached up, simultaneously growing a second, vertical branch for Joren to use to steady himself.

Once in the shadows, he paused. Another branch reached out for her, and she stepped onto it, descending to her window.

"Don't die, Joren," Thali said.

He disappeared without a sound as she slipped through her window. Joren was a lot of things—ridiculous, flamboyant, colorful—but she'd known since the moment they'd met he wasn't an idiot. He did everything with purpose and said everything for a reason. Even his ludicrous proposal had been a test. She'd seen it when she'd looked past her own emotions. However, tonight was the first night she'd seen the real him.

CHAPTER TWENTY-FIVE

T WO WEEKS HAD GONE by since the invisible creature had attacked Joren, and Thali and Joren still had nothing to show for it. She was still searching her threads and had sent word to her parents and Tariq. They hadn't seen anything amiss personally but had heard of some gruesome attacks in the northern lands. Bodies torn to shreds, insides pulled outside, claw marks as wide as the ones Joren had suffered, rural homes razed.

One morning, it occurred to Thali to ask Alexius if he'd heard anything from home.

"Alexius, how is your family? My father wrote me saying he'd heard of more trouble than usual there."

"Last I heard, they're fine. My family lives in a desolate region. We're used to lots of skirmishes, but nothing unusual has happened."

They couldn't chat more as they started to spar, but Thali noticed Alexius looked tired. He was a touch slower than usual, and he was less chatty.

Thali now stayed in the small strip of forest at the edge of the school grounds when she took her animals out. If there really was something like an invisible griffin out there and it was as big as those claw marks on Joren indicated, she didn't want to risk her animals. So now, from the safety of her room and her roof, she spent her time connecting with the animals she *could* detect, hoping one might sense something that would lead to this invisible griffin.

She had been careful to reveal nothing to Elric, though she had asked him from time to time about the state of the kingdom. He hadn't mentioned anything amiss, and she knew he always had a lot on his plate and didn't want to add to it, so she didn't tell him of her worries. If anyone was safe, she assumed it was him with his palace full of guards.

Thali had improved her range with all her efforts to find shimmery threads, but she hadn't caught so much as a glimpse of a shimmery thread since that night Joren had been attacked. He hadn't mentioned his injury since then either and had only continued to push her to train, to push her magical limits farther and farther.

She couldn't help but feel this quiet and lack of events was the calm before the storm. It was eerie.

Chapter Twenty-Six

My dearest Thali,
I was hoping you'd be able to come visit the palace soon.
We have visitors from Cerisa here next week, and I think
this is the perfect excuse to have you here with me.

Please come as I can't seem to remember what you look
like in my dreams anymore and need a reminder.
-E

T HALI LAUGHED WHEN SHE read it. She also couldn't help smiling for the rest of the day. That night, she wrote to her parents to see if they'd allow her to skip her classes for a couple weeks to go to the palace and visit with the delegation from Cerisa. Then to busy herself, she took the specialty scissors she'd had crafted and asked Ana to stand on the table. It was time for Ana's haircut.

Once her room was filled with hair and Ana was naked of her curls, a bat had landed on her windowsill. The letter that came back surprised her.

Thali,
Even as your father, I'm unlikely to stand against a royal
summons.
-Papa

The morning she got the letter from her father, she started throwing clothes together. She could leave as early as the day after tomorrow and be at the palace in a day's time. Refusing to analyze her excitement further, she went to Combat class with an extra spring in her step. She wasn't sure if she was ready to dive into anything with Elric, but thinking about him made her happy and she was excited to go. Besides, it meant missing classes for a couple weeks. What could be better?

Even sparring with Alexius that day was fun. He was a bit more energetic and finally back up to his normal speed. "You'll have to do without me for the next two weeks," Thali said.

Alexius stopped so abruptly Thali whacked him in the arm with her staff. "Why? Where are you going?"

"I'm off to the palace. The prince has summoned me to meet with a special delegation from Cerisa."

"Oh?" Alexius recovered and they began sparring again. "Sounds like an excuse for him to see you," Alexius said.

"Maybe it is." Thali grinned wickedly and hit Alexius a little harder.

After the day's classes, and holding out the royal summons for Master Brown to read, Thali hurried to her rooms to pack some more. She'd practically bounced out of class with glee. When she arrived in her room, she was surprised to see Joren in her chair petting Indi. Ana lifted her head from the pillow, but lowered it and shifted, showing her belly.

"Going somewhere?" Joren asked.

"Yes. When did you and Indi become friends?" Thali asked. She brought her hand to the desk and Bardo slid out into the patch of sun.

"Beauty recognizes beauty when it sees it. Isn't that right, you gorgeous kitty?" Joren purred at Indi, who purred right back.

Thali spotted a corner of butcher's paper sticking out of Joren's pocket. That explained it. "How do you even know I'm going somewhere? I just decided today." Thali opened her trunk to start packing. She glanced over her shoulder at Joren just in time to see him finally tear his eyes away from Indi's to raise his eyebrows at her.

"Fine, spymaster, so you know, is it a problem?" Thali was wondering what lengths Joren would go to to prevent her from going.

"I don't think you should go," Joren said. He continued to scratch Indi's head.

"Why? The palace is probably better protected than the school."

"From normal things, yes. But magical things, no. Someone is both shielding and protecting you here," Joren pointed out.

"I thought we were on the same page. Think about it. If I go to the palace, maybe I'll finally be far enough away from whatever barrier is set up here. Then, maybe I can glimpse something, find something." Thali threw some more things in her trunk.

"Thali, I think someone is *protecting* you by keeping you in the dark. That's why nothing ever happens here at the school. You said the animals can feel you when you connect to their threads? That it's a two-way connection?" Joren asked.

"Yesss," Thali said. She continued packing but slowed her pace.

"Well, what if these magical creatures aren't just magical, but intelligent? What if they can use you? Control you with their own mind?"

"You've been thinking a lot." She sat down in her desk chair and studied him. She hadn't considered that. "I'll keep my mind closed off when I'm there. How about that?"

"I'm not Garen. I'm not going to stop you. But I wanted you to know I think it's a bad idea," Joren said.

Her heart ached as she thought of Garen. "Are you ... are you going to tell him?" Thali asked. She couldn't imagine that Garen would really stop her, but he might put himself in danger for her.

"No, of course not. He'd just come running here," Joren said.

A small sinking feeling settled in the pit of her stomach. Thali knew it wasn't fair to think of Garen. She was supposed to be moving toward Elric. But she couldn't help it. A large part of her wanted Garen to come running. And she wondered if he was happy.

Joren started making kissing noises, and Thali turned to see Indi rubbing his face with her chin.

"Traitor," Thali said. Joren's lips turned up at the corners behind Indi's face. "Well, I'm going. I'll be careful. I'll just peek through once," Thali said.

"Suit yourself. Don't bring anything scary home." And with that, Joren rose, sauntered over to the window, and slipped out onto a tree branch.

Joren

Joren walked along the edge of the forest, not far enough in to catch the attention of a critter, but far enough to use the shadows. He removed his cloak, holding it out for a branch to reach out and take, and stilled as another branch fitted a corset over him and a set of vines pulled the corset's ties to tighten it. Then, a velvet jacket and skirt finished the outfit. He took the piece of mirror a vine handed him and the box another vine held open for him and painted his face to match the whore he'd be playing tonight. A final vine plopped a wig on his head. He would have fun on his last night.

He purposely hadn't told Thali that Garen was on his way back. Their switch had always been temporary, and he was starting to miss his land and his people. The people here were so plain and boring. Though Thali would find out eventually, he hoped he'd planted the seed that he wasn't pleased, so when she got back, she'd assume he was keeping his distance from her and their lessons because he was too busy—or angry—to bother with her. He'd buy Garen as much time away from her as he could.

He dipped back into town under lantern light a few blocks from Ella's and slipped right into character.

Chapter Twenty-Seven

T HALI TOUCHED HER FOREARM to check on Bardo before leaping up onto Arabelle and trotting down the path to the school gate, Indi and Ana traveling next to her. Mia had hugged her goodbye that morning and told her to be safe. Elric had said he was sending someone, but she wanted to avoid the commotion and had left a day early. She was quite capable of taking care of herself.

So now she rode along the deer path just at the edge of the forest so she wouldn't attract too much attention, either from people curious about her menagerie of animals or from invisible creatures. Bardo had settled on the horn of the saddle. It wasn't a long journey, just less than two days, and it gave Thali time to contemplate her feelings for Elric. She knew she should be thinking of the magical creatures, but her thoughts kept wandering to Elric, about how forward and hopeful and consistent he was, how she always found herself smiling when she was with him. When she thought of Garen, she thought of how he had always been there for her, but he'd always had a confidence in her she'd never had herself. It had been hard at times to live up to his belief in her. It still pained her heart to think of him, but she felt less pressure with Elric.

The sun was setting when she arrived at the palace gates the next day. She was surprised to find Elric's personal guard, Stefan, waiting for her by the guardhouse.

"He wouldn't sleep until I said I'd come wait for you. He wanted to come himself, but then that'd mean three more guards would have had to stay up with him," Stefan explained.

"I'm sorry to cause you all so much trouble."

"It's no trouble at all, Lady Routhalia. He's been glowing with antici-pation of your arrival," Stefan said.

This made her heart smile as she handed Arabelle off to stable hands who stared at the tiger next to the horse and wouldn't come near until Indi had accompanied Thali away from Arabelle. Stefan escorted her to a guest wing, where she had a room closest to the exit so her animals would have quick access to the outdoors. At her door, he gave her a note from Elric and bowed, waiting for a response.

Breakfast?

"Please tell Prince Elric I accept," she said.

Stefan let out a breath. "Thank you, m'lady. I think he would have exploded from nervous energy if you didn't."

Thali laughed. "Thank you, Stefan. Now go to bed. I'm sorry to have kept you. I'm sure you had more important things to do."

He nodded and bowed before leaving her to her empty rooms.

Mia hadn't been able to accompany her this time, but she'd sent two full trunks of clothes for Thali and the name of the only person she trusted to handle wardrobe emergencies at the palace. Also in the room, Thali found lit candles and vases of sunflowers scattered around. She smiled at their sunny faces staring back at her. Then she saw Bardo had slipped out of her sleeve and was slithering to the bathing room. He sent her an image of warm water. Thali walked into the bathing room then and almost cried from glee to find a hot bath with rose petals waiting for her.

He knows me well, Thali thought as she stripped off her travel clothes and slipped into the hot tub of water. Letting it slosh and envelop her body in its soothing heat, she closed her eyes and let the warm water melt away her travel grime.

She opened her eyes twenty minutes later to two sets of eyes staring at her. With a big sigh, she climbed out of the tub, wrapped herself in nearby linens, and began the process of using the now-cool water to wash Indi and Ana. They seemed to feel the importance of the palace and wanted to freshen up too.

After wiping Bardo down as well, she returned to her room to find a sliver of bed space left between Indi and Ana, who had sprawled themselves, damp fur and all, over the massive bed. Bardo chose to settle on the nightstand next to the bed. Thali slipped carefully under the covers, careful not to crush legs or catch fur, and quickly fell asleep.

The next morning, she knew there wouldn't be much help from palace staff. There was, after all, a tiger, dog, and snake in her room. She dressed herself in plain linen pants and a loose white shirt with a blue overcoat to take her animals out for a walk on the palace lawns. Elric had housed her in a quieter space so she wouldn't cause a stir with her furry companions, which was just as good for her.

After she returned, she regretfully locked her animals in her dressing room so the staff could come into her bedroom and do what they needed to. They hustled about hither and thither, efficient in their tasks, and were done in moments. As soon as they left, she hurried to let her animals out and change her clothes for her breakfast with Elric. She was just clasping the last eye and hook as he knocked.

When she opened the door, her heart skipped a few beats. Elric's golden hair had grown a little, wavy now as it fell long enough to hide his ears. His foliage-green eyes and infectious smile made her heart skip a beat.

His hands went to his chest as he took her in. "Oh my, Lady Routhalia, it is like opening the door to sunshine." And he grabbed her hand to kiss the top of it before she leaped at him and threw her arms around him.

He squeezed her tight as they breathed each other in before the whine of a dog behind her told her she'd better move so they could greet him too.

She let Elric go and stepped aside. He let the tiger and dog bowl him over into the hall as they licked and batted at him. She wondered if they felt what she felt when she saw him but chose not to check their threads. Animals should have privacy too, after all.

When the animals finally let Elric stand up, Thali led Indi and Ana back into her bedroom, asked them not to scare the palace staff, and promised them a large supper if they behaved well. As she entered the sitting room, Elric smoothed his hair as best he could before offering Thali his arm and guiding her to the palace's inner courtyard.

"Isn't this the inner courtyard for the royal family only?" she asked.

"Yes, it is," he replied.

He continued leading her to the center, where a beautiful little stone table was laden with all sorts of pastries.

She noticed his personal guards, including Stefan, hovering discreetly in the shadows of the perimeter's columns. It was probably the farthest they'd ever been from the prince other than when he roamed his personal forest, which he'd taken her in when she'd visited last year. Thali figured they could keep their distance here because this was one of the most secure locations anyway since there were only two ways to get in and out—except for the open sky.

Looking up, she saw only a sunny blue sky, a few clouds, and some birds flying by.

"So this afternoon, I'd like you to be there with me to greet the Cerisan delegation," Elric began as he handed her a butter knife. He poured her a cup of hot coffee and watched her take her first sip, a grin filling his face at her reaction. The coffee had been mixed with the even rarer chocolate, and Thali thought she was tasting the most wonderful thing in the world as the velvety smooth, hot liquid slid down her throat.

She closed her eyes to savor the moment before replying. "I don't know if that's such a good idea. My mother was dishonored and disinherited after all."

"So?" Elric retorted. He grabbed a pastry after she did and smothered it in jam.

"So, if anyone in the delegation has any relationship with my mother's family—and I'm sure at least their guards will—they'd instantly dislike you if I'm there," Thali said. She was proud of herself for thinking about the politics.

"What would you prefer?" Elric asked.

"Meet them yourself. Tell me about it later. I can be your incognito translator," Thali said.

"Well, you'll at least have to be at supper," Elric said, smiling like an idiot.

"Did you hear anything I just told you?" Thali asked.

"My parents have asked for you to be at supper."

"Oh." Thali was surprised and a little shocked.

"You thought I was using any excuse possible to bring you here, didn't you?" He grinned at that. "My parents actually did send the royal invitation. I can't forge those."

Thali just stared blankly, grateful now that Mia had packed her so many dresses. "I guess I will be there then," Thali said.

"You won't reconsider attending the royal welcome?" Elric asked.

Thali tried to change tactics. "I suppose I could hide in the back, behind your family."

"No, I want you next to me."

"Aren't you worried about what that might say?"

"Not at all." Elric's eyes crinkled over his cup as he took another sip of the chocolate-laced coffee.

Chapter Twenty-Eight

T HALI SMOOTHED HER SKIRT with her hands as she stood behind the royal family. She had agreed to be part of the royal greeting party on the condition she be allowed to stand apart from the royal family for damage control if needed. She now regretted accepting as she stood, uncomfortable, in a daffodil-yellow silk dress. It was one of Mia's hybrid dresses: a corset top with long sleeves and a slim skirt. Even standing behind everyone, she stood out like a sore thumb and wished she'd dressed more plainly.

Elric edged his way over to her. "You look beautiful. Perfect for standing next to me."

Thali blushed as she caught the look in his eyes. "No, thank you, Your Highness." She dipped into a little curtsy as she keenly felt all the eyes on her.

The queen coughed, glancing at Elric. He darted back to his spot. A moment later, two royal carriages rolled into sight of the main entrance to the palace. All the top palace staff had donned their formal uniforms, some with silver and some with gold trim, and had lined up along the grand staircase, ready to jump into action.

When the first carriage door opened, six guards leaped out of the first carriage, and Thali had to bite her tongue to keep from laughing at the thought of how they must have crammed into the tight space. The guards formed a line in front of the palace steps. Thali noted three female warriors next to three male warriors before the prince and princess stepped out of the next carriage. Prince Feng and Princess Suyi were draped in colorful, gold-embroidered silk robes with long, draping sleeves, and Thali wondered if Princess Suyi would tip over as she took tiny hobbling steps. They were older than Thali had expected, closer in age to her parents than her own, and they were both slender and only a little taller than her mother. Prince Feng was a full head shorter than Elric.

Thali's eye was drawn to one specific female warrior, though. She couldn't help but stare at the woman who could have been her mother's twin standing between the two other female guards. The woman's eyes flicked to her momentarily before she replaced her mask of indifference.

Thali had no doubt it was her aunt. Her mother had three brothers and a sister, but Thali had only ever met one of the brothers, Uncle Renshu. She'd only seen him three times in her life, but he secretly kept in touch with them. Her grandmother had mailed an odd trinket to Thali once, but since her mother had married and run away with her father, her mother's whole family was forbidden to have contact with Thali's family. But when she'd met her uncle those three times on their trips to Cerisa, he'd always been incredibly kind and warm toward her. And he'd always brought her and her brother a small stash of dragonbeard candy and other gifts.

Thali bit her tongue to bring her back to the present. She watched the royal couple's every movement as they ascended the stairs, noting that they allowed Elric's family to bow first before returning the customary action and that they spoke the common tongue fluently. As they were led into the palace by the king and queen themselves, Elric glanced at her and offered his arm, obviously wanting her to walk in by his side. Thali kept her chin up but cast her gaze down, knowing the respectful gesture would not be missed by the guards trailing the prestigious group.

Elric waited. Thali didn't want the awkward moment to stretch on any longer, so she delicately stepped over and grasped his elbow but was careful to curtsy low and walk a step behind him. She hoped to convey the great honor this was for her and to show that it wasn't a normal occurrence. She remembered her mother always telling her that in Cerisan culture, one could never be too humble.

"Do my eyes deceive me, or is this the Lady Routhalia in your company?" Prince Feng glanced at Thali once they had all settled for refreshments in a lavish sitting room. Thali had taken a seat in a high-backed chair in the back corner, wanting to use the first excuse she could find to leave.

"Why yes, Your Highness, Lady Routhalia is a dear friend of mine," Elric smoothly answered as he came over to guide Thali to a seat closer to the group.

Thali swallowed as she changed her expression to one of political pleasantness, one she'd practiced many times. She was now grateful that Tariq had taken it upon himself to train her to mask her emotions.

"Your Highness honors me with his attention." She bowed her head, hoping she could escape scrutiny by playing that she was too lowly for attention.

"Your family is quite renowned, even throughout our lands," Prince Feng stated. Thali could feel him studying her and wondered if he was thinking good thoughts or only thoughts of the shame her mother had brought her family.

"Lady Routhalia's family has done great things for our kingdom. They've widened our horizons in both global knowledge and commerce." The queen deftly ended the discussion on that topic, and Thali was touched to hear the queen defend her family as she took command of the conversation and changed the topic instead to Prince Feng's travels.

Thali sighed on the inside. The attention was finally off her. Even though she wasn't new to these situations and knew how to handle herself, she never liked being the center of attention. She couldn't imagine what it would be like to be queen and have to command the conversation as Elric's mother had.

Eventually, the group parted, and Prince Feng and Princess Suyi were guided to their guest wing to rest from their long journey. This allowed Thali to return to her rooms and take her animals out for a walk. Remembering Joren's concerns, she stayed at the edge of the forest, walking with Indi and Ana and combing through all the details she'd recorded. The prince and princess seemed kind enough, and they had surprised her by knowing her name, though she supposed she did stand out. They hadn't been cruel or mean or accusatory, mostly just curious about her presence. Part of her was already a little bored, but she reminded herself that boring was good for these kinds of things. She sighed and enjoyed the outdoors and her momentary freedom. That was enough of those thoughts for one day.

CHAPTER TWENTY-NINE

Q UEEN ADELA

The queen knew what she'd done was risky. As she pulled her jeweled bracelets off and set them back on the awaiting cushions, one of her lady's maids wheeled out the jewels that would go with her dinner dress. Queen Adela looked over the diamond and emerald options and chose the emerald earrings and a diamond necklace. She nodded to her maid, who then went to prepare her next outfit. Another lady's maid started to unlace her dress in the back, and the queen waited for the sweet bliss of stepping out of the stiff dress and into a soft silk robe while she rested. Once the rest of her jewels were also off, they were carted away. Glancing through her door, she could see her husband, Devrain, already in his more relaxed attire and sitting with his tea in their parlor.

She, as queen, had taken a calculated risk and wanted to make obvious what was going to happen. Anyone who saw Elric within ten feet of Routhalia could see how he felt about her. So, as his mother, she had wanted to be transparent and show the Cerisan delegation they had a decision to make, and she hoped it would play out in their favor. Routhalia wasn't like most young women in the kingdom. She wouldn't leap at the chance to marry a prince just because he was a prince. She knew Elric was taking his time wooing her, but she also knew that Routhalia loved her son. She was just more hesitant to show it   and perhaps hadn't completely figured it out yet.

Adela had another purpose for having taken that risk with Prince Feng. She was also hoping she could get the Cerisans to forgive Routhalia's mother, or at least allow her back into her family. Maybe that would help push Routhalia into what would become her new role. Elric was so sure of himself, always sunny and happy, and quick to learn all the things he had to for when his time to take over the kingdom came. She and her husband would hand over a peaceful, prosperous kingdom, and she knew Elric would be at his best with Routhalia by his side.

"What do you think?" Devrain brought a cup of tea to her in her dressing room.

"Thank you, sweetheart," Adela said as she took the cup and her lady's maid finished tying the robe around her waist. Her king guided her back to their parlor, and they sat on the plush velvet couch. Adela took her time stirring sugar into her tea to get it just right before she took another sip. The perfect sip was always worth the trouble of making it so.

Devrain patiently waited for her response. They'd learned how to coexist well over their twenty-five years together.

"I think it's too early to tell," Adela said.

"I know it's too early to tell about Feng and Suyi. Did you see her feet? No wonder she was hobbling around," Devrain said. He sat back with his own tea.

"The custom is to wrap their feet and keep them very small in Cerisa. Small feet are dainty feet," Adela told her husband. She glanced at her own large duck feet. She was lucky she wasn't Cerisan.

"She must not walk much," he said.

"I don't think they're meant to walk much. It's a sign of their wealth to be carried everywhere," Adela said. They hadn't brought people to carry them here though, and part of her wondered why until her husband persisted with his original question.

"I meant, what did you think of Lady Routhalia and our son?" Devrain asked.

"What is there to think? Elric keeps nudging her into position," Adela said.

"I can't believe she's so reluctant. But then, remember when we had to create escape routes for him when we started presenting him in court?" Devrain laughed as he brought the tea to his lips again.

"She's not most ladies," Adela said.

"With his charm and her connections, they could strengthen our relationships with all the other kingdoms. We could extend Adanek's reach, plus we'll be swimming in jewels from Bulstan," Devrain said.

Adela nodded. She knew her husband saw only that the pair could expand his kingdom's influence in the world, improve its trade deals, and exchange more goods, but Adela wasn't sure Routhalia was ready for the restrictive life of the palace. Though she agreed it was a good match, as a mother and a woman, Adela wondered whether the girl would actually accept her son's eventual proposal.

Chapter Thirty

A<small>NA AND</small> I<small>NDI GROWLED</small>, and Thali recognized the signs that a stranger was approaching. A rustle of leaves preceded someone stepping out of the forest before them. Thali calmed Indi and Ana as she recognized the woman that must be her aunt and watched her remove the hood of her dark cloak.

She smiled and said, "I have waited many years to meet you, niece."

Thali nodded. Indi slunk behind her, sitting in the shade of the building, but Ana wagged her tail in excitement. Thali silently asked them to stay where they were as the woman approached.

"My name is Qiao. I'm your mother's sister. I took this trip in hopes that I would have the opportunity to meet you and see my sister again. Renshu is always so terrible at describing you." She smiled, and while so similar to Thali's mother, she was also different. Jinhua was a leader and warrior but looked like a princess. Qiao was stockier, her features sharper, and she had a thick scar along her cheek from her ear to the corner of her mouth.

Thali didn't know what to think. She'd braced herself for hateful words from her aunt. Though she had calmed at her uncle's name, she was at a loss for what to do or say. Surely her mother's family would berate her for her mother's betrayal, for running away with her father.

"I'm sorry for Amah's rules. Mother was just so mad that Jinhua didn't marry Prince Feng."

"What?" Thali's eyes nearly popped out of her head.

"Oh no. She never told you?" Qiao stiffened and cocked her head.

Thali shook her head.

"What *did* she tell you?"

Thali narrowed her eyes at her aunt. This person was unfamiliar to her, but she might be able to give her answers that her mother never would. "Only that she is not welcome at home. I know that Uncle Renshu meets with her only once every time we go to Cerisa, so I've only ever met Uncle Renshu a few times."

Qiao was quiet for a moment. Indi and Ana had calmed and were lying down now, watching and waiting to see what was going to happen. Thali knew they were all out of sight from most of the palace pathways and decided it was probably for the better.

"May we sit?" Qiao gestured to some large rocks nearby.

Thali nodded and sat facing her aunt.

Qiao suddenly dipped her head in her hands, then ran her hands through her hair. it was the same thing Thali's mother did when she was exasperated. "You must think we're horrible people," Qiao said.

Thali shrugged. "I understand that honor and duty are priorities in Cerisa." Thali watched as her aunt's knuckles turned white as she fisted her hands on her knees.

"My mother, your grandmother, was overjoyed when she had a baby girl who was as pretty as your mother was and who was just a year younger than Prince Feng. She was always the hardest on Jin. Jin had to be perfect. The best fighter and the smartest and the prettiest and the most graceful. Mother pinned all her hopes on her. Then when His Royal Highness showed real interest in her, Amah was overjoyed. Jin had been preparing her whole life for this role, but then she met your father and her whole world changed. She just couldn't go back to the life she was supposed to live after meeting your father, after the future she imagined with him."

"That must have been tough for you," Thali said. She thought it was interesting how her brother had been coached in a similar way.

"It was, but I'm grateful now that I was too old for Prince Feng, that it was her and not me that had to live that life. I was one of the boys. I was left alone to follow the path of a warrior," Qiao said.

Thali nodded. She now understood her mother's hesitations about Elric's intentions.

"When your parents are in town, we cover for Renshu so he can go see her, though we all want to meet you and your brother. We all want to see you."

Thali nodded absentmindedly. She didn't know how she felt about all this information. Her mother's family had always been an abyss that wasn't spoken of.

"I have to go, but I hope we can talk more later?" Qiao stood up and waited.

Thali saw the hope in her aunt's face and couldn't help forcing a smile and nodding.

As she walked away, Thali saw Elric with his shadow of guards striding toward her.

"Was that one of the Cerisan guards you were just talking to?" Elric asked.

"Yes," Thali said. Her mind was still reeling from her conversation with her aunt.

"And?" Elric asked as he plunked down on the rock. His guards fanned themselves out, moving out of hearing range.

"That's my aunt."

"You don't sound like you had a happy family reunion."

"I ... it's the first time I've met her. I don't know what to think," Thali said.

Elric's eyebrows shot up, but he crossed his leg over his knee and waited for her to continue.

"My mom's side of the family was never in the picture. I told you she was disinherited when she married my father and left home. That means I've never been to my mother's childhood home, never sat with my grandmother, never even shared a meal with her family. I've met one of my uncles a few times, but that was in secret and never for more than a private meal."

Elric reached for Thali's hand and held it in both of his. "I'm sorry. That couldn't have been easy."

"Not really. I haven't known any other way. But I know that one of my father's greatest regrets was taking her away from her family," Thali replied. Elric rubbed his thumb over the back of her hand, squeezing it reassuringly.

Thali shook her head. "I'm sorry. I shouldn't be burdening you with my family's problems. You have a lot on your own plate."

"Never be sorry, Thali. I'm glad you shared that with me," Elric said.

Thali looked into the rich green eyes filled with kindness and under-standing and warmth. She felt her heart open a little more, blooming like a flower unfurling its petals in the warmth that was Elric. On the outside, she smiled.

Stefan, the captain of Elric's guard, coughed, and she saw Elric shoot him a nasty look before they both looked up to see one of the king's advisers approaching them, ready to usher them off to tonight's sup-per. Thali sighed. At the very least, tonight would be interesting. And part of her wondered if she would have another moment alone with her aunt.

Chapter Thirty-One

THALI HAD DECIDED TO wear one of her favorite blue dresses to the reception dinner. It gave her confidence and made her feel happy. Once there, she waited quietly off to the side until the king and queen had led Prince Feng and Princess Suyi to their seats. Prince Elric took Thali's elbow then and guided her to sit, surprisingly next to him. She had thought to be seated farther down the table given her lack of royal status. Elric himself was seated next to the queen and across from Princess Suyi. Thali reached into her bag of diplomatic tricks and glued on her best pleasant court face while she retreated into her mind. She watched Princess Suyi through lowered lashes, trying to imagine her mother there instead.

In her mind, she put the quiet Suyi next to the vibrant image of her mother. While less outspoken than her father, her mother was always part of the action, always quick to reply with a wise comment. She commanded attention in a room with her beauty but was quick to follow that with a wry smile, dirty joke, or witty saying. As hard as Thali tried, she couldn't imagine her mother as docile as Princess Suyi.

"Yes, yes, Bulstan's jewels are very nice, but given how difficult they are to obtain from there, I mean a diamond is a diamond! We have a healthy supply from the north. Large diamonds that cost us nothing to dig up. We swim in them in the palace. We have an actual pool of diamonds," Prince Feng said.

Thali kept her lips pressed together to avoid saying anything.

The king only nodded politely, but once Prince Feng had a drink in him, he was apparently difficult to stop. "Do you get out to sail much

Prince Elric? I tell you, it does the body good to travel. That is why I offered to travel for my uncle. He is an old man, and he says travel is for the young, so I take it upon myself to travel on his behalf. I told my uncle, 'Uncle, you rest and take it easy. Just take care of Cerisan business. I will bolster our relationships beyond our borders.'" Prince Feng puffed his chest out. "My uncle was so grateful, he offered me another two wives. But I told him I could not have one more than the emperor." He took another drink, and that seemed to raise the volume of his voice. "I know here you limit yourselves to one wife, but in Cerisa, it is representative of wealth. The more wives you have under your roof, the wealthier you appear to others. I have seven others at home, but Suyi here is the only one who can tolerate traveling. All the others are pregnant or have young babies." Prince Feng wiggled his eyebrows as he thrust his hips back and forth in his seat.

Thali thought she was going to puke. She'd developed a headache from all of Prince Feng's talk. He certainly had a lot of opinions. The king and queen agreed politely with their guest, but even Thali could tell he was rubbing them the wrong way.

As their meal finally came to a close, Princess Suyi placed a hand on her husband's arm. Prince Feng ignored the gentle contact as he laughed heartily at his own joke. The queen had thankfully given the signal to stop serving the prince wine in the middle of the meal. Thali dreaded to think of what the prince would have done or said had she not.

"Now, Your Majesty, Your Highness, shall we adjourn to another room and leave the ladies to talk of their frivolous things?" Prince Feng asked.

"Of course, Your Highness." The king signaled the end of the meal and rose.

Prince Feng shrugged off Princess Suyi's staying hand, and she remained staring at her plate as he followed the king.

Elric also rose and walked over to Thali, kissing her hand with a wink before bowing slightly to his mother and following the king and Prince Feng out of the room.

When Thali looked up, she saw Princess Suyi's gaze lingering on the spot where Elric had kissed her. Worried Elric had broken some form of protocol, Thali felt heat rise up her neck and folded her hands in front of her under the table.

"Thank you for a lovely meal. I am quite tired from our travels though, so please excuse me as I return to my room to rest," Princess Suyi said. Not once did she make direct eye contact with the queen or Thali as she spoke, rose, and moved silently out of the room.

Thali waited as the queen also excused herself before leaving. Though the tension that had built in the dining room had fizzled as soon as Prince Feng had left, she was glad to be able to return to her own rooms. Thali couldn't help but wonder what the expectations for her would be if she were to wed Elric and become a princess herself.

Another two nights had passed, and Prince Feng was proving that he was only here for a good time. The king and queen were visibly growing tired of Prince Feng's lack of diplomacy and need for constant attention. He was here for pleasure and showed no interest in trade or strengthening their countries' relations. Thali even saw Elric's weariness at entertaining someone with so few opinions in common with his own, and he was the consummate diplomat. As the men left the royal dining room this evening, Prince Feng was fully into the wine when he stood and initiated their retiring to the antechamber for yet more drinks.

Once again, the king, playing the dutiful host, stood, and Elric again rose, kissed Thali's hand, and kissed his mother's cheek before following his father and their guest.

"Elric! Surely you are just playing with her. She's no more than a bastard mutt!" Prince Feng's too-loud voice rang through the cavernous room as he waved his arm and led the way through the door.

Everyone froze. Princess Suyi only glanced at Thali before dedicating her gaze back to her plate as she turned a bright pink. The room was silent, everyone waiting for Prince Elric's reply. Thali glanced at her hands, wanting to melt through the floor, before reminding herself she was her mother's daughter. So she sat up tall and looked right at Prince Feng.

Throwing a quick glance at Thali and his mother, Elric squared his shoulders and faced Prince Feng. Thali could feel the tension in his body from his voice alone. He clenched and unclenched his fists as the smile melted from his face. "Your Highness, Lady Routhalia is nobility in our kingdom, and I kindly ask your respect in addressing my future bride and this kingdom's future queen."

Thali gasped, her fingers, toes, and nose growing cold as what he said sank in. It took everything she had to stay frozen. Prince Feng laughed it off and they adjourned to the other room. This time, it was Thali's turn to excuse herself politely before backing slowly away from the dinner table and running to her rooms. She suddenly felt the palace walls closing in. Not caring what she was wearing, she let her animals out of their antechamber and led them to the hall. Seeing Stefan turn the corner at the end of the hall and no one else, she ran to the exit with Indi and Ana and made for the forest. Then she ran as fast as she could amongst the trees. She needed out.

Heart pounding in her chest, she ran and ran. She didn't care about her pretty silk shoes or the pretty green dress getting torn by the branches and twigs she ran past. Letting her beating heart drown out every thought, she ran deep into the forest as fast as she could, her tiger and dog running next to her. She had always known she was different, had seen people whispering in quiet corners, the stares from under the brim of a hat or helmet. But today was the first time she'd been cut with such harsh words. And then to hear Elric announce his intentions so clearly to a stranger when they hadn't even talked about it yet was all too much.

Seeking comfort, she opened her mind to the animals around her, wanting to feel the peace and solace of their thoughts and lives. As she ran, she zipped through the lives of the many creatures in the woods and naturally extended her thoughts farther. Her training with Joren was paying off because she could now cover great distances quickly in her mind as she ran. Looking for something else to focus on, she continued to run, searching her threads for anything that could distract her. A faint glittering turquoise thread suddenly appeared.

Thali stopped dead in her tracks, Indi and Ana circling back for her. She sank to the ground, closing her eyes to better concentrate on the glittering turquoise thread, catching her breath as she gulped greedily for air.

In her mind, she saw a faint rainbow of threads, but the turquoise one started glowing as it neared her mind, growing thicker. Thali's instincts told her to back away, to close her mind. Instead, she traveled along the thickening thread to see through the creature's eyes so she could figure out what the creature was, where it was. She saw only clouds flying past. Then, she felt something crawling toward her on the same thread. Like creeping slime, it moved closer and closer as though it wanted to touch her mind. Thali quickly backed away and shut the door to all the threads.

What had she done? Thali thought of the deep claw marks Joren had suffered, of the people that had gone missing, and of how she had this terrible feeling that whatever she'd seen flying was incredibly large and flying toward her. Coming back to herself, she realized that she'd stopped in a clearing. Ana and Indi were laying around her, keeping her warm as they panted, catching their breath.

Thali looked up to see that Stefan had finally caught up to her from across the clearing. He must have heard her leave, but at least he had come alone. He panted as he approached, hands in the air.

"Lady Routhalia, are you hurt?"

She shook her head.

"May I approach you?" He glanced at Indi and Ana.

Thali nodded.

Stefan came over and stood beside Thali, searching the clearing for any threats in their immediate surroundings. "For what it's worth, Prince Feng will no longer be welcome in this kingdom," he said.

The hurtful comments now so faded with the potential threat she had just discovered, Thali was hyperalert for anything that might be approaching them. Words didn't matter right now. "I want to go back to my rooms please," came out of Thali's mouth before she realized she'd said it.

"Of course, m'lady. Please, after you." Stefan bowed and waited for her to lead the way.

Thali rushed back to the palace with Stefan, glancing upward and keeping watch through some of the other animals. She was glad she could now do so without closing her eyes as she hurried back to the palace. Maybe it hadn't noticed her.

CHAPTER THIRTY-TWO

S TEFAN

Stefan had never heard Thali command anything of anyone. And she'd looked terrified when he'd found her in a heap on the ground, dress torn, tiger and dog surrounding her. She looked like she'd dropped right out of a fairy tale with her animals guarding her protectively. His heart had skipped a beat at the sight. Stefan was fond of Lady Routhalia. She was a warrior like he was. And she saw him as a person, not as ornamentation. Besides, he'd watched Elric mature in the last few years, and Thali had brought him out of his shell since they'd met last year. Instead of getting lost in royal business inside the castle walls, Thali made Elric live life.

As they walked back to her rooms, Stefan noticed Thali was vigilant. Overly vigilant. She looked ready to jump into a fight with a dagger in her hand if the wrong twig cracked. Her tiger's and dog's hackles were up too as though they too were scanning the forest, waiting for something to jump out at them. Suddenly, the three picked up their pace and started to run, and Stefan didn't have a chance to ask questions as he kept pace with them over uneven ground.

He clenched his fists, ready to break Prince Feng's bones for what he'd said about Thali. He'd even seen one of Prince Feng's own guards, one of the women, turn pale and let anger flash in her eyes. His heart had almost broken at how Thali had looked. She had gone completely white with shock, and he had half expected her to faint, but she had remained stoic, staring at Prince Feng. Elric and the king were disgusted with their guest and would probably cut his visit short now. On his way out of the dining room, Elric had only given Stefan a single look as he left, but Stefan had known what Elric wanted. So Stefan had dutifully gone to follow Thali, to make sure she was safe.

Following her now, Stefan thought about how Lady Routhalia would make a wonderful queen. She was intelligent and kind and strong. He was honored to have the privilege of watching his prince woo her. Though Stefan was a few years Elric's senior, he'd grown up alongside the prince. Where Stefan had always been more adventurous, the prince had always preferred to read a book instead of swinging sticks at fake enemies or engaging with others his age. But when he'd met Lady Routhalia, it was like a light had turned on and he'd suddenly grown from a reluctant prince to one with vision and enthusiasm.

When they finally made it back to her rooms, Stefan bowed to Thali as she walked into her rooms, her animals following. Then, he stood guard at her door as he knew Elric would want. He fully expected Elric to come to her room to check on her as soon as he possibly could. After a moment's thought, Stefan also sent a messenger to the guard to keep watch in the forest on this side of the palace. He didn't know what Thali had been watching for, but he would take it seriously.

CHAPTER THIRTY-THREE

T HALI WAS BEYOND EXHAUSTED. Maybe she was jumping to conclusions. She hadn't actually seen the direction the animal was flying in, just a lot of clouds. It had just been a feeling, an instinct. She hadn't heard or seen anything amiss when she walked back to the palace with Stefan either, though even Indi, Ana, and Bardo had seemed on high alert. She was too afraid now to open the channels again to check on the thread she'd made contact with. The feeling of someone or something else creeping toward her own mind made her shiver.

Once in her room, she had jumped into bed, but then cringing at what Mia would say about all the dirt and mud, she'd gotten up and carefully taken off the green dress and crawled back under the covers. Now her imagination was racing with thoughts of what had happened.

Elric had been clear he was courting her before, but what he'd said tonight made her face the reality that he wanted to marry her. She'd been shoving that thought into a corner and avoiding it. She tried to picture them together on the throne, her as queen, his queen. Thinking of Elric warmed her heart, but the thought of sitting on the throne chilled her to the bone.

Then there was the animal she'd inadvertently seen. *It was a large flying creature*, she thought.

This was no bird, but there were so many mythical creatures that could fly. She wondered back to what Joren had said, that perhaps these creatures were also intelligent. She'd never felt anything like that creeping up her own thread. She'd never felt anything crawl up her thread.

And buried under all that was Prince Feng and his nasty words. She wondered if that was his thought alone or if the entire Cerisan court thought that of her and her family.

Her thoughts were interrupted by a soft knock on the door. Her heart raced knowing it was likely Elric. Still, she hesitated to open it. Facing him meant facing what he'd said. Perhaps he'd just think she'd fallen asleep. She tiptoed to the door as quietly as she could, placing a hand on it. A piece of paper slid under the door.

I know you're not asleep. Pretty please open the door?
– E

Thali smiled. She wanted to see Elric, wanted to bask in her personal sunshine even if that meant facing what he'd said. She went to put an overcoat on and then tiptoed back to the door to find another piece of paper had arrived.

I'm going to wait here all night if that's what it takes.
– E

Her animals were all fast asleep on the bed when she slowly cracked the door open. Elric had been leaning on the doorframe and when the door opened, he heaved himself upright, shoving paper and pen into his coat pockets. His sunny smile appeared when his eyes found hers.

"Can we go somewhere else? They're all asleep." She nodded at her bed.

He nodded before leading Thali back to the courtyard where they'd had breakfast a few days ago. It was just as beautiful at night with the stars and moon glowing on the stone accents and furniture throughout the garden.

Elric's guards posted themselves along the perimeter and by the entrance and exit just like they had that morning. Thali sat down on a stone bench by a pond, wrapping her arms around herself.

Elric sat down next to her. "Thali, I'm sorry for what Prince Feng said. He was drunk, not that that's an excuse, but I hate that you heard it. My father and I have agreed to send him packing tomorrow. He's no longer welcome here, and Cerisa will have some groveling to do before we welcome anyone else."

Despite everything, she murmured quietly, "I'm from there."

"You and your mother are citizens of Adanek. And we're honored to have you. I almost punched him tonight, Thali." Elric rose and started pacing in front of her. "I even broke a chair in my father's parlor because I gripped it so hard." He produced a wooden knob from his coat pocket, and Thali couldn't help but laugh. Elric dropped the knob back in his pocket and took hold of Thali's hands. She let him. She felt her heart start to race again as his warm hands gently held hers.

"Are you all right?" Elric asked.

Thali nodded.

"I'm sorry I announced my intentions like I did tonight. I was just so angry at him. How dare he be so blind and disrespectful!"

"Don't worry yourself over it. We'll put it behind us," Thali said, staring at their intertwined hands.

Elric perked up. "So, there's still an us?"

"Well, if you want there to be." As much as the prospect of being queen scared her, here, in this garden with Elric, she knew they could have a future together. Everything seemed easier with him next to her. He made her happy. There might not be the same intensity, the same passion, the same connection as she had with Garen, but she was okay with happy.

"I didn't scare you away? I sent Stefan to protect you because I thought for sure you'd pack your things and run," Elric said.

"Well, I did run, but I didn't pack. You've been very clear about your intentions. It was just ... surprising to hear it spoken out loud." Thali glanced up at him momentarily.

"Thali, do you love me?" Elric's voice was just a whisper, and Thali had to concentrate to hear him over the roar of her thundering heart.

She looked up at him, his green eyes and wavy golden hair. She felt her heart swell with happiness. He was joyful and optimistic, and even with the weight of the world on his shoulders, he was thoughtful and didn't mind being silly with her. She nodded her head.

"Marry me," he said, hope and joy filling his expression.

Thali froze.

He continued, "Routhalia, I love you. Will you make me the happiest man in this entire kingdom? Will you marry me?"

Thali felt the world closing in. Her mind reverberated with the words spoken what felt like so long ago, the words Garen had left her broken-hearted with:

You're meant for so much more than just me, more than this underground world ... one day, the prince will ask you to marry him ...

"Thali, you don't have to say yes right now. I know it's asking a lot of you. And even if you say yes, we wouldn't have to get married right away. I know you probably want to finish school, so we could wait a year or so, and you can finish before we make it official."

Against all odds, Thali had found actual happiness with another person after Garen even if it was a different kind of happy. All these opposing emotions swirled within her. Elric made her happy, and she loved him in a way. But she also still loved Garen, was still grieving his loss. She didn't know what to feel.

Elric held his breath as he waited for her answer. Then he pushed something into Thali's hand. She uncurled her fingers to find a ring adorned with a giant rectangular diamond, two slightly smaller rectangular sapphires flanking it. Thali's eyes grew wide.

Movement caught her eye then, and she looked at the pond at her feet just in time to see a dark shadow pass over them. She and Elric looked up and saw an enormous swathe of green fly over them before circling and landing on the far side of the royal courtyard.

In a heartbeat, Elric's guards surrounded them. Thali pocketed the ring before grabbing Elric's hand. He squeezed it tight as they stared at the massive dragon that now stood before them. There was no doubt in her mind that's what this was. His claws were as big as wagons, its immense body completely covered in leaf-green scales. A tail that slowly danced from one side to the other was as long as its body. His leathery wings were as wide as the palace itself and folded neatly behind his back as its keen eyes peered at them down a shiny, scaley snout. To Thali, the creature looked like a palace-sized salamander with scales and wings, except in place of rounded toes that could stick to rocks were sharp claws that could make ribbons of the palace with a single swipe.

Thali then noticed the seven bodies around them. Elric's normal six guards were surrounding them, but the seventh was her Aunt Qiao, now standing in front of Thali. It softened her heart a little to see her aunt standing there in all her warrior glory, for her, for Thali. Maybe she had more family than she'd thought. Maybe her aunt had told her the truth the other day.

The dragon huffed, letting smoke and flames lick his nostrils in stark contrast to the dark night.

Give me the girl.

The voice rang clear in her head, and from Elric's expression, Thali knew it had spoken in all their heads. Before anyone could move, Qiao stepped forward, away from the others, who closed in around Thali and Elric.

"No." Qiao positioned herself between the dragon and the group of guards surrounding Thali and Elric.

The dragon laughed, his whole body rocking up and down with each chuff.

You are no match for me, little human. I could crush this building before the sun finishes its ascent.

No one moved.

Last warning ... And the dragon tilted his head questioningly.

Still, no one moved. Seconds later, Qiao shifted her spear, ready to launch it at the dragon.

Go ahead, little human. Throw your tiny twig.

Qiao threw her spear, aiming for the dragon's armpit, but it bounced harmlessly off like she had thrown a branch at a stone wall.

My turn.

And before anyone could even scream, the dragon shot a stream of blue-white fire at Qiao. Her body crumbled into a pile of ash, and Thali strangled her cry before it could escape her throat as she stared at the scorch mark where her aunt had stood.

A whoosh of wind caught her attention, and they all looked up to see a second dragon, red as blood, land between the green dragon and their little huddled group.

The only thing the group could see now was the red dragon's back. They heard clicks and roars as the two dragons conversed in some unknown language. Thali was tempted to open her mind to see if she could tell what was going on when a familiar voice rang in her head.

No.

The group backed slowly out of the courtyard until they were backed up against the doors. They tried to open them, and they could tell guards on the other side were also trying to pry them open, but they wouldn't budge. By now, the entire palace was abuzz with guards trying to get into the courtyard, alarm bells ringing, and orders being shouted over the din.

Suddenly, they were blinded by white light as the red dragon shot a stream of pure white flame at the green dragon. The green dragon shot up into the sky, and the fire melted a stone wall instead before the red dragon leaped up in pursuit. They flew up and away so swiftly, Thali barely saw them before they became specs in the sky and disappeared.

Finally, the doors gave way and palace guards spilled everywhere. Elric was escorted to his rooms deep within the castle for his safety and Thali back to her rooms, where she had to calm her frantic animals. As soon as the animals were calm, Thali started packing up all her things. She'd go back to school. She should have listened to Joren and stayed put. If being away from the school was going to bring dragons down on her, she needed to get back as soon as possible. Dragons! Of all the mythical creatures she'd seen in tapestries or heard of in stories, she couldn't believe the one they'd been looking for was a dragon. Dragons were truly real! She'd thought of griffons, winged horses, or hybrid horse-sea creatures perhaps, but fire-breathing dragons?! She shoved the thought aside as she focused on packing her things as fast as possible.

She choked up as she thought of her aunt, who had bravely confronted the dragon for Thali. She had barely known her aunt but recognized the act of love she'd shown. How could she have doubted her aunt's intentions? How had she earned her aunt's love? She felt her heart ache as she realized the relationship she would never have.

Ana and Indi squeezed closer on both sides. Thali knelt and petted them both and hugged them to her. She would make herself worthy of her aunt's sacrifice. Ana licked her tears from her face. Taking a deep breath, Thali blinked the rest of her tears away and focused on packing her things.

CHAPTER THIRTY-FOUR

A KNOCK AT THALI'S door interrupted her thoughts, and she wiped her eyes and cleared her throat as she invited them to enter.

She turned, shocked to see Alexius walk into her room, here, at the palace.

"Thali, we need to talk."

Thali's legs gave out as she sank onto the bed. The familiar voice earlier—the voice that had told her not to open her mind to the threads—that had been Alexius.

"You're—"

"Yes, I'm a red dragon."

"But ... but you're human."

"I can take any shape I like."

He hurried to the bed and continued packing where Thali had stopped. "We have to get out of here."

"But ... but I don't understand," Thali said. Her thoughts reeled.

"I've been protecting you at the school. I was hoping you'd come into your abilities on your own, and I wanted to shield you from the others while that happened. But you left my protective range, and they saw you. I thought there was a chance you'd be safe here, but I was wrong. There'll be more coming if we don't leave now."

"Will they ..."

"No, they'll just fly above then leave if they can't find you here. So we need to leave, now."

"Where are we going?"

"Somewhere safe so you can learn about *all* your abilities." He huffed. "This is tiresome." Alexius looked around the room.

Suddenly everything flew into the trunks, packing themselves, then the trunks shrunk to fit in his palm.

Alexius dropped them in his pocket before turning to Thali.

"I know you're confused, and you have questions. But right now, we have to go. We don't have time for you to say your goodbyes, but they can come if you would like." He glanced at Indi, Ana, and Bardo.

Thali nodded. Her world had flip-flopped three times within hours. She thought of all the people at the palace. If she had been the one to attract them here, then she had to leave so they could be safe. Elric had to be safe.

They crept out of the castle and marched into the forest, right into a substantial meadow mostly hidden from view of the castle. Alexius signaled for her to stop before he continued walking ahead, then with a *pop*, turned back into the red dragon she'd just seen.

Alexius the dragon had a pouch around his neck. He pulled something out of it and placed it on the ground. In front of her eyes, it grew to become a stone basket the size of a wagon.

Get in.

Thali hesitated. Her aunt had just died so she wouldn't have to go somewhere with a big green dragon, and now here she was just hopping into the basket of a big red dragon.

Thali, you have to trust me. I will explain everything, but we have to go.

Just as he spoke, there was a shriek in the sky, and Thali, Indi, and Ana leaped into the stone bowl. She checked her wrist for Bardo. Alexius the dragon picked up the bowl and dropped them into the pouch around his neck. She felt him turn his head to look behind him before lunging into the air.

Thali and her animals were pressed into the side of the bowl as the dragon gained speed. He soared higher into the sky and accelerated even more. Thali struggled to reach into her inner shirt pocket and closed her hand around the ring Elric had given her what felt like days earlier. She knew he would be worried. The palace guards had followed protocol given she was a guest; they hadn't yet known what had happened. She knew Elric would have already sent more guards to her room to bring her to him and would be shocked to learn she had disappeared. He'd probably think she'd been kidnapped since the green dragon had wanted her in the first place. Thali felt bad that she would make him worry. She wondered if she'd be able to send him a message from wherever she was going.

Her animals had pressed themselves up against her and were keeping her warm in their unusual transport. Thali was trying to sort everything out in her brain when she felt them descending before they landed softly on the ground. Alexius the dragon pulled the bowl out of the pouch and placed it on the ground. Then with another *pop*, he turned back into Alexius the person. His red hair now made sense to Thali, a muted reflection as it was of his bright scales. His emerald eyes shone brightly, turquoise flecks in the irises.

"Where are we?" Thali managed to squeak as she and Indi and Ana tumbled out of the bowl.

"At school. Do you think you can walk?" Alexius kept his eyes on the sky above them.

"What? I thought we were going somewhere safe."

"We are somewhere safe. This place has been fortified with the magic of many dragons. They couldn't find you before and won't now. No dragon would dare stoop so low as to ask a human where you are. They'll search the skies and move on when they don't find you."

Thali felt like she should feel insulted but held her tongue. She looked around to orient herself before Alexius pointed in the direction of the school.

"So ... am I supposed to just go back to classes?" She asked.

"Yes."

"And not say anything about you, obviously."

"Yes."

"Why didn't you tell me before?"

"Would you have believed me?"

"No. But you could have popped into your dragon form."

Alexius didn't answer. He looked up and she could tell he was using some unknown-to-her sense to search the skies to make sure they hadn't been followed. She shook her head to rid it of all her questions and walked toward the school, but Alexius stopped her.

"Not yet. The school is a day's ride from the castle. Even at your fastest, you wouldn't be back until tomorrow morning. We'll stay here until then so no one thinks it's strange you got here so fast. Once I'm sure we haven't been followed, I'll answer your questions," Alexius said.

Thali flopped down on the grass. Her world spun around her, and she was glad to have her tiger and dog with her. She focused only on breathing, trying not to think of anything else, trying to calm her mind.

Everything was silent in the meadow where they had landed. The minutes seemed to drag on for hours until finally Alexius turned back toward her, sat down cross-legged across from her, and grinned.

Thali could only stare. She'd seen Alexius every day for the last several months. How had she missed the pointed teeth, the too-red hair, the emerald eyes that were too green to be human?

"Tongue-tied now, are we?" he asked.

"I ... we ... how ... why...?" Thali clamped her lips shut to try to form a coherent sentence.

Alexius sighed. "I am from a family of dragons that have long protected this world. Until recently, we guarded a gate to your world. But when you opened it, magical creatures flooded into this world. I was sent to protect you."

Thali's heart sank into her stomach. She'd been denying it all this time, but after moving those gems on Star Island last year, seeing those sparkling threads flood off the island, and Joren's warning, she'd feared she'd opened some kind of door, and now Alexius had confirmed it. "Why me?"

"Do I really need to tell you why?" Merriment danced in Alexius's eyes as he raised a single eyebrow.

Thali felt her throat closing, and she stared at her hands. "What now?"

Alexius let out a big sigh. "You go back to class. You train with me at night. You need to learn more about your ability, more than that plant man can teach you. He's done well so far, but I don't think you realize you've only barely scratched the surface of your abilities."

"How am I supposed to go back to class after all this?"

"It will be a singular incident. My brothers and sister will help ensure the others behave while you stay hidden. Routhalia, you need to re-alize that there are forces at work here that are going to change the world. Like it or not, you are going to be a factor, but until you are able, you have to stay hidden."

Thali deflated. "Is this all my fault? Is this all happening because I opened the portal?"

Alexius shook his head. "No, it is not your fault. This day was meant to come."

"What do you mean? Meant to come? What forces are working to change the world?"

Alexius looked at Thali. Thali looked at Alexius. She felt a thread slide in and knock on the door to her mind. Alexius nodded ever so slightly. "We might as well start tonight. There are things I can only show you, and you need to let me in so I can do that."

Thali looked at Alexius again. Could she trust him? He had saved her life, and the lives of everyone in the palace—save for her aunt. Taking a deep breath and making a choice, she cracked open the door in her mind and let her thread slide to the other side where the glittering turquoise thread connected with it.

Routhalia, dragons live a long time. My parents were there when humans rounded up all the magical creatures and sent them to another world before sealing the gates between our worlds.

Thali saw a shimmering, rainbow-colored portal as big as her school and all the mythical creatures she had ever seen in tapestries flying through it, even a large sapphire-blue dragon with green eyes flying above it.

But nothing stays gone forever. The prophesy states that when the gates open, the greatest forces of evil that have ever been seen will be unleashed.

Now, Thali saw an old woman in pink and gray rags, diamonds sparkling on the hems, huddled over a wide bowl of water.

My aunt is an oracle. The one part of the prophesy she did not tell anyone but my family was that there would be a girl, a human, who could cross the boundary of the worlds and would determine this world's demise or rebirth.

Thali now saw a muscular man with blue hair the same color as that flying blue dragon holding the old woman's hand as she whispered something to him. Thali wondered whose perspective she was seeing.

The voice was soft in her brain, the images vibrant, reverberating in her mind. She squeezed her eyes shut to focus on the images. "So ..." Thali started to say.

Alexius shook his head. He tapped his temple.

Thali thought about what she wanted to say. But Alexius shook his head. She closed her eyes to better see the glittering turquoise thread and the softness of it attached to her mind. She let her thoughts flow through the attachment.

How do you know the prophesy refers to me? Thali thought.

Alexius cringed. *Try not to yell in my head. But we don't. Not for sure. But I believe it's you. That's why I'm here. And someone else thinks it's you, too. That's why they're looking for you.*

Thali found herself reaching for the ring in her pocket. *Did you see everything that happened? Before you chased off that green dragon?*

Alexius tried not to cringe so obviously this time. But she could tell she must still be yelling in his head. *If you're asking about your prince's proposal, I heard it.* He glanced at Thali's hand closed around the ring. *I've been protecting you since you opened that portal. I thought it would be easier if I were a fellow student. I'm hoping now that you know, you'll go easier on me.*

Thali thought back to the conference she'd been to before school had started. Her eyes grew wide.

I do not care about people politics. Thieves or royalty, it does not affect me.

She shivered. Alexius had guessed what she'd been thinking about. Or could he read her mind? She thought about her life since the portal had opened. It seemed like years ago. Suddenly, she wondered if Garen would know what had happened at the palace, then she wondered if he would even care. She thought about Elric, who was probably beside himself with worry. How could her life have changed so dramatically in the span of a year? She was only her father's daughter a year and a half ago. She'd been about to embark on a journey with her own ship. Now, her brother was dead, she had nearly died, she had attended a thieving conference and been accepted as a prince of thieves, she had found and lost her true love, she might be betrothed to the prince of Adenek, and she had a dragon as protector and teacher. Oh, and she had an ability she'd been trying to hide her whole life that the world might now need to survive.

Alexius stood and retreated to the other side of the meadow. She could feel the glittering turquoise thread that was Alexius retreating, but a tiny strand of it remained in her mind, similar to her connections with Indi, Ana, and Bardo.

Thali looked at the ring Elric had given her. It was one of the biggest jewels she'd ever seen. She couldn't imagine wearing it every day. It would likely feel cumbersome. But the way it sparkled reminded her of Elric and his sparkling smile, so she tried it on. Examining it, she decided the sparkling ring looked like it belonged on the well-manicured hand of a fancy lady, not on her hand with its crooked finger from a rope accident and dirty fingernails.

Pulling a piece of paper and a pencil out of her pocket, Thali wrote Elric a note. If she could tell him she was okay, he'd stop worrying. She could have done that from the road, and she mentally kicked herself for not doing so. Not knowing quite what to say, she simply wrote:

> *I'm okay. I've gone back to school. I figured it would be easier to slip out during the hubbub. I'll be safe here.*

She called for her bat then and tied the note to his leg before sending him off. Alexius had watched her do it and hadn't tried to stop her, so she figured it was safe.

Ana whined softly to let Thali know someone she knew was coming toward them. Thali looked up to see that Alexius had disappeared. Thali scanned the meadow for who the visitor could possibly be and wondered why Alexius was letting them walk right up to her if she was supposed to be on her way back to school.

Spotting movement finally, Thali's heart stopped beating when she recognized who was striding across the field.

Chapter Thirty-Five

INDI AND ANA CIRCLED him as he got close enough, rubbing against him to show him how much they had missed him.

Thali rose to her feet, knees wobbly as he approached. It was like seeing a ghost come back to life. The polished-wood brown hair, the turbulent blue eyes, the lithe movements like he was a stalking panther. She could tell he was angry. But she was still trying to wrap her mind around the reality of what was happening. She hadn't seen Garen since he had broken her heart and left the broken pieces for her to do with as she pleased.

Suddenly, she felt her own anger jump to the surface. How dare he? When he reached her, she punched him in the stomach. Surprise crossed his face as he doubled over. She crossed her arms, narrowing her eyes as he recovered. A small part of her ached to hold his face between her hands, but her anger simmered above that.

When he stood up again, she saw the hurt in his eyes, and it softened her anger. "A dragon, Thali? Did you really call a dragon?" he asked.

"Who told you?" Thali countered.

"Everyone knows," Garen said.

"I didn't call it. At least, I didn't mean to."

"Didn't Joren teach you—" Garen started.

"I screwed up, all right, Garen? I promised Joren I wouldn't open my mind, but then I got overwhelmed, and I made a mistake." Thali felt a pressure on her chest ease as she said it out loud.

"And now?" Garen asked.

"I'm safe." Thali crossed her arms.

"How?" he asked.

She touched on the thread in her mind. She tried to send her thoughts delicately this time so she wouldn't yell in his head. *He knows about me. He won't leave me alone until he knows I have this under control.*

She heard a laugh through the thread. *Under control?*

Before she could reply, Alexius stepped out of the woods to Thali's left.

"Your sparring partner?" Garen looked confused.

Ignoring how he knew who her sparring partner was, she gestured to Alexius. "Alexius, let me officially introduce you to Garen. Garen, Alexius. Alexius saved me. And he's protecting me here and will be training me."

"And what special power does Alexius have?" Garen narrowed his eyes, suspicious.

Knowing Garen the way she did, Thali could see that his thieving instincts told him Alexius wasn't what he said he was.

"What did you hear about the attack on the palace?" Thali asked.

"Only that a green dragon landed and fried one of the guards before a red dragon came and chased it away."

Thali's heart filled with anguish at the thought of her aunt being gone, but she swallowed to continue. "Alexius is the red dragon."

"Oh?" Not a stranger to new and shocking things, Garen only lifted an eyebrow. His eyes flicked to Alexius, then he adopted his heaviest drawl. "Pleasure to meet you, great red dragon."

"Enough," Thali said. She could feel Garen gearing up for a fight.

Hurry it up. We have work to do, Alexius said in her mind before he melted back into the woods, leaving Thali and Garen alone again.

"How did you find me anyway?" Thali was trying to hold on to her anger because if the anger disappeared, she feared to feel what was underneath it.

"I knew you'd likely head back to school, so I waited for a bat to fly out solo and figured you'd be where he landed."

"Why?"

"I wanted to make sure you were safe."

Thali felt her anger crumbling.

"So ... when's the big day?" Garen grumbled through clenched teeth.

Thali's eyes opened wide in shock. Garen, who didn't miss a single detail, was now staring at the ring she had forgotten to take off her finger. Her beloved Garen now hid behind a mask of indifference.

Thali could see the hurt in his eyes. "Garen, it's not ... we aren't ... I haven't ..."

"What, you aren't getting married? You aren't currently betrothed to the wonderful Prince Elric?" Garen's bitter words almost sounded like a snarl. She knew he was trying to protect himself and it broke her heart. She hadn't meant for him to find out this way.

Thali hung her head. "I haven't said yes. It's not official." She wanted to reach out to him, to hold his hands and tell him he would be all right. That she would be all right. That this is what she wanted, what he'd wanted.

Garen laughed dully. "I don't know what you're waiting for. This is what was supposed to happen."

He started to turn away, but she reached out and grabbed his hand before he could leave. "I loved you. *You* broke *my* heart, not the other way around," she said.

"I broke both our hearts," Garen murmured before slipping out of her grip and walking away.

Thali felt empty. She was emotionally drained and stared after the spot that Garen had recently occupied. Fumbling, she carefully removed the ring and put it away in her shirt pocket.

Ready to go back? Alexius softly prodded her mind.

I thought we were staying here? Thali let her thought drift past the base of his thread like it was a peripheral thought instead of aiming it directly at the thread.

At least you're not yelling in my head anymore. Alexius offered her a soft smile as he reappeared. *I think you need the comfort of familiar surroundings right now. We'll sneak you in.*

At her nod, Alexius flew as a dragon back to school, Thali and her animals secure back in the bowl. Then he popped back into his human form at the edge of the forest before walking Thali to her rooms in the middle of the night.

She was exhausted. Grateful not to encounter Mia in the common area, she nodded to Alexius as he turned to leave, and she, Ana, and Indi slipped into her room and straight into bed. Without changing or pulling up the blankets, she fell into the deepest sleep she'd had in a very long time, not even noticing when Bardo crawled out of her sleeve and slithered up to his usual spot by the window.

CHAPTER THIRTY-SIX

I T WAS MID-AFTERNOON BEFORE Thali opened her eyes. She stared at the ceiling, remembering all the things that had happened yesterday, not believing all of it had happened in a single day. She noticed that her animals had been let out to relieve themselves and were back in bed with her. Mia must have done that and not woken her.

Thali changed her clothes, grateful for the warm bowl of water in her room so she could wash her face and wipe some of the dirt and grime off. Mia must have done that too.

Feeling a little more refreshed, she cracked her door open.

"Finally awake, sleepyhead?" Mia looked up from her sewing with a grin only a cat who'd caught a mouse could have. She knew.

"Heya, thought we'd welcome you back properly." Daylor grinned. Daylor and Tilton were hanging out in her common room, too, and they'd looked up from the books they'd been reading when she'd opened the door. Tilton clamped his lips together, dipping his head briefly, before joining the cats-who-caught-a-mouse club. Daylor wore a smile to match Mia's.

Thali looked around the room to make sure there was no one else in the common room before putting her hand on her hips.

"How do you know?"

"Well, *I* found the ring in your pocket while trying to get you out of your dirty clothes," Mia offered.

"And, well, Thali ... um, you should probably look outside," Tilton piped up.

She rushed to the window of their common room. Her jaw dropped when she saw royal guards posted every five feet along her building.

"He didn't ..." Thali started, feeling the heat climb up her neck.

"It's the same in the hallway." Daylor could barely contain his laughter.

"I didn't even say yes ... he said he was going to wait until I was ready. They must have raced all the way here without stopping," Thali squeaked.

"Whatever you did, I think he took it as a yes. And I'm sure his idea of discretion changed when you were attacked by a *dragon*." Mia returned to her sewing like she'd asked what they'd had for supper.

Daylor's eyes widened like a little boy seeing his first bear. "Was it really a dragon?"

Thali just swallowed. Tilton rose and gently guided Thali to a chair. "We were just at the wrong place at the wrong time," she murmured.

Mia caught her eye, asking her with a simple glance if it had been because of her ability. Thali gave an almost imperceptible nod and Mia understood. They would need to talk about it later.

"It's a good thing you sent him that note. He'd sent me a desperate message asking if you'd returned. He'd even sent search parties out in all directions."

"When ...?" Thali asked and pointed out the window.

"Oh, the cavalry descended on the school late this morning." Daylor now sat back in his chair, feet up on the table. He was clearly enjoying watching Thali sink into an abyss of embarrassment. "And before you make any excuses, if he had sent just the army, it would have made sense, but those people out there are royal guards. They're meant only to guard the royal family. The whole school knows."

Thali's eyes went wide. "My parents," she whispered. Even Mia's eyes went wide. Thali's parents would be furious if they found out from rumors and not her. "Quick, Mia, grab me some paper. I have to write to them." Thali blocked every thought in her mind and tried to compose herself enough to write a note to her parents. She sent it by bat and hoped they would get it before they heard the news from someone else.

As she sent that bat off, she saw another bat come flying at her. She opened the window for her, gently took the note from its leg, and unrolled it.

Sorry about how we're making this official. I know I said I'd give you time, but I thought you'd been kidnapped. Then when I told my parents about the proposal, they sent out royal guards immediately. They take safety very seriously. I'm not even allowed to come to you myself, but I've convinced them to let you stay there until we have a better handle on things here.

Sorry about all the guards. Mom and Dad really like you, by the way.
– E

A soft knock on the door pulled Thali's attention back to the present. Mia went to answer it and let Stefan in.

"Hello, Lady Routhalia." Stefan bowed deeply.

"Stefan. Thank goodness. Can you make them all go away?"

A smile twitched at his lips before he regained his stoic composure. "I'm afraid we're here on the king's orders, m'lady."

"So, that's a maybe?" Thali said hopefully.

"Unfortunately not." Stefan finally cracked a smile at that.

Thali cringed. "What are your orders, exactly?" She hoped she wouldn't be forever trailed by the two dozen guards now within a mile's radius of her.

"Myself, Amali, and Derk are to be your personal guards, and we have two squads to cover the campus and your general whereabouts."

Thali's face fell. How was she going to have any privacy with three guards following her everywhere? She was at least glad that she knew Amali and Derk. They had been part of Elric's personal detail. She'd even trained with Amali at the palace. "Can't I count as my own personal guard too?"

"Why do you think you only have three personal guards to Elric's six?"

Thali swallowed, her shoulders sinking as she sighed. She looked over at Daylor, Tilton, and Mia, who were all trying to hold in their laughter.

Daylor rose and went to offer Stefan his hand. "Well, since we'll be seeing a lot of you, I'm Daylor." Then gesturing, he added, "And this is Tilton. I'm sure you've met Mia."

"Stefan." He nodded his head as he shook Thali's friends' hands.

Thali then thought of a way she could wipe the smiles off their faces. "Don't you even start laughing, you three, because I'm dragging all three of you into this circus whether you like it or not."

Daylor swept into a ridiculous bow, made more ridiculous by his enormous size. "Well, of course m'lady, we would be honored to serve you."

Thali grabbed the nearest thing she could find and chucked it at Daylor's head. Thankfully, it was just a pillow.

Stefan was conveniently looking at a tapestry on the wall at that moment, one corner of his mouth twitching. He dipped his head, turned to leave the room, then stopped suddenly and asked, "M'lady, would you like us to get you something to eat?"

"You could do that?" The thought of going into the dining hall with her own set of guards made her not want to eat anything.

"Of course, m'lady. Today, there's no need for you to leave this room. We still have to brief you on protocol and procedure from here on out anyway," Stefan said.

The color drained from Thali's face, and she swallowed. She nodded and Stefan left the room to send the message down the line.

Noticing her friends trying to preoccupy themselves, perhaps unsure of how to treat their new princess-to-be, Thali sunk into a chair and looked them all in the eye. "You know, I'm no different from when I left. You all have permission to be yourselves. In fact, I hope you'll be yourselves for my sake. I'm going to need as much normal as I can get."

They all sighed as a group, then Daylor and Tilton put down the books they'd picked back up and Mia dropped her sewing. They scooted to the edges of their seats to get closer to Thali, excitement written all over their faces.

"Tell us everything!" Mia demanded as she crossed her legs, clearly settling in for a good story.

So, Thali settled in, too, and told them about her time at the palace, of how she'd met Prince Feng, Princess Suyi, and her aunt. Finally, she got to the part about Prince Feng's comments, Elric's reply, her trying to make a run for it in the forest, the proposal in the courtyard garden, and the dragons showing up. There, she had to clamp her lips together. She couldn't bear to think of Garen, let alone say anything about him, and she definitely couldn't tell her friends about Alexius being the red dragon. So, Thali had to make up the ride back to school on the spot and wondered how she would get Arabelle back into the stables without raising suspicion.

The guards were the only interruption that day, eventually bringing enough food to feed all of them for the rest of the day. After Thali finished her story, she asked about the local gossip at school and what she had missed. Mia happily obliged, while the others added bits and pieces here and there.

It was late into the evening when Daylor finally squashed her in a hug and he and Tilton left Mia and Thali alone. Stefan took the opportunity to brief Thali and Mia on the protocol from then on: who would be with her when, certain codewords they should be familiar with, and where there would always be guards. Thali could only think of how difficult it was now going to be to train with Alexius, but she figured the great red dragon could figure that out.

Once Stefan left her and Mia alone for the night, Thali finally had the opportunity to fill her in on all the things she couldn't tell Daylor and Tilton.

"Spill it," Mia said. She went to make them another cup of tea.

"Where do I even start?" Thali asked. She was bursting to tell Mia what had really happened. Alexius hadn't told her to keep his identity a secret, but who would even believe her? She wasn't about to label herself as crazy. But this was Mia. So, she jumped in and told Mia everything: how her reaction to Elric's words at dinner had called the green dragon, how Alexius was the red dragon and had been sent here to protect her, and how he now would train her here. The only thing she couldn't bring herself to share was that she'd seen Garen. That, she just couldn't bring herself to recount.

"You know ... if you really wanted to, you could surround yourself with friends, even as princess of the kingdom," Mia volunteered.

"What do you mean?" Thali asked.

"I mean that if you're going to be princess, and eventually queen, I'm sure you can appoint whomever you want to positions closest to you."

"Would you want that though?"

"To be able to dress you every day and make fabulous dresses with an unlimited budget? YES!" Mia threw her hands up in the air.

"And what position would that be?"

"Royal dressmaker to the princess? Head lady's maid?" Mia pondered the titles.

"If I accept Elric's proposal, the position is yours if you want it. I'd love to have you with me."

Mia turned to look at her straight in the eye. "Why *are* you hesitating anyway?"

"I ... it's a lot," Thali said with a sigh.

Mia watched her carefully. "You'd be a great queen. You know that right?" she asked quietly.

Thali smothered the laugh in her throat. Of course her best friend would think that.

"Well, at least a great Princess Routhalia to start. So if you accept his proposal, I accept the position." Mia said.

"Good ... wait, do you think Daylor and Tilton would want positions in the palace?" Thali asked.

"I don't see why not. Though they might want to finish school."

"We're all going to finish school."

"Really? I thought you'd be sent off to princess school as soon as the word 'yes' came out of your mouth."

Thali rolled her eyes. "There's no such thing. And that was part of the deal. I get to finish school," Thali explained. Her head was spinning as she thought about all the implications of being a princess again.

Mia laughed. "For what? You're not going to be allowed to sail off into the sunset now."

"I'll get to sail off at least two more times, for the final exams." Thali crossed her arms. She would be adamant.

"Do you really think they'll let you?"

"I hope so," Thali said. She thought about the chaos that was last year's exam, then wondered if she'd be able to sneak onto the ship if the powers that be said no. She sat quietly thinking about that as she sipped her tea and Mia continued her sewing project.

Thali fell asleep curled up in the chair she had been sitting in and only barely came to wakefulness when Mia gently laid a blanket over her. Her animals curled around her feet, tired from the excitement of the last few days and glad to be home. She slept the night through after that, at peace for at least a little while.

Chapter Thirty-Seven

THALI WOKE TO MUFFLED yelling on the other side of the door. Metal clanging in the hallway pulled the cloud of sleep off, frightening her before she heard Stefan's booming voice. "Halt! Let them through."

Half the building would be awake now, Thali thought, cringing at the thought of how much her classmates would appreciate the early morning wake up.

Indi and Ana were already at the door, excited to greet whomever was on the other side. Thali recognized Ana's whine and barely had time to smooth down her hair before the door flung open.

"She was my own daughter before she was your princess, so I will damn well see her when I want to."

Thali grinned at the sound of her mother's voice.

"Honey, they're just doing their job." Her father's soothing did little to calm his wife.

"At least this one knows who we are. Goodness' sake."

Thali leaped at them with as much ferocity as Indi might as they walked into the room. They both caught her in a group hug.

"My darling girl," her father whispered, pressing his cheek to her forehead.

She eased slowly away from the comforting circle of their arms and led them to the little brown couch. The commotion had woken Mia, too, so she bustled about making tea for everyone as Thali and her parents caught up. Her father wouldn't let go of one of her hands, so she sat between them, telling them everything that had happened, though a redacted version of the tale she'd told Mia. When Thali got to the part about her aunt, Qiao, she found she couldn't look at them.

"Qiao was always so stoic. She always wanted to do what was right. I'm glad you got to meet her."

Thali saw her mother's deep brown, almond-shaped eyes filling with tears, yet she held them at bay, filing away her grief for another time. It was yet another reason for Thali to admire her mother.

Still unsure of what she could and could not say about Alexius, Thali decided to omit the part about his identity as the red dragon, how he'd brought her back to school, and how he would be training her. When she finished her story, her parents sat back, her father finally deigning to let go of her hand.

"Here I was, assuming school would be a safe, steady place for you, and here you are, finding excitement at every turn." Her father shook his head, making Thali realize there was more gray than brown in his thick hair now. He was no stranger to adventure himself.

"Are you sure this is what you want, Thali?" Her mother searched her face, looking for any sign of doubt.

"Which part? I could have done without the dragon."

Her father laughed, and Lady Jinhua shot her husband a pointed look. "I mean it, Routhalia. We would be just as happy to have a merchant daughter as a royal one."

"Actually, I think I'd prefer it," her father murmured so quietly Thali almost couldn't hear him.

"Papa!" Thali exclaimed. She paused for a moment to check in with herself, to make sure she was being honest with herself. "I haven't said yes, but I think this is what I want. I'm just sorry I couldn't give you more warning."

Lady Jinhua nodded, looking to her husband as he somberly nodded too.

"Then, if you choose to say yes, you will be the most beautiful princess bride this world has ever seen." Lady Jinhua rose and gave Thali a smile full of pride.

"We wouldn't be getting married until after I finish school though," Thali said.

Her parents nodded. Despite the great honor to their family, Thali knew that her mother understood the pressures of joining the ranks of royalty and didn't wish such a public life for her daughter. Thali, for her part, wondered how she would handle the pressure of everyone's competing agendas.

"Has Alexius been around?" Lady Jinhua suddenly asked as she sat back down and looked at the door expectantly.

"Sorry?" Thali's jaw dropped. "What—"

"Has he properly introduced himself yet?" her mother continued.

"How do you ...?" Then, Thali dropped her voice to a whisper. "Do you know ... do you know about him?"

Lady Jinhua had a mischievous glint in her eye as she whispered equally quietly, "You mean, do we know Alexius is actually a dragon?"

Thali's eyes practically popped out of her head, and the clang of ceramics beside her told her Mia had heard Thali's mother too.

Thali's father puffed out his chest and sat straighter. "Routhalia, did you really think we'd abandon you with no help after your near-death experience on that island last summer?"

Too shocked for words, she just looked from her mother to her father, her mouth agape.

"We've been searching for someone who could better understand you and help you since you were six. It's one of the reasons we've been traveling the world."

"But ... he said ... he ..."

"We asked him not to tell you until we could ourselves. We'd long heard legends of a family tasked with protecting humanity, of dragons legendary in their magical ability and intelligence. We've been searching and asking and learning but could only find solid leads after you opened that portal letting the magical creatures through. Then we tracked them to a far corner of the world and explained your abilities. Turns out they'd been searching for you too."

Thali could feel the tears well in her eyes. All this time, her parents had been trying to help her, setting things up so she'd be safe and trained at the same time. "So, you knew about the portal too? I just learned about it." When they just smiled knowingly, she recounted the real version of how she'd gotten back to school, leaving out the part about Garen of course. They nodded, looking satisfied.

Mia coughed. "Speaking of Alexius, if you want to make it to combat class, you're going to have to leave soon, Thali." She had started gathering her own things as Thali had finished that last part of the story.

Thali went to hug her parents and asked, "Will you be staying?"

Her mother frowned. "No, we could barely scrape together enough time to come see you this time. Soon though. When you finish your final exam, we'll sail the Bulstan route together."

Thali smiled; she would get to visit Tariq.

"That is, if you're allowed to?" Thali's father glanced at the door, on the other side of which the royal guards would undoubtedly be standing.

Thali's smile vanished. She'd never thought about whether she'd be allowed to join her family when she wasn't at school.

With one last hug, her father whispered, "Your exam destination will be Kadaloona." He wiggled his eyebrows as he pulled away from Thali.

Thali smiled and shook her head. She squeezed her father's hand gratefully, thinking about how he must have asserted himself with the school's authorities after last year's disastrous final exam. Kadaloona was a town between Lanchor and her home province of Densria. It was a decent-sized town that had blossomed as the intermediary between the wealthy merchants to the south and the larger markets further north.

She led her parents outside and watched them ride away before she headed to combat class. The merchant students would learn the details of the final exam in the next few days, and she hoped Elric would hold true to his word. Thali wanted desperately to sail with her friends. She was always happiest on the ocean. However, that happy thought was short-lived as she tried to push down the unease she felt at the three shadows following her.

At least I don't have an army of them following me, she supposed.

When she got to the edge of the training ring, she turned and said, "I can take it from here. Please don't follow me onto the field."

Stefan nodded his head and that was good enough for Thali. She walked up, blissfully alone, to Daylor, Alexius, and Tilton.

Barely containing his grin, Daylor acted like it was the first time he'd seen her. "Thali, what's with all the security? Did the prince propose or something?"

Thali couldn't help but laugh and roll her eyes as she reached up and punched his shoulder.

"Hey, Thali, can we see the ring?" Ari ran up and joined them. She was a stockier brunette girl who was fierce with daggers.

Seth, with his strawberry-blond hair and freckles across his nose, came up on her other side. "How did he propose?"

"Oh, I don't have it with me," Thali said. They were all acting like she'd already said yes. She smiled as she did her best to recount the public version of the proposal. When she glanced over at Daylor, she caught his wink, and she realized he had diffused the whole situation. Her classmates were still calling her Thali and were curious about everything instead of keeping her at arms length and addressing her formally. She really hoped Daylor would agree to come with her to the palace. He was much better with people than she could ever hope to be.

The rest of day looked exactly the same as she tried to catch up on two weeks of missed work: her guards attending classes with her—always trailing a few feet away and standing in the back of the classrooms—her classmates asking questions, and her giving modified answers. She could tell the guards' presence made her teachers a little nervous, but they continued as if nothing was out of the ordinary. Even her classmates treated her no differently, despite their questions, and Thali was grateful for that, at least.

CHAPTER THIRTY-EIGHT

T HE AIR HAD A crispness to it as the students neared the end of their school year.

"This year, we've decided to openly announce everyone's destinations to prevent any confusion." Master Kelcian stood on a raised platform in front of the crowd that had gathered. All the merchanting students had assembled in one of the main halls to learn the details of their final exam. Thali had snuck in just before the teacher had started speaking, sitting with Daylor and Tilton near the back, her guards sitting behind her.

Some of the first-year students seemed wary of the guards, but it had been a week since she'd returned, and the excitement that was the royal guards was already dying down.

"This year, we've decided to change the format of these practical exams, so you'll all be sailing to the city of Kadaloona. You'll have three checkpoints, at which you must wait for all ships to arrive before you will be allowed to depart in the order you arrived. You will also each have an instructor with you for each leg of the trip. The instructors will switch ships for each leg, evaluating your performance according to their specialties and combining their scores to give you a total score. While speed is a factor, you will also be tested on culture, product, and combat at each checkpoint, with challenges that each crew must complete. Each challenge is specifically aimed at different years, and you must complete each task to succeed and move on. The final challenge at Kadaloona will involve trading that which you've collected from your previous challenges for a profit. Whichever crew returns with the highest profit will be awarded extra points. All ships leave tomorrow, so you have a day to prepare."

Thali's blood thrummed in her veins. The sea called to her, and she was excited to get on the ocean again, smell the salty air and feel the wind whip through her hair. She said goodbye to Daylor, Tilton, and some of her other friends before running to her rooms to pull out the familiar waxed canvas bag she always used on board. In her excitement to prepare for her final exam, she forgot all about training with Alexius.

Suddenly, a knock on their door surprised her and Mia let the visitor in. Thali momentarily abandoned her packing, expecting to confront Stefan and defend her need to go on this sailing trip, but was surprised to see Alexius instead.

She knows, yes? Alexius asked into her mind as he glanced at Mia.

Thali nodded. Guilt came rushing to the fore. Since her return, she'd struggled to find time to train with Alexius alone, though he'd resumed being her sparring partner in class.

"Then, enough is enough. We will train here, at least to start with," Alexius declared.

Thali was flabbergasted. "Don't we need more space? And what about during the trip?"

"You will have chambers of your own as first mate, yes?"

Thali nodded again.

"Good enough. Come and have a seat. Cross-legged. Yes, that's it. The first thing you are going to do is meditate. Every morning from here on out but only for an hour for now." At Thali's incredulous look, he said, "It's one hour. One hour to focus on your breathing and keep all the doors in your mind closed. Today, I want you to begin examining these doors from your side. What do they look like? How well sealed are they? What can you sense from your side of the doors? And that wall you inadvertently built in your mind to separate yourself from the animals, are there any weak points? Cracks? Holes? Gaps?"

Thali sat stunned as he sat down across from her. She realized that Alexius had put some sort of silencing bubble around her to help keep the noise in the building from distracting her. With all the packing everyone had to do, the whole building was abuzz with energy. Why Alexius had picked this very moment to start their first lesson boggled her mind.

At least Mia had gone back to her room to work on her own final project as a seamstress. And if Thali was being honest with herself, she supposed that though the others might be panicking with their packing, Thali could finish packing quickly. She'd been doing this a long time and knew exactly what she needed to bring. Maybe that was why Alexius had come now.

"I told you to think of nothing, just focus on your breathing, in and out."

Thali shook her head and cleared her mind this time, focusing instead on inhaling and exhaling. She felt Indi and Ana come and lay down beside her, surrounding her, and she let out a sigh as she melted into their warmth.

"Interesting. They're helping you by strengthening the walls around your mind. I've never seen anything like it."

She ignored Alexius and continued to focus on her breathing. With every inhale, she brushed along the wall that separated her mind from the chaos of the threads. With every exhale, she gently prodded the wall, testing for weak points. Anytime she felt it waver even a little, she strengthened it, mentally slapping on more mortar. She felt Indi, Ana, and Bardo next to her as she traveled along the wall, and she focused harder, even sensing Alexius's turquoise thread, barely a shadow, standing watch in her mind.

"Why is it that Indi, Ana, Bardo, and your threads are on my side of the wall?" Thali asked as she opened her eyes.

Alexius stood before her now, arms crossed, eyebrow raised.

"They are your family. You've inadvertently put them on the inside of the wall so you'll always have contact with them. Luckily, they accept and welcome your presence. I jumped through the crack in your door before I told you to close it. I'm hoping you'll let me stay on this side from now on so I can help you. But all you have to do is push me back through the door to block me out."

Thali started chewing on her lip. The other side of the wall could be chaos and she wasn't sure she'd be able to find Alexius's thread again if she did that. "Does everyone see magic like I do?"

"Magic is different for everyone. It's difficult to explain how I see this singular aspect, but I see how you see it, so I've been trying to explain it in your terms. I see it more like light echoes, or waves, that approach or depart from me." Alexius sat down again and crossed his legs.

"So why are we strengthening the wall that separates me from magic? Shouldn't we be diving in?"

"Your magic has the unique ability to affect other creatures. I want you to strengthen the wall first so we can control unintentional effects."

Thali nodded. She thought back to the animals she'd inadvertently hurt or sent into a panic without meaning to. It was something that ate at her whenever she let it.

As she closed her eyes, Alexius piped up again. "Receiving this magic was not your fault. It was not your desire. The best you can do is learn to control it so it does not control you. Whatever happened in the past, before you had control, is not your fault. Do not let those ghosts haunt you." He paused before adding wryly, "You'll have plenty of ghosts in your future that will result directly from your decisions. No need to start early."

Thali closed her eyes and cleared her mind, filing Alexius's bitterness away for later, and focused again on breathing in and out.

CHAPTER THIRTY-NINE

T HALI WAS SNEAKILY TRYING to look over the charts and maps Seth had prepared and Jethro had approved. Jethro would be their captain on this, their final exam, and Thali was grateful he'd appointed her first mate.

Jethro was average on the outside—rail thin with mousy brown hair and a pointed nose—but extraordinary on the inside. He was a talented healer; he'd saved Isaia's life last year during their final exam when they'd encountered a sea monster. Thali knew he was hoping to improve his community of healers by becoming a merchant specializing in medicines and medicinal products. She also knew he wasn't decisive. As a healer, he was one of the best. But as a captain, he lacked confidence. She'd seen him make good decisions, but they often took time they didn't have. He needed confidence. But then Isaia, as last year's captain, had also needed improvement, and he'd gotten that in real time. So, maybe all would go smoothly this year.

Thali had held her breath as she had been about to board the ship, nodding to Stefan before joining her classmates. Her guards hadn't stopped her there, so she'd continued walking. She'd later determined they'd taken rooms near her, and there were only three of them. Not believing it was real until she was sailing, she had breathed a sigh of relief when the ship had left the dock and started meandering toward the open ocean.

Stefan had handed her a letter that morning, and she'd been afraid of opening it. She'd thought it would be a royal summons again or perhaps a letter saying she wasn't allowed to go. So, she'd waited until they were well out to sea before breaking the seal to peek at the letter. Now,

Stefan, Amali, and Derk were nearby, standing at attention while she stood quietly on the bow of the ship, taking a deep breath before she read the letter.

My dearest Thali,
A promise is a promise. Have fun and I can't wait to see
you when you return.
Stay safe and don't be too brave.
– E

Thali smiled. She folded the letter and tucked it in her inside pocket. She should have had more faith in Elric. It must have been difficult for him to convince everyone that she should be allowed to go on this trip, though she imagined the nearness of their route to the kingdom helped too. She truly hoped not to see an army of guards at every port, but she shook her thoughts away. For now, she was on the ocean with the salt breeze in her hair. She'd enjoy this moment as it was.

Their first port, the town of Licata, was very much like the bay they'd been practicing in all year. It was a smaller version and about half a day's sail away from the school. A town built on local trading, it was a common stop for smaller ships before they headed up the coast to the larger town of Lanchor and its abundant markets. Thali knew the school had probably picked this place because it was easy to get to, and it would be much easier to maneuver their ships to the dock than in most other ports. Licata's dock was unusually large for a town its size, so they often saw travelers who could not afford to dock in the larger port farther north or accommodated the overflow of ships from that same port.

Thali's ship had been host to Master Kelcian during their first leg, who had quietly watched them and taken notes in a little book.

She thought they had done quite well. While every ship was a mix of first-, second-, and third-years, their group worked well together this year. They mostly knew their knots and performed their tasks just as they had practiced. Jethro had maintained a calm, aware demeanor, quick to assign tasks and keep everyone busy. This leg hadn't been much of a challenge in Thali's opinion. They hadn't and probably wouldn't face any rough waters so close to land. The waters along this entire coast were mild, sheltered as they were by the peninsula that jutted out farther south. Thali's heart twinged at the thought of that peninsula. Almost all the land south of Licata was her family's land of Densria. It had been gifted to her family long ago. It had once been an abandoned but defensible post, and the king at the time had given it to her father's mentor in return for the business he brought in that improved the kingdom's economy. Later, her father had housed a few families in the southern end, paying them to warn him of anyone approaching. From the roof of her home, she could see the coast from practically every vantage point.

"Ready sailors?" Jethro shouted from the helm, making Thali refocus on the task at hand. She jumped off the ship to tie one of the ropes to the dock. As soon she landed, she moved aside a little as she maneuvered the rope, knowing full well that some first-years were watching how she tied her knot before tying their own. Derk had jumped off the ship with her, standing watch on the dock as she did her work. Her crewmates had been kind enough not to say anything about her guards.

Theirs was the second ship to arrive, and after disembarking, they walked down the dock, following Master Kelcian as he guided them down a couple side roads that opened to a wide dirt square in the middle of town. Thali had been there before, usually on a market day, when it was bustling with activity and stalls and goods overfilling the space. But today, the square looked more like their school.

"Third-years, you will be heading to the far right. Second-years to the middle, and first-years to the far left with me. You will need items from your shipmates to complete your own tasks," Master Kelcian said.

By the looks of it, the first-years were to be tested on Goods and Textiles, and the third-years were taking some kind of Combat test, so that left her class with Global Culture.

Inwardly, Thali groaned. She and two of her fellow second-years, Ban and Ari, stood before a burlap curtain, waiting for the first ship to finish their test so they could take theirs. She hoped Alexius, who was with the first-years, would steer his cohorts correctly; surely a magical dragon would know the right answers.

Thali hated waiting when she could be doing something productive. When they had arrived, the first ship was already at the third test, and Thali wanted to catch up as quickly as they could. Ban sat on the ground, flicking the contents from under his nails into the street. She pulled a face, and Ban flicked one in her direction when he saw her watching. He'd mostly made himself scarce since she'd returned with a royal contingent. Ari stood stock still, waiting. Thali looked around, trying to sneak a peek behind the curtain from any reflective surface. Stefan, Derk, and Amali stood with their backs to her, scanning the open space for possible threats. Just as Thali was trying to think of what it must be like to have to constantly be on alert, waiting for the worst to happen, Alexius, Kesla, and Meelo ran up to them, each carrying an object.

Ban jumped up and joined Thali and Ari as they all pushed past the burlap curtain. Thali had immediately recognized the objects the first-years held. They were each from a different culture, of course, and mildly valuable. The first-years stood behind Thali and her fellow second years, looking at three raised platforms. Master Brown watched the students. Thali glanced at the various objects on each platform and back at the objects in each of the first-years' hands.

"I think we have to perform the ceremonies that each of these objects are for," Ari suggested.

"I agree," Thali said.

"I think I know this one," Ban said.

Thali nodded. She'd done this ceremony so many times, she could do it blindfolded, but they would each have to perform one ceremony, so if her classmates knew one, she'd let them do it.

Ban took a gold-rimmed cup from Meelo's hands and approached a low table and a cushion on a raised platform. He looked around and found a teapot and tea leaves. With shaky hands, as delicately as he could, put the leaves in the pot, found hot water in a pitcher on an adjacent little table, and poured the water into the teapot. He waited—Thali could see him mouthing the seconds before he could pour the tea into the small cup—then he brought it to a plainly-dressed woman standing behind the platform before bowing and serving the tea as Thali had done many times before.

The woman nodded and gave Ban a two-foot length of chain before motioning to the second platform.

Thali's crew rushed to the next platform, where Thali looked first at the platform, then at the objects Alexius and Kesla held. Alexius's item held her attention. It was a thick roll of leaves carefully rolled into a thick stick. Thali looked up and caught Ari's gaze, who also looked at the stick of leaves and nodded. Silently, Ari took the stick and stepped onto the second platform, upon which beautifully woven carpets adorned the floor in a circle around a firepit with no fire. Thali watched as Ari looked around for something to ignite the leaves. Thali bit back a smile as she thought of how Alexius, standing next to her, could help in his other form. However, she shook the thought off as she saw the panic in Ari's eyes when she couldn't find anything to ignite the leaves.

There are embers in the firepit, Alexius's voice whispered in her mind.

Thali stared hard at the firepit, trying to communicate with Ari the only way they were allowed to. Ban looked over then and saw Thali and Alexius pointedly staring at the fire, so he joined them. When Ari finally looked up, she saw her teammates staring at the firepit and thrust her hand in to try and find whatever they were staring at.

Pain flashed over Ari's face as she discovered the embers underneath were still hot before she used a dagger to dig up what was underneath and shove the roll of leaves into it. When they started to smoke, Ari gently shielded them with her hand as she rose and carefully waved the stick of leaves in small circles. She slowly eased away from the center of the round fire pit before walking its perimeter, continuously waving her smoking stick of leaves. Soon, there was a rising ring of smoke. Ari descended the stairs, and still waving the smoking leaves, she circled the person standing there before climbing onto the platform once again and placing the stick reverently in the firepit.

The second man nodded and handed Ari a wooden stick three feet long before waving them on to the last platform.

Thali already had Kesla's object in her hand when Ari looked back at her and gestured at the third platform. Trying not to smirk, Thali climbed up to the third stage. Her object was a wide shallow bowl, and Thali remembered the summer she'd met Tariq's future bride. They had been young, about eight years old, when Bree had insisted Thali go to lessons with her that morning. They had gone to the back gardens by the pond, and Bree had shown her two similar bowls.

"To show our grace and humility, we must balance these bowls of water on our heads, then walk with them still balanced before bowing before those we respect," Bree had begun.

Thali and Bree had become fast friends that afternoon as they had soaked themselves in pond water in their attempts to bow gracefully to the floor with the bowls on their heads.

It had taken them an entire day to stop giggling long enough to perform the task. Now, every time they met, it was a challenge to see how far they could increase the challenge without spilling a drop. Last time, they'd been able to ride their horses and jump over a log with the water still in the bowls on their heads.

Thali filled the bowl three-quarters full, more than was necessary, and placed it gently on her head. She turned gracefully and descended the stairs toward the hooded man at their foot. Keeping her eyes downcast, as was customary for this ritual, Thali carefully lowered into a bow. Then, lowering first to one knee and then the other, she respectfully touched her chin to the floor before slowly rising once again. She removed the bowl from her head and handed it to the hooded man. As he reached out to take the bowl, Thali swallowed a gasp when she recognized the hands. He turned and placed the bowl in a box next to him before turning back to her again holding a heavy iron ball. Giving him a slight bow this time, she glanced up from her lowered position, and her heart raced as she took in the mischievous sparkle in the dark-blue eyes watching her carefully. Her skin tingled at the contact as he placed the heavy ball in her hands, and her eyes narrowed when she felt the piece of paper between the ball and her hand. Garen glanced down to hide his face again, then swept his arm to the side, indicating they should exit.

Thali had to tear herself away from him when Ban shouted, "Hurry Thali, the next team just walked in!" as he raced off to the next test.

Thali, carrying the heaviest object, ran behind her classmates as they approached the third test. She snuck the paper into her pocket as she transferred the ball to the other hand and caught up as her shipmates joined the third-years.

Jethro glanced at Thali as she jogged over to him. "We got here just in time to watch a bit of what the previous crew figured out. We have to use a mace, so I hope you lot brought the stuff to make a mace."

Thali, Ban, and Ari dumped their winnings on the ground. Sure enough, Jethro had found a pin and an open chain link to connect the iron ball to the chain. A mini forge stood at one side of the platform, and the third-years went to work forging the chain together.

The second- and first-years just watched as Master Aloysius surveyed the third-years. This far into their studies, students had to create weapons and be able to use them. As Thali observed carefully, she saw that while the second-years had been busy at their own tasks, Jethro, Monk, and Seth had been busy sharpening the dull blades of two swords and an ax. They had also found a long staff. She looked around the small area and noticed a sturdy but tall wooden stump next to two sheets of parchment strung up on a tree, and even—was that a paper-mache ball hanging from the tree?

As soon as the three were done forging the mace, Monk strode over to the ax and tossed it at the stump. It took a few tries, but on the third try, he finally hit the stump square on. The ax finally stayed put. Once Master Aloysius nodded his approval, Jethro took one of the swords and approached one of the parchments. As Thali looked more carefully, she saw a shape drawn on it; in fact, one piece had a star on it and the other had a heart. Jethro carefully sliced his way through each point of the star. He switched to the second sword halfway through. The swords would have to be very sharp to pierce the parchment without ripping it. Once Jethro handed over the paper star, Master Aloysius nodded for them to proceed.

Seth, being the biggest of the third-years, grabbed the mace and walked over to the hanging ball. He started swinging. In five swings, he'd hit the target perfectly three times.

"Why didn't he use the sword for this one?" Kesla asked.

"They're probably only allowed to use one weapon for each challenge. For that matter, that hanging paper-mache ball could have something inside it, and a sword may not puncture it," Thali answered.

Alexius added, "Look, see how it's finally bent and dented, but it hasn't yet blown open? It must have a very thick wall. Maybe it's even lined with something more solid."

Thali could see the sweat on Seth's brow as he beat the ball with the mace for an eighth time. Finally, on the ninth time, a crack appeared in the ball and the whole group cheered. He hit it once more, and a few coins rained to the ground. Before gathering the coins, of which Thali counted ten, he grabbed the staff and poked at the ball to make sure there wasn't anything left in it.

"That'll be enough for us to buy a table at our last stop," Thali remarked. Ten silver coins was exactly the cost to buy a table in Kadaloona.

Seth handed the coins to Jethro as they gathered.

Master Aloysius broke into their celebrating. "I'm with ya next leg. We won't be allowed to leave until tomorrow mornin', but I want everyone back on the ship before the sun starts to meet the horizon, understand?"

They all nodded before going their separate ways. Thali was glad for the break but knew that as first mate, she'd have to go back to the ship to debrief with Jethro first. Jethro had invited Alexius to join them to fill the captain in on the first-years' challenge. Jethro had been too busy with his own test to watch the first-years' challenge.

The note in Thali's pocket was burning a hole in her trousers, but she resisted even touching her pocket before she was alone.

They gathered in Jethro's quarters and shared the details of each challenge, reported on any incidents, and disclosed which crew members had struggled with their challenge. It wasn't long before Jethro dismissed them given the lack of any worrying incidents or struggling crew members. Thankfully, Stefan, Amali, and Derk had stayed on deck, allowing her to attend her meeting alone, though Thali had noticed them nod to another three royal guards near the ship as they had boarded with Thali. She figured Stefan had likely set up guards at every port to safeguard the ship.

After she left the meeting with Jethro, she ducked into her own room so she could read the note Garen had handed her.

Be wary of Alexius.

A knock sounded at her door at that exact moment, not giving her time to wonder what Garen knew. "One second, just changing."

She shoved the note in the pouch where she kept the medallion Garen had given her. Though she hadn't worn it lately and felt guilty about the promise she was breaking, she wasn't even sure if she was supposed to wear it anymore. She also thought it silly considering she had three full-time guards, anyway.

Thali went to answer her door and was surprised to see Daylor standing there.

"What did you change? I saw you jumping off your ship this morning, and you were wearing the same thing," he said.

"And here I thought no one ever noticed what I was wearing," Thali said.

Daylor grinned. "Notice? You are going to be the trendsetter! Isn't that one of your jobs as royal princess?"

Thali rolled her eyes.

"So, any plans yet? We thought since we have the afternoon here, we might as well go explore."

"Sounds good to me."

Stefan, in the hall behind Daylor, cleared his throat.

Thali's heart stopped. "Do we have plans, Stefan?" She rose on her tiptoes to glance over Daylor's shoulder at Stefan, who looked a little cramped in the small space.

He motioned for her to proceed to the ship's deck. "We have an appointment to see someone in town, m'lady."

"Who are we going to see, Stefan?"

"An artist. Their Majesties have commissioned an artist to paint a portrait of you."

Thali's head reeled. Daylor snorted behind her, and she turned to glare at him.

Daylor pressed his lips together. "Forget sightseeing. There's no way I'm going to miss this."

Once they'd disembarked, Stefan led the rather large group that now included Daylor, Tilton, Thali, Amali, and Derk through town to a famed portrait artist.

Amali helped Thali into her favorite blue dress that had been waiting for her when she had arrived at the little studio. Thereafter, she spent the afternoon frozen in place as the artist cooed at her to pose, gaze, and smile this way or that. Tilton even had to drag Daylor out of the studio a couple times because he was laughing so hard. Finally, Thali was done, and she breathed a sigh of relief. All she wanted now was a little freedom. She was sad to leave her dress behind, but the artist assured her it would be returned to the school by the time she got back.

Having a couple hours before they had to head back to their respective ships, Daylor, Thali, Tilton, and the ever-present guards went to one of the local eateries for supper. The cramped place was mostly filled with their classmates, so no one stared too much as she walked in with her three guards. Thali insisted they join her and her friends for dinner, so they grudgingly took shifts, one eating as the others stood guard.

After dinner, Daylor recounted his own test experience, and Thali leaned back to listen in on the local gossip. A few locals had seated themselves behind her, and it was habit for her to listen to what they were saying.

"He was an old man, but it got his son too. Wife says she don' know what to do next."

"Send 'er 'ere. We could use more help this season," The barmaid said as she came back to refresh their drinks.

"Did ya see the bodies? Torn to shreds all o'er the field. They found the hoss jus' runnin' 'round laying seed willy nilly."

"I don' need ta see no more body parts. That's seven bodies this year. Or parts of seven bodies, more like."

Thali was jolted back to reality as her shipmates prepared to leave and Daylor stood up. She had just stood up and reached for her coins to pay for their supper when she felt a looming presence next to her. She felt Stefan tense.

"No need, m'lady. It's on the house. Just remember us when you're up in the big castle." The barmaid curtsied to her.

Thali nodded, though she saw the barmaid forcing her friendly, warm smile. *I'll have to find a way to fix this divide in classes as princess*, she thought.

Daylor and Tilton thanked the barmaid, and Thali did the same before they left the eatery and walked back to their ships, laughing and joking the whole way. However, the barmaid's words replayed in Thali's mind as they walked. She guessed she hadn't been as inconspicuous as she had thought.

Thali had just settled in bed when she heard her door scrape open. Grabbing the dagger under her pillow, she looked at her door. It was already closed, and Alexius stood there expectantly. She remembered a guard stood on the other side and wondered how her dragon friend had gotten in.

In your head, Alexius's voice said in her mind.

What are you doing? How did you get past the guard?

They were switching and I was quick. If we're going to do some training, this is the best time. It's the only time your guards aren't at your side.

Thali was getting used to sliding into her brain, so she allowed her thoughts to drift through the thread that was Alexius. She thought of Garen's warning. Her family had found Alexius. Surely that meant he was genuine. How was she supposed to choose who to trust?

I've been meditating when I can. I don't exactly have a lot of free time, she said.

You never will.

Fine. What are we learning today?

You're going to learn about magical creatures.

And how are we going to do that?

Like this. Then she felt something mentally sliding toward her on Alexius's thread and recognized it as a large creature that looked like Indi but was all blond fur, massive claws like an eagle, and bird beak.

This is a griffin. They are very strong and very powerful, but their magic is limited. They like to eat meat. But only intestines. They will leave the arms and legs.

Thali swallowed, thinking of the claw marks in Joren's side.

Alexius spent the next two hours sending her images and memories of different magical creatures. She was awed at how accurate many legends she'd heard around the world were. The physical descriptions matched those she'd seen in murals and tapestries, but their behavior and intelligence were misrepresented in legends.

The training session stole the last remnants of her energy, so the minute Alexius slipped out, Thali closed her eyes and drifted off to sleep.

CHAPTER FORTY

T HE NEXT MORNING, THALI's ship was allowed to leave an hour after the first ship. She and her crewmates hoped to catch up to them, and everyone was feeling motivated and encouraged as they went through their tasks as quickly as they could. They had all performed well in their challenges, and now that they had some idea of what they would face in their exams, they were excited to speculate about the possibilities.

Thali herself wondered what challenges lay ahead, but Garen's note, besides sending a minor pang into her heart, puzzled her. She wondered if he knew something more than she or her parents did about Alexius and was trying to warn her, if he was just speculating because Alexius was getting so close to Thali, or if there was just more she needed to know. A small part of her wished she could talk to Garen; she missed talking with him.

She pulled the ring out of her vest pocket and slipped it onto her finger. She looked down at the ring on her finger, feeling guilty that she hadn't been thinking of Elric. The ring made her smile; it was almost comical to think of the places she took this beautiful ring. She felt a little bad that it was trading silk pillows for dirt and sea water. Then she thought of Elric; he was sunny and cheerful and devoted. Her soul swelled to think of him and his smile, and she longed to be with him again. Even though she always loved being on the ocean, Thali realized she had a lot more pulling her back to land than she ever would have thought.

"Destination ahead, Captain!" A shout from above made Thali look up from her ring to see a fuzzy green strip along the blue ocean ahead of them. She tightened and checked knots and ended up having to grab

Kesla by the neck to shove her down so a beam wouldn't knock her unconscious. Afterward, she returned to her position next to Jethro.

"Good save, Thali."

"Thank you, Captain."

They stood silently, Jethro carefully maneuvering closer to land and gently adjusting their position according to the water depth. This port had two exposed sides, unlike the tranquil inlets they'd sailed into the previous two days.

"I imagine this is pretty boring stuff for you," Jethro said.

"The moment we get bored is the moment things go wrong." Thali quoted Crab's favorite saying.

Jethro laughed. "I'm finding this too easy. Especially with what happened last year."

Thali smiled at that. "I could jump off the ship. That might cause some drama." Thali glanced behind her at the three armed guards.

Jethro pressed his lips together, trying to smother another laugh. After a moment, he murmured, "I can't believe you'd give up the open ocean."

"Who says I'll have to give it up completely?"

Jethro glanced back again at the guards standing just out of earshot. "Well, whatever happens, I'm indebted to you, Thali. Who knows what would have happened to the ship without you last year."

Thali nodded. She was touched that Jethro thought so much of her. "It's unnecessary, but thank you."

The maneuvering got a little tricky then as the open ocean pushed their ship around a bit more than the inlets they were used to. This was a small fishing village, and aside from the delicious fish they would eat tonight, they would have to take the smaller longboats to shore.

When Jethro had successfully dropped anchor, they piled into the longboats, though Derk stayed on board to ensure the ship remained secure. While they rowed to shore, Thali saw another longboat of royal guards make their way toward their ship. She prayed no one commented on it. It was embarrassing that they would make such a big deal over her.

The school had picked this port specifically because of how quiet it would be. However, as soon as they stepped foot on the beach, a cheer went up, and Thali's stomach fell to her feet when she turned and saw what must be half the village lined up.

Alexius sidled up next to her. He looked more tired today than he usually did. She mentally asked if he was all right, and she caught a glimpse of the protective barrier he was emitting around her to protect her.

Sorry, I didn't mean for you to see that.

Wow, that looked ... expansive. Can I help at all?

No. It'll be better at the next port. I'll have help there.

She didn't have time for a more thorough conversation as they approached the small crowd of people. Suddenly Thali was very conscious of the two-day-old clothing she was wearing. She smoothed out her vest as best she could, thinking she was glad to have put her long hair in a braid this morning. At least her hair would be presentable. Stefan sidled up on her other side. She felt Amali come up behind her, and Thali prayed the village was gathered to welcome all the students.

"Any chance this is your hometown, Jethro?" Thali asked to his back. She realized then that he was in part shielding her from the crowd.

Once they got closer, he glanced back at her and said, "Not at all. Make it quick if you can, Thali, then meet up with us by the flags as soon as you can."

Leading her ship's crew, Master Aloysius veered directly right as soon as their feet touched the road, abandoning Thali and her two guards to the people lined up to the left. Thali looked beyond the crowd and saw this was a typical fishing village. The hilly land was dotted with small wooden structures as close to the water as they could get. The homes were all well taken care of but simple and small. They had all recently received a fresh coat of white paint. She hoped they hadn't done that for her.

Thali plastered on her best smile and a little girl in a dull pink dress was the first to greet her, handing Thali a purple flower with a yellow middle. As Thali bent over and accepted the flower, she saw the little girl didn't have any shoes on. She took the little flower and tucked it into her braid.

"How does that look?" she asked, turning around so the little girl could inspect it.

She was too shy to talk, so she just nodded before running back to the safety of her mother's legs.

"Lady Routhalia! Thank you for visiting us!" someone shouted. Thali shook a few more hands, listening as the people of this small village started to ask if she could send them wood to repair their houses and more clothing. Merchants only ever traded minor, inexpensive goods in their small village because they would not find large profits, and the townspeople could not travel far from their fishing boats to buy goods. She wondered if these people were asking Thali the merchant or Thali the soon-to-be princess. Then she heard a bugle to her right and used it to excuse herself from the crowd, filing away what she had learned for another time.

Amali, Stefan, and Thali ran up a small hill to a bunch of flags in their school colors. Her ship had caught up to the first ship's crew, who looked well-rested as they stood dressed and waiting for them. Then she saw the first-years donning protective gear. *So this would be their Combat challenge*, she thought.

The two groups of first-years from the first two ships would challenge each other: If you were knocked down or someone drew blood, you were out. The team with the last person standing would go on to the next challenge while the losing team would wait for the next ship to arrive and go through the challenge again. Thali knew the other ship would be gunning for Alexius. He was by far the best first-year, so all three of the first-years from the other crew would try to knock him down first.

She looked at Kesla and Meelo. Meelo was quick and agile, and Kesla was clever in her fighting. Meelo and Kesla ran to flank Alexius. At least they also knew what would happen. Then, one of the opposing first-years charged the three, hoping to knock one of them down with sheer force; however, all three dodged out of the way. Alexius darted behind the initiator and tripped one of the other first-years with his staff.

Thali looked around for the next challenge, her challenge, wanting to be ready to run to it as soon as she could. Her challenge was to be Goods and Textiles. The first-years had had to pick out the most expensive items among an array of goods at their last port, and Thali imagined the second-years would have to do something similar.

A crash turned Thali's attention back to the first-years, and she saw Meelo on the ground, caught between two bulky boys from the other ship. Kesla jumped on the opportunity and stuck her staff strategically next to the bigger boy's foot, causing him to trip and fall.

Now it was Kesla and Alexius versus one boy on the other team. Alexius charged the last boy, and they began exchanging blows. Alexius hit the boy several times in the arms and legs, but the other boy was built like an ox and didn't look as if the smacks bothered him much.

Another ship had caught up by then, and Thali was glad to see Daylor and Tilton among them.

"Did you get mobbed by your fans?" Daylor could barely contain his glee. Thali kept her eyes on the combat but responded by smacking his shoulder. The first-years from Daylor's ship were already getting dressed, likely hoping to capitalize on the losing team being tired from the first round.

"That's my cousin." Daylor looked at the boy taking every blow Alexius had dealt him.

"Of course he is. Are all of you built like oxen?"

"Why yes, thank you for noticing." He flashed her a falsely cheerful smile.

Kesla's hand whipped out so fast no one saw it, and she tossed a knife that grazed the boy's shoulder.

"Wow, she's awfully good at that." Daylor looked impressed. Thali had to admit she was surprised. She hadn't known about Kesla's skills with knives.

"That's *my* cousin," Ari said as she came up next to them.

Thali's ship cheered as they'd gained first place with Kesla's knife trick. They ran to their next challenge, leaving the first ship to fight against the third ship.

Thali, Ban, and Ari tossed aside the curtain as they stepped up to their challenge. They saw tables and tables of objects from all over the world.

"Welcome! Pick the two that would fetch the highest price if all these objects were for sale at the local market," an old woman dressed in a plain dusky-rose dress said.

Thali caught the hint in the way the instructions had been said. These objects were from all around the world, but in a town like this, an object was only as valuable as its use to the buyer. The students were allowed to talk to each other, so they went around each table, discussing the merits of each item and trying to pick something.

"Nothing with jewels or precious metals. Those aren't of much use here, so they wouldn't be worth much," Thali said.

Ban and Ari scanned the other two tables.

"What about something wooden?" Ban asked.

"Probably. But nothing that would be useful as an everyday implement," Ari chipped in.

"So, something useful, but not too useful. Something meaningful only to here," Ban murmured. "Like this?" He pulled out a drawing of instructions on how to make an ancient northern teapot.

"Yes!" Ari agreed.

Meanwhile, a shiny glass that was chipped and cracked had caught Thali's eye. She recognized it as one of the finest glasses in the world, even with a chip and a crack in it, it would be useful in this town.

Ari pulled out a small, tightly woven basket among many large and loosely woven baskets. "The weave is too small for fish to escape, but still loose enough to let water pass."

Thali nodded and they headed over to Master Caspar. He nodded with a glint of pride in his eye and swept his arm at the exit. They brought their goods with them, realizing from the last exam that the third-years might need them, or they might need them for the final challenge tomorrow.

As the trio joined the first-years, their shipmates cheered and ran to the third-years' area. Thali spotted an actors' caravan peeking out the side of the curtain and wondered whether the third-years would have to dress their parts and act out ceremonies like she'd had to in her first exam.

All the first- and second-years could do was wait outside the curtain while Jethro, Seth, and Monk faced their challenge. Soon, the waiting crewmates heard players delivering their lines, and as the crew listened quietly, Thali knew the third years would have to identify the inaccuracies of the play they were watching. She heard a line that would have been considered quite rude in Cerisan culture and hoped her shipmates had picked up on it, too.

Eventually, they must have gotten something wrong because ten minutes later, she heard the actors start over again from the beginning. Thali hoped her team got it before another group arrived. Bored now, she let her thoughts wander to her animals. Jethro had not allowed Indi and Ana, or even Bardo, to come with her, and as much as it had saddened her, she knew Mia would take good care of them. It was just a strange feeling not to have them with her.

Please don't open the door. Not here. I'm not strong enough to protect you here. Alexius's voice sounded tired in her head.

Sorry. So what exactly are you protecting me from?

Detection. It's like casting a giant bubble around you so you're undetectable. Here, come have a look.

Thali laid back in the grass with her arms beneath her head. Her part was over, so it would seem reasonable that she might take a nap on this sunny hill. Closing her eyes, she followed Alexius's thread to the images he was showing her. It was as if he was pulling back a curtain and letting her view his magic flowing out of him as he created a sphere around the town.

Why the whole town?

Because people talk. This town is so excited for you to be here, the dragons wouldn't need to scent you.

Scent me?

It's like smell, but with magic. Magical creatures are always drawn to others with magic. Yours is still wild and not under good control, so you'd attract them in droves.

Sorry.

The meditation is helping. The more aware you are of your magic, the more control you'll have because you'll know where it reaches or touches.

"We did it!"

Thali's eyes flew open. Jethro was bounding toward them. She jumped up and cheered with them.

Jethro told the whole crew the story of the third-years' challenge before gathering Thali and Alexius to debrief. Then, they all had their afternoon to themselves. Thali just wanted to stay on the hill, away from the townspeople, for as long as she could. She decided to sit there, meditating, trying to feel her magic around her. Ban and Ari had fallen asleep on the hill, and she was glad for their quiet company. Daylor and Tilton eventually joined them, too. Daylor chose to take a nap like Ban, and Tilton joined Thali in meditation. Once, Thali glanced behind her and saw that Ari had woken and had also crossed her legs and closed her eyes to meditate. Alexius stayed at Thali's side and guided her in her mind, teaching her to feel the magic she emitted.

Now that she was focusing on it more, she was starting to see her magic almost as thin strands that reached out away from her.

Alexius, how do I bring the magic in? Should I twist the threads together to make a rope? Should I cut them off?

You should reel them in. Like thread on a spool. Try to imagine keeping the spools tightly wound and close to you instead of letting the threads roll out away from you.

Thali learned that afternoon to pull in the threads on imaginary spools but had difficulty keeping them close to her while multitasking.

It's coming along. We should probably go eat something.

Thali allowed herself a moment to come back to herself after checking to see if the walls in her mind were fully shut off from the rest of her.

Then she looked around and saw that her friends were still there. The sun was starting to set, and just as she opened her mouth, a giant growl came out of Ban's and Daylor's stomachs at the same time, waking them and making everyone else erupt in laughter.

"Food?" Daylor asked as he jumped up from his snooze.

Thali had no idea how he could be so awake so suddenly. The sky filled with bright oranges and pinks as the group walked back into town, Thali's two guards trailing them.

Thali was glad there wasn't another secret appointment her guards had planned for her. As the group walked back toward town, they debated where they would go to find their supper. But to their surprise, a delightful smell wafted into their nostrils just before they crested the hill to see the beach dotted with light and people.

They followed their noses to the beach that fronted the little town but was tucked behind a low hill that protected the town, and the beach, from the worst of the storms. The townspeople were all there and had built three large bonfires along the beach. From what Thali could see, they must have dragged all their kitchen tables out onto the beach and lined them up to make one long table close to the hill. As she and her friends got closer, they saw at least two giant pots on each bonfire. Smiling faces pressed warm mugs into their hands, and her group gathered around one of the bonfires, curious to see what was in the pots. Thali peeked into one and was excited to see that the pots were filled with all sorts of fish, crayfish, clams, mussels, and potatoes.

"Ya got good timin'," one of the local fishermen said, looking up from his stirring.

Whatever they had put in the water made the food smell heavenly, and Daylor was quickly enlisted to help carry one of the pots to the long table. Everyone pitched in though because some pots needed four people to carry them up the beach. Following the townspeople's example, the students helped lug the pots to the table and unceremoniously deposited them on the edge, some of the soup sloshing out. Without thinking of proper manners, Thali sat down and jumped in. Her mother loved seafood, and Thali had known how to disassemble a crayfish since she was five. She'd had to learn quickly—and to eat quickly—or her brother would have eaten it all. He still often had.

"Wow, slow down there, Thali. I see you've eaten this before. Care to share with the rest of us how to get the ... ah ... meat out?" Daylor interrupted Thali halfway through her third crayfish.

She looked up to see half the table staring at her, juices dripping down her face.

"It's good to know our efforts are appreciated." A jolly woman with red cheeks waddled over and squeezed herself between some of Thali's classmates. "Now, 'ere, let me show you how you get at the meat."

The townspeople took her cue and dispersed themselves among the students to show those who had never seen a crayfish before what to do with it.

Thali swallowed, then took the time to show her friends what to do with the various shells in front of them. Soon enough, they were all eating, elbows deep in seafood. Once they were done, all the merchant students helped gather the shells, and as directed by the cooks, put them back into the pot. They would make soup from the shells for the next day.

Sated now and with dinner tidied, everyone present gathered around a bonfire. Thali appreciated that her fellow students and her teachers didn't congregate in a group but mingled with the locals.

Thali sat on a log between Daylor and Tilton, Alexius on Daylor's other side. Her royal guards joined the festivities but remained a watchful five feet from her. Thali was glad she'd convinced them to wear normal clothes instead of their uniforms. It helped everyone relax.

"Excuse me, miss lady." Thali turned to see the little girl in the dull pink dress pulling at her sleeve.

"Hi there. Thank you again for my flower earlier today." Thali smiled.

The little girl turned a deep shade of pink and nodded, clearly trying to screw up the courage to keep talking.

"You know, when I'm a little nervous, I take a deep breath and then I imagine that my friends are right next to me, helping me."

The little girl nodded her head, closed her eyes, and took a deep breath. Then, she opened her big blue eyes and looked Thali right in the eye and asked, "Miss Lady, can I sit with you?"

Thali's face cracked into a genuine grin as she said, "Of course you can!"

The little girl then scrambled over the log and right into Thali's lap.

Tilton stuck out his hand. "And who might you be, new friend?"

"Riley Dorothea." The little girl looked at Tilton and immediately looked like she was falling in love with him. She giggled as he took her tiny hand in his and shook it.

Tilton grinned. "Well, Riley Dorothea, I'm Tilton, and this is Daylor and Alexius. And you know Miss Lady." Tilton smirked at Thali's new name.

Riley, turning back into her shy self, simply nodded and retreated into Thali's lap. She was so small, she simply curled into a ball on Thali's thighs and stayed there, listening to the group as they continued to chat.

Take a second to look at her in your mind.

Alexius was conversing with Kesla on his other side, making Thali wonder how he could maintain two conversations: one out loud and one in his head.

So, as Daylor and Tilton were arguing about something, Thali took a moment to go inside her mind, to the door where she was trying to reel in the spools of her threads. There, she saw a thin, light-blue sparkly thread that led to the little girl in her lap.

She's harmless. She's half mermaid. Don't connect with it, but I thought I would point it out so you know what mermaids look like, magically that is.

Will she be all right? Thali's brow creased in concern for little Riley. Thali hid her own gifts as a child, her parents always telling her that people would be scared of her abilities and that she wouldn't be able to fit in or make friends.

She will be alright. She doesn't have much mermaid magic. Nothing that would make her stand out. But she has a way with the ocean, can feel the weather. She'll see that soon enough, and it will be up to her what she wants to do with it. She might be a very good fisherman. Or she might even come to school to be a merchant.

So, mermaids, huh?

It's safe to assume that every mythical creature you've ever heard of exists, Thali, Alexius said.

She nodded ever so slightly. Thali wondered if the stories about them were also true.

It wasn't long before Riley fell asleep in Thali's lap, and Thali held her so she wouldn't fall even though her own legs were numb.

It was late and completely dark when Jethro rose and signaled for those on his ship to leave with him as they would be the first ship to leave tomorrow morning for the final part of their exam. Thali was trying to decide what to do with the little sleeping girl when the same round woman with rosy cheeks who'd taught her friends how to eat crayfish walked up to her.

"Mighty kind of ya to let her be."

Thali shrugged. "She seemed comfortable."

"Y'know, she don't take to strangers well. Yer the first I've ever seen her so comfortable with."

Thali was surprised to see tears in her eyes. "Well, we special ladies have to stick together." She smiled at the little girl who was now trying to use her scarf as a blanket.

The woman gently took Riley from Thali as the rest of the students were thanking the town for their generosity, some even exchanging names and ways to get hold of each other.

Tilton held out his arm for Thali as she tried to get up and nearly fell over. Her legs had pins and needles from sitting in one position so long.

Tilton smiled as Daylor grabbed her other side and helped her to her ship's longboat.

"Thali, where are your boots?" Tilton noticed Thali's bare feet in the sand as they approached the ocean waves.

Thali just shrugged. "I have others."

Thali saw Stefan, always within a few feet of Thali, looking back at the retreating form of the woman with the little girl, whose newly-booted feet hung over the woman's arm. She held her breath, hoping he wouldn't say anything. To his credit, after a glance at her, he remained mute.

CHAPTER FORTY-ONE

O NCE SHE'D RETURNED TO her ship, Thali was all too grateful to sink into her bed and go to sleep. But then she felt the creak of the door in her mind, and she was about to groan when she felt Alexius's exhaustion.

Okay, today I want to show you more magical creatures, and we'll review the ones you've already seen. You need to know them so when you see them, you'll know how to react.

Thali scrubbed her hands up and down her face a couple times before sitting up, cross-legged. She knew it must be taxing on Alexius to teach her while he was maintaining a bubble of protection around her, so the least she could do was be an avid learner. They spent the next few hours reviewing images Alexius showed Thali. He even showed her memories of fights or interactions with the magical animals so Thali had a better idea of how they moved or behaved.

It was morning by the time Alexius left her, and Thali had just shut her eyes when they were roused to prepare the ship to leave for their next location.

Master Caspar was on their ship this leg, and unfortunately for them, it would be the most difficult of the three ports as it was the busiest. While Lanchor, their school's town, was a thriving and busy market town, Kadaloona was a city. It was the closest city to Thali's home, and she was excited to be in familiar territory.

Kadaloona was only a few minutes' ride from her home, and whenever she was home, she visited the city. It thrived mostly because of her father's business. Though Jethro had never been there, Thali could navigate into the marina blindfolded. Together, they'd be fine.

As the ship set sail, Thali was exhausted, and she realized she was anxious about their last stop. She wondered, too, if her parents were home and if she'd get the chance to see them. Suddenly, the excitement of being in her home city in just a few hours reinvigorated Thali, and the rest of the ship took notice. Everyone started buzzing with nervous energy.

They sailed for a few hours before spying the famed rock wall that had been built to create a wave break for the ships in the harbor. Thali's father had paid for most of that wall to protect his armada of ships while they were docked.

"Is there anything I should know about sailing between the breakwaters?

"Be careful of your momentum. The waters in the harbor are dead calm, so there's nothing opposing the ship's movement. As soon we get past the breakwaters, we'll move faster than you'd expect," Thali said.

Jethro nodded as he began giving the order to decrease their forward momentum. Thali's heart swelled when she saw the line of her father's ships tucked along the left of the massive harbor. She noticed three docks completely void of ships or boats. She smiled as she could imagine her father giving them the order to move the boats in case the students crashed their ship into the dock. Jethro guided the ship in a touch slower than he should have, so he had to send most of the crew off to help pull them into place.

Once docked, they followed Master Caspar off the dock. While most of her fellow students gawked at the armada of ships, Thali searched the ship decks for familiar faces. Her family's ship was docked, but none of its crew was around, and she was surprised at how quiet the harbor was.

They walked through the city to a big grassy clearing usually used for children to play in, lovers' picnics, or overflow market space. She barely had the time to stare at the wares displayed outside the shops they passed or take in the hubbub of the citizens' daily routines before they reached their first challenge.

First-years would take their Culture challenge, second-years their Combat challenge, and third-years their Goods challenge. The first-years dashed behind their curtained challenge, and Thali, Ari, and Ban started gearing up for their combat challenge, seeing nothing to suggest what they would be doing. It was a long, grueling hour before Meelo, Alexius, and Kesla returned to them, breathless from running over, papers flapping in their hands.

Thali had noticed that Alexius looked relaxed and rested this morning, with a sparkle in his turquoise eyes and a slight flush in his pale face that highlighted his bright red hair. She hadn't had a chance to ask, but he almost looked happy.

The second-years grabbed the papers in the first-years' hands just as a commotion by the docks pulled their attention in that direction. Thali's guess was that someone had almost run aground. She looked at her paper, Ari's, and Ban's before taking off at a full run. She knew what they had to do.

"Follow me!" she shouted over her shoulder as she ran toward the long strip of grass outside the city walls—toward her home.

On each paper was a clue to their next destination. Thali's paper had a picture of a long rectangle with a thin foot at the bottom, Ari's had a picture of a horse, and Ban's had a picture of a long lance that Thali'd seen used before in games on horseback. Knowing immediately where they were to go, she had taken off, not waiting for her classmates. However, Ban and Ari only took a couple moments to catch up to Thali.

Thali used to pass by this particular grass strip on her way to the city each time she'd left her house as a child. It was the perfect size and shape to race someone on horseback. Or just to run on. She had often taken Indi, Ana, and Arabelle there to run the length of it.

Ari, Ban, and Thali ran to that strip of grass, which was now decorated with flags in her school's colors. Horses were lined up along one side, and there were three marked lanes on the field. The second-years had just learned how to handle weapons on horseback, and Thali was nervous for Ban, who had been struggling the most. She didn't like Ban, but he was part of their team.

Squinting to better see the challenges, she saw that one required getting a long stick through a tiny hoop suspended from a tall tree. The second had a rotating dummy that you had to throw something at, mostly likely an ax. Depending on where the ax landed, the dummy would keep rotating and knock you off your horse if you weren't quick enough. The last was the most difficult, involving hurdles with targets the rider would have to hit as their horse jumped over the hurdle.

"I'll take the axes," Ari said.

"Ban, do you think you can get the little ring on the stick?"

Ban scoffed. "I've a better chance of that than shooting while sailing through the air."

Thali went to inspect the row of horses, thrilled to see she wouldn't even need her ability as she recognized a few of her father's horses among the choices. She laughed when she saw her father's old bay gelding: whoever picked him would have their work cut out for them trying to get over the hurdles. Next was a young chestnut horse Thali recognized as having only two speeds: fast or grazing. Then she saw her father's flea-bitten gray mare. She wasn't terribly pretty to look at, but she was Arabelle's favorite friend, and Thali had ridden her a few times. The gray mare was reliable and quick and also superbly clever at knowing what the rider wanted. Without waiting for the others, Thali walked right up to the gray mare and brought her over to the first lane so Ban could mount her.

Ari knew Thali well enough to leave the animal choices to her.

But Ban looked doubtfully at the gray mare, shook his head, and said, "I'm going to take the bay gelding."

Thali clenched her teeth, hoping Ban's decision wouldn't cost them the final exam. Ari was happy to take the chestnut horse. She handed Ban a stick, and then ran ahead to the next challenge. Thali stayed with Ban.

"Go slowly if you need to," Thali said. This was about their team, so Thali was determined to put their team above her disgusted feelings for Ban. She'd never forgiven him for gossiping and spreading terrible untruths about her last year when she'd thought they were friends.

Ban nodded, so she went to strap on a quiver of arrows and a bow before turning back to watch him. He squeezed and kicked the bay gelding, finally getting the horse to trot a few steps before the horse resumed his sauntering. It took forever for Ban to finally raise his stick and reach for the hoop. But by the time he got to the ring, his arm had tired, and he missed the ring by a couple inches. He circled back, holding the stick with the other arm, trying to steer with his legs. Thali knew his legs must be tired by now. The gelding fell back into his usual walk-trot pace as he went along, but this time, he started to zigzag.

"Hold the stick upward! Like a flag!" Ari called.

"Keep your legs straight while you sit on him!" Thali yelled. The bay gelding started looking confused and pinned his ears back in frustration, swishing his tail to show his displeasure.

Thali felt like it would be cheating to use her ability, but she saw the next group running up to join them and she wanted to win so badly. The bay gelding was getting frustrated with Ban and would either stop or try to toss him soon. Alexius was still down with the others, waiting for the second-years to run back.

Thali cracked the door in her mind, hoping to get a glance at the gelding's thread. She found it quickly and started coaxing the willowy brown thread to the other side of her wall. She saw a few other threads reaching for her, and before she realized what she was doing, she'd thrown up a woven tapestry of her own making, guiding only the thread she wanted through a hole she'd made.

Sending calming thoughts, she showed the bay gelding what they wanted. The gelding nickered when he felt Thali's thoughts touch his own.

Despite Ban's flailing, the bay gelding seemed to grit his teeth, then trotted back around a third time and started toward the ring again. The second group was already starting down the adjacent lane. Thali saw another second-year from the third ship run up, so the third ship must have arrived, as well.

The bay gelding maintained a steady trot toward the ring. This time, Ban only raised his stick a moment before so as not to tire his arm and finally got the ring. Unfortunately, the second group had gotten theirs on the first try, and now both teams were galloping to their teammates.

"Take the gray! The chestnut will help me catch up." Thali shouted, swapping the gray mare's reins with the chestnut's and running for the last station as Ban hopped off and gave Ari a leg up to mount the gray mare.

Ari was a much better horsewoman than Ban and tied the reins into a knot before urging the mare in a straight line. Both Ari and Daylor galloped toward the rotating dummy.

Thali made it to her spot and turned around just in time to watch Ari throw the ax at the dummy. She was off center, but Ari had known that as soon as she had thrown the ax, so she ducked, laying flat against the gray mare as the dummy's arm swung around, just missing hitting her on the back of the head.

Ari galloped up to Thali, who was pleased to see the second-year from the third ship turning back around to try the ring again.

Daylor had passed the first challenge easily enough and now handed his horse over to next member on his team, who threw the ax perfectly on the mark, keeping the rotating dummy stock still. Thali groaned.

Ari jumped off the gray horse, and Thali leaped onto the chestnut, grabbing her bow with one hand and an arrow with the other. Then, after Thali showed the chestnut mare what she wanted her to do, the horse took off at a run toward the first hurdle: a log. As they sailed over it, Thali prepared to loose the arrow. It hit the target with a heavy *thwack*, and Thali reached behind her to grab a second arrow. The track for this challenge looped in a circle, and Thali galloped around the bend, ready with a second arrow. As the mare jumped, Thali loosed a second arrow into another bag marked with an "X." But as she approached the third log hurdle before the straightaway back to the starting line, Thali sensed something coming at her head. She ducked just in time. A weighted bag swung down, hitting only the bun she'd thrown her long dark hair up in this morning.

The second target must have set it off, she thought. As she sailed over the third log, and hitting her target with a third satisfying *thwack*, another bag on an invisible line above their heads came zooming at them from the right. Thali felt the mare's muscles bunch as she shied away from the surprise bag and leaped to the left. Thali kept her seat, having felt the moment of fear in the mare's body before she had shied away.

They were now out of the second bend and racing down the straight-away. She saw that Tilton, from the second ship, had caught up and they raced to the finish line. Thali closed her eyes for a moment, enjoying the wind in her face and whipping her now-loose hair. Once past the line, Thali leaped off the chestnut mare with a pat on the neck before she and her crew raced back down to the grassy clearing, cheering their win, to the waiting third-years.

Thali shoved the threads in her mind back to the other side of the door and closed it tight, checking to make sure that another thread hadn't snuck around her guard.

Alexius wasted no time popping into her mind. *Well, that was reckless. And cheating, I might add.*

I was concerned for Ban's safety, if you must know. Thali stood straighter as the third-years dashed behind their curtain.

Good job with the net of threads. That's new.

It just happened.

Why don't you try putting a little net like that around the spools of your magic once you've reeled in your own threads?

Once she'd caught her breath, Thali sat down, pulled in her threads, and conjured up a little net to wrap around the spools.

That's a lot better.

Do I have it completely sealed?

Yes, for now. Let's see how it holds up over time.

Thank you.

Alexius nodded. "I have a feeling this is going to take a while." Alexius said out loud. They watched as the fourth ship streamed past them to the dock. The first- and second-years sat and rested, taking the time to look around. Thali was hoping to see someone she recognized from her father's ships or from the city. When she saw no one, she couldn't help but think it odd.

Thali woke up to Ari shaking her shoulder gently.

"Thali, they're back."

Thali shook her head to clear it. Jethro, Seth, and Monk were walking over with a large tapestry draped over their arms.

"Thali, can you help us fold this properly?" Jethro asked from afar.

She looked around and her heart sank when she saw that only the last ship's crew was left waiting with hers. Two ships had already finished and left.

Thali helped roll the delicate tapestry, and they all carried it back to the ship as Ari filled Thali in on which order the ships had departed in.

"We could always catch them on the way back," Meelo added optimistically.

Once they had stored the tapestry carefully in the captain's quarters, they met on deck to regroup.

"At least we'll be sure this journey is safe, what with Thali's armed guard on board," Seth said.

Thali laughed but turned away as Jethro nodded and moved on. She supposed he probably didn't want to remember last year's exam when a sea monster had nearly taken his friend and their captain, Isaiah's, life.

As with the two previous ports, once Thali's ship had docked, a squad of royal guards had inundated their ship while Thali, Stefan, Amali, and Derk had disembarked.

"So, where to now?" Thali asked. She hoped she sounded casual, but she was desperately hoping to be released so she could go home if only for a few hours.

"We're off to your house," Jethro said.

"What?" Thali thought she'd misheard.

Jethro handed her a paper he'd tucked into his vest. "They gave it to us when we completed our challenge."

When she looked at the invitation, Thali was surprised, but she supposed it made sense that a founding member would welcome their own branch of students to their home for supper.

"Then follow me, I guess!" Thali leaped back off the ship and walked, trying to keep her pace reasonably slow as her heart raced at the prospect of going home. By the time her home came into view, Thali was running. She didn't care anymore what her fellow shipmates thought; she just wanted to go home and hug her parents.

As Thali approached her home, she saw planters with bright flowers and extra oil lamps lining the main path leading around back; her parents had put a lot of effort into this evening's supper. Thali ran up and hugged their house steward, who'd been with her family since before she was born.

"Congratulations are in order, miss." His warm brown eyes glanced inside the house. Thali looked away. She felt guilty for not having thought of Elric's proposal in days. "They're in the main hall. Big banquet tonight," the steward said, bringing her back from her thoughts.

Thali nodded at the rest of the house staff lining the back entrance as she ran in, her shipmates following her at a distance. She could barely contain herself as she threw the doors open to the massive hall only used for parties or formal occasions.

Familiar candles lined the walls as she took in the decorations. Her mother had decided to decorate in the school's colors, and Thali saw flags and ribbons swirled around the columns in the room, with bright swathes of fabric draped along the walls. The chairs had been reupholstered in bright red, while the tablecloths were indigo beneath plates of sky blue and white. The students from the two ships ahead of them were already there, looking awkwardly at the formal setting and sitting in their dirty three-day-old clothing.

Thali ran over to her mother and father, hugging them fiercely before her mother leaned back and pinched her nose. "Really, Thali, couldn't you have changed your clothes?"

Thali just squeezed them harder, and they squeezed her back. When she finally let them go, she turned to find Stefan, Amali, and Derk bowing to her parents.

"Lord Ranulf, Lady Jinhua, it's an honor to be invited to your home." Stefan rose.

"Oh, so now you bow." Lady Jinhua raised a brow as she referred to the last time she'd seen these three and they'd barred her entrance to her daughter's room.

"Many apologies, Lady." Derk bowed his head again, turning a bright shade of red.

She waved him off. "No harm done. Please, join us and be seated."

As the students from the last ship arrived, Thali took her place next to her mother, and Jethro sat on Thali's left. She admired the simple silk dress her mother was wearing as her father gave a speech welcoming the merchanting students and thanking them for not crashing into his docks. She saw her mother gently touch her father's arm, silently telling him to move on from his bad jokes and start the meal. They had their own language of touches and sighs and looks. Thali wondered if she'd ever have that level of communication with Elric.

The students were all starved, so they devoured the food before them. Thali was proud to have only earned two pointed looks from her mother as she stuffed her face with delicious food.

"Where's Crab?" Thali asked her mother.

"He'll be back tonight. If you can stick around, he'll want to see you."

Thali turned to Jethro. "Captain, permission to stay on land tonight?"

"Of course." Jethro bowed his head to her mother. Then, her father called him over.

"Shouldn't you ask them too?" Thali's mother motioned to the three guards keeping watch from the walls.

Thali got up, swallowing her nervousness and holding her head high as she strutted up to Stefan. "Stefan, would it be all right if we stayed here tonight?"

"Of course, m'lady. We've already secured the building and your room."

Though she felt a little violated at the royal guard roving through her room and all over her home, she thanked Stefan and returned to her mother's side with a nod. Lady Jinhua watched Thali carefully after that, so Thali smiled and conversed with her fellow students with her best manners.

When the meal was finished, the table was cleared and a musician began playing her favorite stringed instrument, a pipa, softly in a corner. The students and teachers, now sated and relaxed, were happy to converse among themselves and with Thali's father and mother. Eventually, everyone drifted out and back to their own ships for tomorrow's final leg back to school. They'd have to sell their tapestry and the other goods they'd collected over the course of the exam at the market before the exam was over, but most of the exam was over and all the students were shaking off the stress of the journey.

"Thali, be back on board by the time the sun's up. We'll be leaving third, so no need to be early," Jethro said before he led the rest of the crew back.

Thali nodded. "Thank you, Captain."

She walked her shipmates to the door, and when Alexius told her to enjoy her night, she remembered she had questions for him about why this place seemed easier on him than the last port, but they would have to wait. She just couldn't think of a good excuse to get Alexius to stay behind with her without raising suspicion. When the door clanged shut, Thali breathed in deeply, finally able to be herself. Well, herself with three armed guards always within five feet of her.

Grateful to be home, even for a night, Thali headed for the indoor courtyard. Visitors often thought the koi pond within looked awkwardly placed, given its location just off the main entrance, but Thali loved it. She kneeled at its edge, dipping her hand in the water, letting a couple koi swim up under her hand, one even nipping at a finger.

She sat at the pond's edge for a while, knowing her mother and father were still entertaining her instructors, who had been invited to stay in the guest wing for the evening. The peace of home restored her soul as she breathed in the familiar scents. She eventually made her way to her rooms, only to be greeted by another royal guard standing outside her room, who opened her door for her. Inside, she took in the shelves of strange objects she'd collected over the years, smiling as she reminisced. They were a mix of worthless bobbles and honored gifts from her travels around the world, and they reminded her of the people she'd met and the places she'd been to. She smiled at the trinkets Elric had given her when she had visited the little hidden town he'd taken her to last year behind the palace. Then, her gaze landed on a couple tokens from Garen, and she wondered how he was and if the warning he'd given her was indeed true. There was so much he didn't know about her life now. Her heart twisted, but the pain felt ... well ... further away.

Thali's gaze moved to her satchel, placed there by one of her ever-present guards. She dug a hand in to remove a cloth pouch containing a thick letter. Glancing at the door, she opened the trunk at the edge of her bed. She looked at the pouch and glanced at the door. If her grandmother had written to reconcile, she would have written to Thali's mother. Thali didn't want proof that her grandmother really was a terrible person. In fact, she didn't care to know her grandmother at all. So, she hid the letter at the bottom of the trunk, between some old journals.

Sitting on the bed, she made an impulsive decision and changed into some old but clean clothes. The pants were a touch tighter than before, and she made a mental note to get Mia to stop altering her clothes to fit the latest fashion when she wasn't looking.

Chapter Forty-Two

W HEN THALI BURST BACK out of her bedroom, Stefan looked surprised to see her.

"I'm off to see my animals," Thali said, wide-eyed and awake now.

"There's more of them?" Amali blurted out.

Derk nodded as Stefan issued new orders. From the sounds of it, he'd thought Thali would be in for the night.

She didn't wait for them as she strode down the side hall to the door, then outside to a long building no more than fifty strides away. She stopped short of the doors and turned to her guards.

"You may look inside, but you are not permitted beyond these doors. Is that understood?"

She'd never issued such a command and was pleased when Stefan nodded his head. They could secure the building from the outside. He was halfway through requesting that he alone could go with her when she cut him off.

"Only you. There are weak animals recovering inside, and I don't need anyone dragging in any illnesses. We will undergo a strict cleaning before we can enter the rest of the building."

Stefan nodded. He would learn that when it came to her animals, Lady Routhalia was not to be told.

She opened the doors. Inside was a room with a small, low-walled bathing cubicle, clean clothes folded on a shelf. Beyond that was another set of clear glass doors. Stefan had only seen pure glass doors once before and marveled at them to Thali. Beyond the glass doors were row upon row of half-walled rooms of all sizes like stalls in a barn, but with a greater variation of widths and depths.

Once she had closed the doors, Thali started to strip down and Stefan abruptly closed his eyes. "I told you we would be undergoing a vigorous cleaning. After me, you are to strip down here and wash, then step into the next room to don the tunic and pants on the shelf. Every inch, understood?" Thali asked.

Stefan nodded, his eyes shut tight. She had to try hard not to giggle as she washed herself, then dumped the bucket and refilled it for him.

Thali stepped out of the cubicle, and as she closed the glass door behind her, she saw Stefan counting to himself before finally opening his eyes. Thali waited for him until he too started to strip down. As she turned away to dress, she was glad for the first time that the bottom half of the door was not clear glass but tinted.

Thankfully, Stefan wasted no time, and in moments, he had opened the door and walked in, Thali returning the favor and turning to give him time to dress.

When he gave her the all-clear, she opened the last door and said, "Welcome to the barn," as she walked up and down the aisles, acquainting herself with the inhabitants.

As a child, Thali had always brought home strays, but only those who needed care. Then she'd let them free when they were well again. Soon enough, sick animals were showing up on her parents' property constantly, so her father had built her a barn of sorts where she could tend to the ill animals. Eventually, there were so many and she was so often not home, she ended up hiring help. That had been probably the most thorough interview she and her father had ever done since it was likely that whomever they hired would discover Thali's gifts eventually. But they'd been lucky when they'd met Deshi on a trip. Deshi and his family loved animals and were the gentlest, most patient people. They may have been shy and didn't like meeting new people much, but they were Thali's kind of people.

As Thali allowed a spool to unravel in her mind, she imagined her mental door thinning like fabric stretching, letting the threads nearest come through. She went to the door of each animal's stall, determining what hurt, or what had happened, and showing them comfort and healing and freedom when they were better.

She had made it halfway through the stalls when a cough caught her attention. She turned to Stefan, but he was watching a young man of thirteen or so hovering at the door with a bucket. Thali wiped the sweat off her brow and glanced up from her kneeling position as she gently put a baby owl back in the makeshift nest.

"Oh, wow, Jito. You've grown."

"Hi, Thali." Jito was Deshi's son, a thin wisp of a boy and shy to the nth degree. It had taken two years before he had been brave enough to say hello to Thali. But he, like his parents, had a knack with the animals.

"I mean, Lady. Ma and Pa said you'll be the royal princess soon." Jito, turning beet red, glanced at Stefan.

"Please, just call me Thali like before."

"Yes, Lady."

Thali raised an eyebrow.

"I mean yes, Thali." He smiled.

"Where's your mom and dad?"

"They heard you were coming, so they cleaned up all the animals for you. They wanted to stay up to see you, but sleep got the best of them."

Thali nodded. "I added some notes to the ones you made." She nodded at the aisle she'd already gone down.

"And this little owl, what does she have to say?" Like the rest of his family, it was apparent he knew her secret, but he and his family had always been discreet.

"He's been hiding a broken bone back here. I wrapped it, so you'll see what I mean once you see the bandage. He's also sad. He lost his mother and two siblings," Thali said, ignoring Stefan. He'd figure it out sooner or later anyway if he was going to be around likely for the rest of her life, and part of her wondered if he would dare to ask. As she put the owl away, she thought about how strange it was not to have to make excuses for her gift.

Jito nodded earnestly, studying the notes hanging outside the owl's cage. For the next few hours, Jito assisted Thali as she went from animal to animal, helping them tell Jito what hurt and what was wrong.

Thali was getting an excellent grasp on letting only a tendril of her threads go out and only allowing one thread to come through the mesh door she'd created in her mind's barrier. Finally, feeling exhausted, she was nearly done, glad to have made it through almost all the animals.

"You're stronger than before, miss," Jito whispered, blushing. "And we've even got more animals than usual."

"Can I tell you a secret, Jito?" Thali glanced at the teenager in time to catch his serious nod. "I've been training." Thali winked.

"Glad to hear it, miss." Jito nodded again. "Are you ready for our special friend?"

Thali smiled. "She's still with you?"

"She hasn't wanted to leave, so Pa's just let her set up her home." Jito led them through a hall to an adjoining building where their more permanent residents stayed.

They walked up to a low stall, and Thali peered inside carefully. She kept her spools wrapped up tight and a solid wall between her and the threads as she studied the white, feathery bird she'd met when she was home last summer. She was a little bigger, but not by much, and

Thali wondered if it was just that her feathers had grown or become more abundant. Her white tail was almost as long as a peacock's, but not quite, and the white of it was as pure as wave caps.

Suddenly, a loud whooshing came from above, and a soft, warm breeze slithered across her cheek from the open window. Looking around to find the source of the wind, she saw Jito holding the bird now, but before she could connect with it, shouting from outside echoed down the aisle. Before Stefan could stop her, Thali ran out the nearest door.

Chapter Forty-Three

T HALI DARTED OUTSIDE AND saw two of her guards, swords drawn, shouting at something above them. She followed their gaze and gulped. An orange dragon, this one more snakelike than Alexius, hovered over them. He opened his mouth and Thali cringed, bracing herself for the flames to turn her two guards to cinders. Then she flew sideways, hitting the ground hard.

Before she could recover, strong arms wrapped around her and carried her around the side of the barn.

She fought the arms—*I have to bear witness to their deaths!*—and they finally let go as a voice said, "I'm sorry, my lady. It's my duty to protect you at any cost." It was Stefan. He had tackled her and carried her to safety.

She didn't bother to look at him. Her other two guards were about to die because of her, and the least she could do was honor them by bearing witness, no matter how terrible the sight. The dragon's bright-blue flames screamed through the air. But instead of turning Derk and Amali to cinders, they bounced off an invisible barrier, shooting straight up into the sky.

"Wha—" Thali started to say before Stefan clapped his hand over her mouth. Thali glanced at the docked ships, her crew, the other crews, her friends, the town below ...

As if reading her mind, the dragon turned his head. Thali could have sworn she saw the corners of his lips turn up before he flew to the town below. Landing, he tried the docks first. He blew fiery blue flames at the fleet of ships from her school, and again, a barrier protected them.

Thali wondered what kind of barrier Alexius had put up to withstand so much.

Then, the orange dragon turned and aimed its maw at the town. Thali slipped out of Stefan's grip and ran to the fastest way to get down there: the rope her brother had long ago rigged to the cliff so they could scale down faster. She grabbed the rope and leaped, letting the rope cut through the skin of her hands like a hot knife through butter as she squeezed periodically to slow her descent.

Her guards ran behind her down the switchback stairs, and as she got closer and closer to the docks below, the same warm breeze she'd felt at the barn caressed her cheek. Dropping to the ground, she turned just in time to see the orange dragon inhale.

Suddenly, a red dragon shot up from between buildings and leaped into the space, making the orange dragon back up, away from the town and back up into the sky. It strangely took Thali a moment to recognize Alexius, but remembrance dawned as the dragons started to speak in an unknown language that sounded like swishing silk and grinding, clicking rocks.

Thali's guards finally caught up with her as they shielded her with their bodies and scanned the sky above them. Stefan grabbed her hand and grunted at her shredded skin.

Thali couldn't take her eyes off the two dragons above them. Nor could she believe no one was running out of town screaming; in fact, the town looked like it was still asleep. No one came out to see the commotion; no one screamed or shouted to rouse their neighbors. If this creature did raze the town, it would be gone in seconds, and the people would become ashes as they slept.

"We have to get the townspeople to safety," Thali said.

Wait. A voice floated by her ear, or was it in her mind? Had she said it aloud? Her guards froze as if they were actually waiting. She remembered the warm breeze that had touched her cheek, twice now. She stood, confused, as she delved into her mind to look for a thread.

A milky-white sparkling thread dangled like an invitation. She hadn't even opened the door to her mind yet, so this had to belong to something familiar to her. She let her own thread unspool and join with it, and suddenly, as she looked up into the sky at the still-posturing dragons, it all made sense—as did their words.

"... just because you are a royal, you do not have authority over us ..." she caught the orange dragon saying.

"Leave now or I *will* make you leave," Alexius demanded.

"She deserves to know the truth," the orange dragon replied. "I am only a messenger, here to give her options and lead her—"

"LEAVE NOW!" Alexius said before he shot a stream of blue fire.

The orange dragon dodged it. "They will send someone else," the orange dragon warned.

"I will not repeat myself." Alexius flew closer to the orange dragon. He blew a short stream of blue fire again, and this time, the orange dragon flew up and further away.

"Your family will pay for this," the orange dragon growled before it flew away.

"They already do," Alexius said as he flew into the space the orange dragon had left.

They conversation ended, and the orange dragon flew away. As he did, he breathed fire on the little town's outer buildings, and Thali saw the barrier, now milky white like the thread in her mind, that protected the flames from catching the buildings.

The milky-white thread in her mind receded, snapping away from her.

"Thali, are you all right?" Stefan broke into her thoughts. "I don't know what protected us all, but we should go in case they come back," Stefan said.

"They won't," Thali said. But because she had only whispered the words, Stefan didn't hear them. So, he ushered her closer to town, close, in fact to where Mia's family lived.

Thali was too lost in her thoughts to notice. Garen was right. He'd been right all this time. What was it that Alexius should tell her? Where was he from? What was Alexius hiding from her?

"She gets like this sometimes," she heard Mia's mother say. In her haze, she was guided to sit in a bed, and a cup of water was placed in her hands. "Best to leave her be with her thoughts a minute."

Thali felt the warm breeze on her cheek again, and it was all she could do to put the cup of water on the table before falling asleep.

It was the sun's first rays that finally woke her. How had she fallen asleep?

Thali leaped out of bed, suddenly remembering where she was. She threw Mia's bedroom door open and ran smack into Stefan.

"Slow down," he said.

"We have to get back to the ship," Thali said. She needed answers from Alexius, and he would be on the ship.

"You mean, allow you out into the open ocean where there are no solid structures to hide in when there are dragons in the sky?"

Thali looked at him hard. She knew he was just doing his job, but she didn't need guards right now. She needed answers.

"You saw that we were all protected yesterday?" Thali asked. Stefan nodded, so she crafted her lie. "I can't say how I know, but we need to be on the ship. That's where the source of the protection is."

Stefan studied her as if wondering whether he should trust her. He clenched his teeth, then unclenched them and nodded.

She ran down the stairs and found Mia's mother in the kitchen. "Thank you," Thali said, giving Mia's mother a peck on the cheek.

"I sent word to your mother that you're here and safe," she said.

"Did you see ...?" Thali asked, flicking her eyes to the sky outside.

"No, I didn't have a clue what was going on until your guards started beating down the door. We were sound asleep. Best sleep I've had in a long while," she said.

Thali nodded. She would have to write Deshi and Jito to confirm her suspicions. There was no trace of a milky-white thread in her mind now.

Mia's mother shoved a basket of baked goods into her arms but then abruptly took it away and put it in Stefan's arms instead. "Be safe."

Thali nodded and burst out the door between Derk and Amali, now standing guard outside the house.

Mia's brothers and father must already all be at the forge by now, she thought. She wished she had time to see them, but she looked up to the bright-blue, cloudless sky, and ran for her ship.

CHAPTER FORTY-FOUR

T HALI HAD JUST MADE it to the dock when she was crushed in familiar, corded arms. "Crab!" she squealed.

"Lassie. It's good to see ya." He let her go and eyed Stefan and Amali, who had their hands on their swords, clearly unsure of whether this was a threatening situation or not.

"Relax, this is Crab. He's family," Thali said.

Crab walked her back to her ship, chattering away. She really wanted to talk to Alexius, but she was also desperate for the normalcy of family gossip.

Crab eventually demanded to know what his cousin, Master Aloysius, was teaching them. She could see the exercises forming in his head as he thought about what he would add when she returned from school. Then he turned serious. "I know ya got protection now, but ya let me grab ya without doin' anyfin'," Crab scolded gently.

Thali looked at her feet, wanting to say that she'd recognized him, but the truth was she'd been completely distracted and allowed herself to be surprised.

"My own little lass, goin' ta be the queen of the kingdom. It's makin' me mighty proud. Though don' tell yer pa that." Crab beamed as he hugged her one more time before leaving. She gave him a tight smile with her farewell. She hadn't thought of Elric much this entire trip, and now that guilt was growing. Part of her was even angry as she hadn't even said yes to his proposal, but everyone already assumed she had.

Thali put it away to sort out later when she saw her mother and father standing by her ship talking with Jethro. When she approached, he nodded to her and left her alone with her parents. She hugged each of them. "Do you think they'll let me go see Tariq this summer?" Thali whispered in her mother's ear.

Mischief twinkled in her mother's eyes. "Oh, I think you'll see Tariq this summer. Especially if he has anything to say about it."

Thali cocked her head in question, but Lady Jinhua didn't respond. So, seeing an opportunity, she asked, "Mother, how deeply did you look into Alexius?"

Questions flitted through her mother's eyes as she eased back and looked at Thali, making her wonder if her mother had seen the orange dragon last night. After a moment, she said, "You can trust him, Thali. A dragon's oath is stronger than anything else, and he's taken an oath to protect and guide you."

Thali nodded. She wasn't sure if that made her feel better or worse. The second ship was leaving the dock, the emptiness of which reminded her that her father had ordered his fleet to anchor farther out for now.

"Controlling what I can," her father said as he followed her gaze.

She smiled and squeezed him tight once more. Then his words sank in. Though he had no idea what she was thinking, his advice made her realize she would have to exercise caution if she approached Alexius. He was a dragon after all, and much more powerful than she was.

"Thanks, Papa," she whispered in her father's ear. He grinned and hugged her one last time before she finally said goodbye, boarded her school ship, and ran off to find Jethro.

After going over their route home with Seth and Thali, Jethro dismissed them so they could complete their tasks. The crew was working smoothly now, so they were all ready to go when they were told they could leave the harbor. They launched themselves into the open ocean to head back to school.

Thali settled into her task as she coiled the rope landing on the deck as they pulled the anchor up. She would have to be smart about how she approached Alexius. She didn't want him torching her school because of her temper.

That was quite something you did last night, Alexius said into her mind.

That was quite something you did this morning, Thali replied.

You saw? Alexius sounded surprised.

Oh, you know, I just happened to be outside. Orange dragons and red dragons are pretty hard to miss.

I was glad for the caladrius's help.

The what? Thali asked.

The fluffy white bird that resides in your barn, it's a caladrius named Vitafera. Alexius pulled up an image of a bird that looked like the one Jito and Deshi were caring for, but this one's tail feathers and crown feathers were much longer, it was much whiter, and it had a pearlescent shimmer.

Thali was curious. *How did it help?*

It kept the town asleep and protected. You saw the barrier the dragon's flames hit?

Yes.

That was Vitafera. They're cherished where I'm from, Alexius explained.

And here I thought it was a kind of silky chicken.

It's worshipped as a deity in some places.

Understood. Thali decided to take a chance here. She wasn't sure if Alexius knew she'd been able to understand his conversation with the other dragon. *Was that dragonese you spoke last night?*

It's an old language, but I suppose you can call it that. He paused before continuing. *Last night, I watched through your eyes. It's the first time I've seen a place of healing for animals.*

Thali noticed how abruptly he changed the subject but decided to play along—for now. *Sorry I didn't warn you.*

Vitafera has grown fond of your home and helps protect it now.

Is that why you look more rested?

Yes, though I would have loved to have seen this glass-doored building myself.

Next time.

Alexius nodded ever so slightly from across the deck as he returned to his menial task hoisting a sail. Thali returned her attention to making sure no one got injured while they sailed north as fast as possible. She would have to wait to get more answers from Alexius, if he ever deigned to give them to her that is. She clenched and unclenched her jaw as her frustration built.

"Letting everyone else do the work, I see," Master Brown said as he wrote something in a book. Thali clenched her fists. It was bad luck they ended up with Master Brown for the longest journey. They would sail a full day and night to Lanchor and their school.

To distract herself and put her mind back on her task, she went to the helm and traced over the route again. Thali, Jethro, and Seth had discussed the swiftest route north earlier, and thus far, the plan was unfolding smoothly. Thali thought momentarily of how she could have asked some whales to give them a tow and smiled as she imagined her crew members' faces when they saw whales pulling the ship.

It would take them roughly a day to sail back to school. They would constantly be in sight of shore, and the first ship would arrive before nightfall. They were to spend the night on the ship and then sell their goods tomorrow at the market before racing back to the combat field. And, she remembered, the first group back would win extra points for their final exam.

The ship was making its way steadily back toward school, so Jethro, Thali, and Alexius had gathered in the captain's quarters to go over the goods they had to sell. Thali was busily gauging both their true value and the realistic price they could expect to sell them for. She was also trying to determine whether there were other uses for the objects they'd gathered and whether they'd bring in more coin that way.

After working out their strategy and deciding who would sell what when they finally arrived, they stood on deck and watched the sun set. Their ship had managed to catch up to the second ship and sailed alongside it now, slowly inching their way ahead of them. They all took a moment to watch as the sun sank below the horizon and the sky filled with orange, yellow, and pink.

"Nothing better than a sunset on the ocean," Thali murmured as they all beheld the sun's last rays sliding beneath the horizon. She wondered where the orange dragon had gone and where it had come from.

To the dismay of the second ship, Thali's passed them and approached their home bay as the torches in the distance lit their way. It would be more difficult to maneuver in the dark, but they were more familiar with this dock and managed without too much difficulty. They were the second ship to arrive; therefore, they would only have to wait a half hour after the first group left in the morning to go to the market.

Now safely docked, Thali's crew had gathered belowdecks to discuss their strategies and talk about the finer points of how best to present themselves and their products to passersby, ending with a chat about the ideal customers for each product given their final group challenge was to sell the wares they'd collected at their home market. Thali only hoped that the right people were there to buy what her crew had collected.

The first-years would sell the basic items they'd gathered: just bowls and cups. The second- and third-years would sell the weapons, but only after polishing them to a high sheen. They would demonstrate the weapons' sharpness with some rotten food from the ship. Finally, it was decided it would be best if Jethro, Thali, and Seth focused on selling the tapestry that had been the final challenge for the third-years: they'd had to make a quilt-like tapestry. Her team had kept the design simple, with waves of blues and greens and patterns of white swirls. Since Thali was the most experienced with markets, she would help with its sale though she wasn't a third-year.

Lying in bed that night, Thali tossed and turned, her excitement at selling their wares at the market tomorrow warring with her dread at questioning Alexius and her guilt at having thought little about Elric and his proposal the whole time she'd been away. Finally, just as the moon was about to find its rest, Thali fell asleep.

CHAPTER FORTY-FIVE

T HEY'D MADE GOOD TIME through the night and by the next morning, arrived in Lanchor. Thali and the crew made their way to the market. They arrived extra early to secure a table near the entrance. After laying bright cloths to draw attention to their table, they placed their wares on the table, keeping some underneath so it didn't look too cluttered. The team worked together smoothly since they'd run through their plan last night. Thali was busy hanging the tapestry with Jethro when she turned to see the first-years already pulling out the extra bowls they'd stashed.

"You've already sold something?" Jethro asked one of the first years as he followed Thali's gaze.

"Yeah, a guy my age startled me nearly out of my trousers and bought a bowl, cup, and plate," Kesla said.

"But vendors are still arriving," Jethro said, looking around. Some of their classmates walked by and waved on their way to find their own table.

Thali kept a more wary eye on the market then and noticed a woman with red hair making a beeline for their table. She wore a pretty pink dress but kept a drab-looking brown cloak over it. Thali narrowed her eyes. She knew she'd seen that woman before. The odd woman came up to their table and bought three cups without even trying to negotiate before melting back into the growing crowd. Usually, only bread and tea sold this quickly this early in the day. The red-headed woman had never even looked up. It niggled at Thali. Where had she seen the woman before?

The stream of people to their table remained steady, and if Thali hadn't been so busy putting on a show to sell the tapestry, she might have figured out how it was they had sold all their wares in the first two hours of the market opening.

"That was a lot easier than I thought it'd be," Jethro said.

"Seems too easy," Thali murmured. She wasn't going to question their good luck, but she'd had much tougher days at easier markets with better products.

As soon as they were finished with their last transaction, which was the tapestry, they ran to school, having left all their bags on the ship. The first ship still had a few items left to sell when Thali's crew took off at a run. Kesla had turned her ankle on the ship last night, so Alexius was carrying her over his shoulder as he ran with the rest of them back to school. Jethro had wrapped her ankle as best he could, but it would take time to heal, and at this moment, they didn't have time to wait for her or seek additional care.

As they arrived at the combat field, it dawned on Thali who the red-haired woman was and where Thali recognized her from.

She was from Garen's court. It was Ella, a thief Thali had met when she'd met Garen's family last year. As she thought back to the people she'd met that night, she realized each one of them had bought something today—not directly from her, but from the other second-years and the first-years. That would explain why their things had sold so quickly. And she would put money on the fellow that had startled Kesla was Garen's second: Fletch. She tried to rack her brain to see if she'd met the person who had bought their tapestry, though she was pretty sure she hadn't. For that matter, given the amount of haggling and selling they'd had to do, Jethro and Thali had really had to push that particular sale. At least they'd sold that on their own.

Shoving it in the back of her mind to think about later, Thali focused on the report they had to give to their instructors on the items they'd sold. Once the other crews had arrived, they'd given their reports, and all the coins were counted, Thali's crew was deemed the winner. The whole crew cheered and hugged and congratulated the other crews on a job well done by all, though they did puff out their chests and walk taller as the winners. Then they returned to their ship to gather their bags; they were now free to return to their rooms at school.

"Congratulations, Jethro," Thali said as they disembarked.

"Thank you for your help, Thali," Jethro replied. As the winning captain of this year, Jethro was guaranteed a position with one of the top merchants. "If you ever need anything, or anyone, please let me know," Jethro said. "We couldn't have done it without you." Then he nodded at her before being swallowed up by some of his own friends as they left the dock. Indi, Ana, and Mia were laying in the grass at the end of the dock, and Thali ran over to meet them.

CHAPTER FORTY-SIX

THALI HAD JUST ENOUGH time to drop her bag on the ground before her tiger and dog, and even her snake, leaped at her. Once they had finished with their crazy, high-pitched cries of welcome and Thali was coated in saliva, Mia gave her a side hug, not wanting to be covered in saliva herself. "This came for you." She could barely hide her smirk as she handed Thali a letter as they walked back to their rooms.

Opening it, she scanned the contents, and her heart raced as she realized Elric was here and wanted to see her in the ballroom. The girls hurried back.

As they ran into their rooms, Mia said, "You really need to bathe first." Thankfully, she had guessed at the contents of the letter with the royal seal and had prepared Thali a hot bath in their shared bathing room.

"You're the best, Mia!" Thali ripped her clothes off and jumped into the bath. She could have died of happiness at the warmth of the water cleaning the salt and saliva off.

Not wanting to keep Elric waiting, she scrubbed herself as best as she could, trying to rub all the dirt out of her hair. Tired of braiding it so much, Thali let her wet dark hair drape over a fresh tunic as she ran down the hallway to the ballroom.

She tried to calm her excited heart before walking through the doors, but the moment she crossed the threshold, she immediately felt tension. The ballroom was empty except for a blanket in the corner and Elric.

He strode up to her, but Thali recognized the fake smile he put on for strangers and felt the tightness in his hug when he went to embrace her. She also noticed his glance at her left hand. Thali's uncertainties heightened.

Elric had set up a little picnic off to the side for them, and he led her there. They both sat and he poured her a refreshment.

"How was the final exam?" he asked, not looking at her.

"Fine. Uneventful." She looked at Elric, examining the tension in his body, the slight shake of his hand when he poured a drink for her. She felt like an insect waiting to be squished. "Elric, what is it?"

He looked up, surprised, before forcing a half smile. He licked his lips. "So, you know Stefan and I practically grew up together." Thali nodded. "Well, Amali and I and Stefan actually grew up together."

"All right …" Thali wasn't surprised. She knew Amali had been training at the palace as a guard since being orphaned at a young age, so that made sense.

"Well, Amali is a good friend of mine. And she sent me a letter that was more like a warning from a friend to a friend than a report from a royal guard to the prince."

"Okay …" Thali was trying determine what that could possibly mean. Had Amali developed a crush on Elric at some point? They had spent so much time together growing up after all.

"She was on night watch most of the time during your final exam." Elric slid his gaze her way briefly before looking away.

Thali finally realized what Elric was trying really hard not to say, so Thali did it for him. "And she saw Alexius come to my room on one of the three nights."

Elric looked up. He was scanning Thali's face, clearly wondering if he'd missed something, as if he hadn't expected her to admit it.

Thali took a deep breath, and the resulting sigh echoed in the cavernous ballroom. Then she looked down at her hands, scared to tell Elric the secrets she'd been keeping from him. To explain Alexius being in her room, she'd have to tell Elric about her special talent. It felt like she'd been telling her secret to a lot of people in the last two years, the secret she'd kept hidden her entire life until now.

Alexius, can you come here, please? We have to tell Elric everything. Your late-night visits didn't go unseen, and now my respectability is in question.

Elric looked panicked when she snuck a glance at him. She sucked on her front teeth, trying to think of a way to start.

Fine. I'll be there shortly, but put a protective bubble around you like we've been practicing. And no comments on my smell. I was about to go bathe.

Alexius didn't sound happy, but he should have known they'd have to explain their spending time together eventually. She wondered yet again what Alexius was hiding.

Thali took a deep breath in, closed her eyes for a moment to weave a bubble around her and Elric with her magic, then looked Elric straight in the eye. "Have you ever noticed anything strange about me? About how I have a tiger, dog, and snake that treat me like family?"

Elric's eyes narrowed. "I've considered it, but some people have a way with people, and I just figured you have a way with animals."

"Well, it's more than just a knack or a *way* as you call it." Staring down at her hands, Thali recounted to Elric how when she had been a child, animals had flocked to her, and that was why her parents had taken her with them on their travels. She recalled how her parents had realized she had more than a knack when she told them about the camel dealer mistreating his camels and their babies. And then she told him about how she had learned to put up a wall between her and the animals she sensed for her own protection and sanity.

Initially, Elric backed away. That was the reaction she had expected, but then he surprised her by moving in closer and taking the hand that she'd been staring at, holding it between his. He squeezed it gently and stroked the back of it with his thumb, waiting for to her finish.

Encouraged by the action, Thali sat a little straighter and told him about how she'd truly met and taken in her tiger, dog, and snake. It was like a dam had broken, and Thali let it all flow through her as she told Elric about how scared she had been to come to school and how she'd tried to hide her abilities for so long.

"I'm sorry I didn't tell you all this before. If you don't want me anymore, I understand." Thali had taken the ring out of her pocket and rested it on her open palm. She felt her eyes burning with tears but refused to let Elric see them.

"Ah, of course," Elric said.

Thali looked up quickly. Elric was looking at their hands. Had she heard him correctly?

"That explains the bats," he said then. Then, he gently cupped the side of her face with one hand. "Lady Routhalia, I've always known you were special. If this is part of the package, then I welcome it. I can't say I understand it yet, and I have many questions. But it does not change my love for you." He closed her hand with his, ring still inside.

A tear rolled down her cheek. Thali had always expected her secret to be met with anger and fear. And even though she'd told more people in the last two years than she had her whole life, she was surprised by how accepting Elric was.

"Now, I assume this has to do with Alexius. So before I kiss you, I'd like to hear the rest of it. Please." His voice was gentle, but she could tell he was still holding on to some scandalous image in his head. He gently squeezed her hand, encouraging her. She glanced at her closed fist, the ring cutting into her palm.

"Remember when you proposed?" Thali asked.

"Of course."

"Remember the red dragon that came and chased off the green one?"

"Wait, the green dragon. He said he wanted the girl. Did he mean you?"

"Yes. But I'll get there later." Thali waved off the question Elric had opened his mouth to ask. "Well, when the red dragon arrived, I heard a familiar voice shout, 'No!' in my head. When I was ushered back to my room, there was a knock at my door, and I thought you had come to check on me. But when I answered the door, it was Alexius. And I remembered why the voice in my head was so familiar. Alexius is the red dragon. He's here to protect me." *I think.* "Since that day, he's been helping me learn about my ability and training me. So, on those nights he snuck into my room on the ship, he was giving me magic lessons. Nothing else."

"Really?" Elric seemed a little surprised.

May I come in now? Alexius's voice was gentle in her mind.

Yes, please. Thali sat back. "I know you don't believe me, so I've asked Alexius to come and show you himself."

Elric cocked his head to the side, asking with his eyes how she had called for Alexius to join them. Alexius walked into the room at that exact moment. For a second, he scanned the room, looking for them.

Interesting. Where are you? You must have woven your magic quite tightly. I can't even see you.

Oops, sorry. Thali gently pulled her magic back into the imaginary spools so Alexius could see them.

He nodded his head at them, then looked around the grand ballroom, trying to judge the amount of space he had to take his other form, Thali assumed. Elric glanced between Thali and Alexius a couple times before his gaze stayed glued on Alexius as his skin started to turn red and scales took the place of skin. Then a pop sounded, and where

Alexius had been standing was a smaller version of the dragon Elric had seen in the courtyard that day.

Another pop sounded and Alexius shifted back to his normal human-looking self before striding toward them. Elric's eyes were as wide as saucers as Alexius bowed. "Your Highness. It's an honor."

"Wait. So Thali, can you control Alexius?"

"No!" Thali and Alexius replied in unison before Alexius elaborated.

"Thali's magic is strong, but right now, she only has enough control to make suggestions to others. Animals willingly follow, but for the magical *and* intelligent, like dragons, it's like one person demanding something from another independent, free person."

Thali pressed her lips together, holding in a laugh as she thought about how she had yelled in Alexius's head when she had first tried to communicate with him in thought.

Elric turned to Thali. "Wait, does that mean you can read my thoughts?" His eyes bulged.

"No. I don't get much from people. Just their general feeling," Thali said.

Elric breathed a sigh. He seemed a little less anxious than before. "Would you show me how your ability works?" Elric looked intrigued and she was glad to see curiosity, not fear.

Thali glanced at Alexius, who nodded ever so slightly. She could feel Alexius put a protective barrier around them so prying eyes would not see if they peeked into the room. There were about a dozen guards just outside the doors.

Thali searched her mind for threads of any kind. There were ants nearby, marching from a hidden store of sugar to their home out in the garden. She redirected them to her. Elric watched her as she directed the ants through Alexius's bubble and asked them to march in a line right between her and Elric. Then she drew a pattern for them to walk, and they formed a heart shape as they continued marching.

Thali glanced at the ants but watched Elric's face carefully. She expected him to reject her, to reject her ability and storm off.

"That's amazing." Elric looked up instead, his eyes filled with awe. "How many can you control at the same time? Is it like hundreds of ants but only three tigers?"

Thali shook her head, eyes narrowing. "No, it's not like that. I make a suggestion, and they can choose to follow, or not."

"But you can force them."

Thali nodded slowly.

"You could command an animal army?"

Thali sat up, pulling her hands away from Elric's. "No. I could, but I will not. Never."

"But why not? We could win any battle with an army of tigers, or horses, or ... you can control any animal, right?"

Thali stood up abruptly. "No, Elric. Absolutely not. I am tied to them. I am responsible for them. Don't you understand? I will not ask them to die for a cause that doesn't involve them." Fear wrapped her insides. She remembered the pain of watching an animal's life slip away because she couldn't help them in time.

Elric shook his head as if clearing it. Then he rose to take hold of Thali's hands ever so gently again. "I'm sorry," he whispered, standing so close Thali could smell the sunshine that radiated off him.

Gently, Thali felt soft fingers tilt her chin up and the pads of his thumbs brush away the tears on her cheeks. "I won't ask again. I promise. I understand what it's like to feel the responsibility of so many lives on your shoulders."

Thali nodded, finally raising her head to look into Elric's eyes. There, she saw warmth and understanding, and his green eyes reminded her of a grassy field on a sunny day. All she could think of was Elric's eyes and how soft his lips were as his head dipped toward hers.

"Ahem." Alexius coughed.

Thali and Elric froze. Then Elric straightened but took Thali's hand.

"What, are you a traditionalist?" Thali raised an eyebrow at Alexius, annoyed that he had interrupted.

Alexius ignored her question. "Your Highness, it would make our lives a lot easier if we could avoid future suspicion when we train."

Elric pursed his lips. "What if we told people you two are related somehow?"

"That could work. I've told people I'm from the Highlands, and Routhalia's father has family there."

Where are you actually from? Thali asked in Alexius's head.

"What do you think, Thali?" Elric turned to her.

"I think that would work." She turned her attention back to Elric. "So, you're all right with all this?"

"If there's anything I know, it's that the key to the future is learning. The more we know, the fewer mistakes we might repeat. And given how many lives could be affected by your gifts, you owe it to them to learn as much as you can."

"Thank you, Elric." Thali squeezed his hand to emphasize her words. The ring still rested in their joined hands.

Elric raised her hand to his lips and kissed it in response. "If we're all done with the surprises, I did pack us a little picnic if you're hungry?"

Alexius took his cue and bowed.

"And thank you Alexius, for keeping her safe." Elric nodded appreciatively.

Alexius nodded before turning and leaving them. Thali could feel the faint barrier Alexius had put around her and Elric. She rolled her eyes. Of all things, the dragon was offended with a little public display of affection. A twinge in the back of her mind made her wonder what Alexius's goal was.

What was he getting from teaching her and staying here?

Well, she wasn't going to get any answers today, so she turned her attention to Elric. But when they returned to their little picnic, they discovered the ants had gotten bored of their heart-shaped marching and turned their attention to the food in the basket. Thali sent the ants away, and Elric thankfully managed to salvage most of the food, except the dessert.

As they started to pick at what was left, Thali felt the weight of his questions still lingering between them. She felt the wave of all that was coming: dragons, griffins, other magical creatures she didn't even know about yet. Then, she heard the oracle's voice in her thoughts and the dragons' last conversation. She felt like her future was already laid out for her, as if she didn't have a choice.

"Here, I saved this for you. I think it's ant-free," Elric said as he presented her with a perfect strawberry tart. "I had it brought in from Densria. I know there's that little bakery there that's famous for them and didn't think you'd have a chance to visit while you were there." He smiled. He was clearly proud of himself for bringing the perfect little strawberry tart all this way.

"Yes," was all Thali said. She held her hand out, revealing the ring on her palm.

Elric looked in her eyes, clearly confused. His gaze dipped to her hand and the ring, and a grin spread across his entire face. Thali grinned too when she saw realization dawn. "Really?" he asked.

Thali nodded. A giddiness filled her chest as Elric's sunshine filled the room. He gently picked up the ring with shaking hands, a huge smile lighting his eyes. He slid the ring on her finger.

"Thank you for not pressuring me to answer all this time," she said.

"It's a big decision," Elric said. But he was beaming.

Still not quite believing what she'd just said, Thali blurted out, "I'd like to go visit Tariq."

Elric smiled. "Well, that's good because you can show me around."

Thali's face contorted. "What do you mean?"

Smiling, Elric pulled a letter out of his inner pocket. "This came to me a few days ago. I'm a little scared to tell you the truth."

Thali reached for the letter and immediately recognized the royal seal of Bulstan.

> *Dear Prince Elric,*
> *It is customary in Bulstan for the royals of our kingdom to approve the marriages of our court. We are willing to forgive your ignorance if you can present yourself with Lady Routhalia, who is by extension a member of our court, to us formally within the next two months.*
>
> *We expect to see you soon,*
> *His Majesty, Mupto Shikji of Bulstan*

Thali's eyebrows rose. "Wow."

"Did you tell Tariq of our betrothal?"

"Of course."

"But you didn't tell me you were a member of his court?"

"I didn't know I was."

"Well, it's practically a royal summons. His father must be awfully fond of you. We're leaving in a week with your parents."

Thali broke into an enormous smile. So, that's why her mother had been so cagey when they'd said their goodbyes. She secretly thanked Tariq for arranging things so she had to visit him.

CHAPTER FORTY-SEVEN

T HALI HAD LEFT HER guards behind with Elric when they had parted ways after their picnic so he could explain their updated situation. She couldn't help but smile a little when the next morning, Amali blushed and couldn't seem to look her in the eye whenever Thali looked at her. She was glad that Elric had friends looking out for him, but she would never forget now that she was always being watched.

She also knew it would only make things more awkward if she tried to say anything. Amali would always look out for Elric, and Thali was honored that Elric had asked not only his most trusted guards, but his most trusted friends to keep her safe. She still felt it was unnecessary, but if it let her live her life a little more normally, then she was all for it.

The night before they were to leave for Bulstan, Thali was packing her things. Many of her classmates had already gone home to help with the holidays before coming back for the next school year.

Suddenly, Stefan rushed into her room. "Stay here. There's something going on in the courtyard."

Thali nodded, surprised since there were so few people left at the school.

When Stefan ran out, she heard a soft thud on her desk. Turning, she saw a note tied to a rock that had been thrown through her open window.

Thali's heart skipped a treacherous beat when she recognized the handwriting.

Roof

She thought of the last time she'd seen Garen as she asked her animals to stay in her room, and to give a warning if someone tried to come in. Indi moved to lay behind the door, blocking it from opening.

Then, he had been hooded, and their eyes had met for a moment as he passed her a note. She wondered how he'd known about Alexius. Then she wondered if he had news for her or if he had something else to say to her. A small part of her wondered whether he'd ask her not to marry Elric. She loved Elric, but she would always wonder what may have happened with Garen if he hadn't pushed her away. While Elric's love was warm, sunny, and made her insides want to burst with happiness, Garen's had been immoveable and solid as stone. Her soul and her body reacted to him, sharp heat flying up her limbs to melt her insides. She had thought he would always be there.

Thali swallowed her emotions as she climbed onto the roof to their hidden spot behind a large chimney, out of sight from anywhere on the ground and the other rooftops.

Garen was leaning against the chimney, hidden in the shadows with arms crossed. He stood stock still.

Thali stepped before him and examined his face, finding more worry lines.

"Is Alexius holding you hostage?" Garen asked. Thali could tell he was trying to remain stony-faced as he watched her carefully.

Feeling awkward, she kept her hands in her pockets. "No, he's not. He's teaching me." She looked up but couldn't stand to look into his dark-blue eyes without feeling the pain he'd caused, so she stared at his feet.

"And do dragons make good teachers?" Garen's voice was soft but strained.

Thali nodded. She wanted to tell him everything. But he wasn't supposed to be part of her life anymore.

"What are you not saying?" Garen asked.

She answered before she realized what she was doing. "When I was
home, I overheard Alexius and another dragon talking, and the other
dragon said, 'She deserves to know,' and I learned that Alexius must
not be just any dragon, but perhaps a very important one. The other
dragon backed down to his challenge."

Garen was quiet for a time. Then, still unmoving, he asked tonelessly,
"What are you going to do now?"

"He's a dragon, Garen. I wouldn't stand a chance, the whole town
wouldn't stand a chance, if I pushed him too far. I have to be careful
about how I even approach questioning him," Thali whispered softly.
"He's taught me a lot already." She hoped she sounded confident, able
to take care of herself.

Garen went mute again. Thali was surprised at how comfortable the
silence was.

Then he broke it with a dart to her heart. "I didn't think you were one
to break your promises."

"What? I didn't ..." Thali, in her surprise, looked up into his eyes and
saw the pain flicker across his features.

"The medallion," Garen said.

"Oh." Thali looked back at his feet. "I ... I wasn't sure if I was supposed
to anymore ..."

"Of course you are." Garen's voice softened.

Thali wanted to look up, to touch him, to hug him, to know that he was
at least all right. But she didn't know if he wanted her to, didn't know
if he hated her now, or if he would even want her to touch him, to care
about him.

"Does Elric make you happy?" Garen's voice was so soft, she wasn't even sure he'd said anything.

Without taking her eyes off his shoes, she nodded gently. Garen's feet moved toward her, and she froze. He was so close now, she could feel the warmth radiating off his body, smell the familiar scent of oiled leather from his soft boots. Garen's lips hovered above her head.

Thali was concentrating so hard on the silence and the electricity, she heard him barely whisper into her hair, "Wear the medallion, please." And then he was gone.

Thali stood there for another full minute before quietly climbing back down into her room and crawling into bed. She reached into the drawer by her bedside and wrapped the ties of the medallion around her wrist before pressing it to her chest. Then, blowing out all her lanterns and letting her animals surround her, she let the silent tears fall into her pillow. She knew without a doubt that she loved Elric, but she would always love Garen.

Garen

Garen sat in a tree in the forest. Their tree. He came here often to think, to mourn her, to mourn the life they could have had. He let his own tears fall as he looked up to the sky between the branches, his back leaning against the sturdy tree trunk. It had been all he could do to keep a straight face and keep from touching her. He had wanted so badly to hold her, embrace her again, but he knew it wouldn't be fair. The oracle had warned him, and the effects of the sleep deprivation remained starkly in his mind. She had chosen someone else now. It wouldn't be fair of him to create such conflict for her. Yet, his resolve had been moments from dissolving. He had been so close to her, feeling her warmth, smelling that wonderful lavender scent of hers. He had wanted so badly to kiss her, to break that barrier between them.

He shouldn't have come, he knew that. But he'd been getting so many conflicting reports, he had to know the truth. He knew Alexius was a dragon. But there was something else about it all that bothered him. Growing up with a brother that could manipulate plants, then knowing how Thali was with animals, it was an easy truth to accept, that there were magical creatures in their world now. But he didn't know if Alexius was here to help or if he was here to control her. His instincts told him she was safe for now, but there was something bigger going on.

He had been compelled to see her in person, to make sure she was safe, that she was being taken care of. He'd had to see her answer for himself.

It had almost killed him, but at least now he knew she was all right for now. He would learn what he could about dragons and get the information to her if he found something. Fletch would help. Garen wouldn't contact her again. He should leave her to live her life. When she moved to the palace, it would be too difficult to contact her anyway. She was the royal princess-to-be now. Garen grabbed his chest as the pain squeezed his heart. He took another moment to gather himself, to pick up the broken pieces, put on his stony face of indifference, and return to his court of thieves.

CHAPTER FORTY-EIGHT

E LRIC MET THALI OUTSIDE her building the next morning to accompany her to the docks to board her family's ship. He waited while Thali stuffed the last few things into her small canvas bag. Before she let Thali go though, Mia kept insisting she bring this dress or that dress to show Bree. Eventually Thali ended up with two extra trunks before she could hug Mia goodbye. Thali would see her in a couple weeks at their home in Densria.

Hefting her own trunks toward the entrance, Thali stopped at the top of the stairs leading down the hill, then laughed and dropped everything when she saw Elric give a sweeping, exaggerated bow in front of a carriage.

"Princesses don't carry heavy trunks." Elric leaped up every other stair to embrace Thali. He glanced meaningfully at Stefan, who shrugged as if to say she hadn't given them a choice.

"Really? A carriage? We can walk, you know. It's not that far."

"Princesses don't walk when there's a carriage to be had!" Elric beamed a huge smile, and Thali's heart swelled at the smile that was always just for her.

He helped her into the carriage before climbing in himself. Someone had already handed her luggage up to the roof.

As soon as the door was closed, Elric sat next to her, holding her face in his hands.

"Are you all right? You look sad."

Thali thought a moment of last night on the roof. She nodded. "I'm a lot better now, here with you." She smiled as best she could and squeezed his knee. She looked away as she changed the subject. "Have you ever been on one of my father's ships?"

"No. Isn't it like any other ship?"

Thali laughed. When the carriage rolled up to the dock, Crab was there waiting for them. Thali had figured there would be a few extra ships going with them since they undoubtedly had to bring guards, but her eyes grew wide as she saw twelve ships ready to sail waiting for them.

"Wow, Papa's really pulling out all the stops." Thali leaped past Elric and out of the carriage, running over to give Crab a hug.

"Glad to have ya, lassie. But don' let yer ma see ya. Gotta be ladylike now, princess-to-be an' all." Crab set her down and beamed at her.

Elric finally caught up to them, and Crab bowed low, looking more formal than Thali had ever seen him. "You're Highness, welcome."

"Please, anyone who is family to Thali is family to me. Elric will be fine."

"Yes, Your Highness." Crab bowed again, then ushered them onto her parents' ship. Thali hid her smirk as she recognized that even the Prince of Adanek would be treated as a stranger until Crab approved of him.

Thali had her old rooms again and was happy to find Indi and Ana there already. Her parents had given Elric their own spacious rooms while taking one similar to Thali's.

It was mid-afternoon by the time all twelve ships had left the dock and were on the open ocean. Thali had been mildly surprised to see Alexius on her ship, apparently hired as a deckhand by her father specifically.

The guards were given rooms next to the prince's, though a few chose to sleep on the floor in his chambers. Thali hoped no one would sleep in her room and was glad to see that Stefan, Amali, and Derk had been given the room across from hers, while her parents occupied the room next to hers, between her and Elric. Even with a dozen guards on board, Thali's parents still wanted to chaperone her time with Elric.

After checking her animals over, she had taken them to the bow of the deck. It was her favorite spot, and she was glad to have her animals with her as the ship launched into the open ocean. She sat, cross-legged, before hearing faint steps approach from behind.

"It's certainly beautiful." Elric sat down next to her.

Thali nodded, taking in the ocean and feeling like she was home.

They sat in silence for a while. Thali was in her happy place. She'd undone her hair to let the ocean air whip it around her head, and now she breathed in the saltiness of the air, just staring ahead at the horizon. She wanted to go into her head to feel the calm of the lithe creatures below but restrained herself. Thinking she would have to ask Alexius what manner of magical creatures roamed the ocean, she sat with Elric quietly, watching the sunset. When the deckhands had all disappeared beneath for their meal and their chance to sleep, Crab took the helm and she felt his eyes on their backs, watching Elric's every move.

Elric leaned back on his hands, slowly inching his hand closer to Thali's. The ship took a sharp turn to the left, forcing Elric to move his hand to catch himself from falling over.

Thali bit down on her lip to hold in her laugh. Royal or not, Elric was going to have a rough month.

"I think I'm starting to see why you've never really had many romantic partners before," Elric said.

"And how would you know that?" Thali asked.

"It's obvious. I think every single male on this ship has bumped into me on purpose and given some sort of 'I'm watching you' signal."

Thali thought of the crew, most of whom had indeed watched her grow up. She had always imagined she would eventually lead this crew when her father decided he'd rather stay at home with her mother and grow crops or find some other pastime in his old age. Funny how life worked.

"Avoid the nightly games then," Thali said.

"What games?" Elric asked.

"You'll see."

They stayed on deck until the sun disappeared completely before Thali led Elric below to the galley. It was dark and quiet in the cramped corridor as everyone was still enjoying the delicious meal the cook had prepared for their first day at sea. Thali led Elric by the hand but stopped suddenly, pushing Elric into a pitch-black alcove. Before Elric could say anything, Thali grabbed his face and pressed her lips to his. He wrapped his arms around her, and they lost themselves in the kiss before Thali pulled away. She hoped he could see the enjoyment in her eyes as she pulled him back into the main corridor.

When they entered the galley, every eye turned to them and Thali let go of Elric's hand, finally relieved not to have all the attention on her for once. She grabbed a bowl, and their ship's cook spooned in a heaping scoop of rice and a beefy stew before she grabbed some bread and headed toward the table she always sat at, right in the middle of the ship's crew.

They scooted over for her, and she looked closely at their faces. They almost looked relieved. Maybe they were glad to have their girl back, to see she hadn't changed into a fancy princess.

Elric followed suit, his guards suddenly keeping a closer eye on him as the entire crew seemed to tense. He came up behind Thali, but no one budged to make room for him.

"Come on boys, make some room, please," Thali finally said.

They groaned and shifted over enough for Elric to join them. Thali introduced them all with nicknames. "Elric, this is Mouse, Raffe, Chip ..."

Elric nodded, but his forehead wrinkled as if he was trying as hard as he could to remember the names of all the men that had in truth raised Thali.

Thali grabbed four sticks from a cup that had been carved into the table, handing two to Elric before using her own to eat the stew. Elric stared at her. Every other eye stared at him as he watched Thali bring her food to her mouth with the two sticks. Thali finally realized that Elric still held both sticks the way she'd given them to him.

"Instead of utensils, it's a lot easier to clean and store sticks to eat with. Here, like this." Thali showed Elric how to hold both sticks, then how to move one without moving the other.

Elric stumbled with them, dropping them numerous times before Thali finally reached over and put the sticks in his hands the right way again. Elric grabbed a chunk of meat and moved his face closer to the bowl so his fingers didn't have to work so hard.

After a few pieces of meat had successfully made it to his mouth and stew dribbled down his chin from all the misses, he dropped the two sticks and stretched his hand.

Laughter rippled around the table as he tried to pick up the two sticks again.

"You'll get used to it," Thali said, helping him adjust them again. Elric would be hungry later that night.

Knowing her parents were busy in their rooms planning and organizing the upcoming trades, she felt her heart rate increase when all the bowls had finally been washed and put away. Everyone was still gathered around the table, and she waited for one of her favorite parts of being on the ocean to begin.

"What'll it be tonight, lassie?" Mouse asked.

"I get to pick tonight?! Cards, please!" Thali sat up a little straighter.

Elric watched in amazement as the men pulled out dice and cards and the dining table became a games table.

As Mouse started to deal the cards, Thali put her hand in front of Elric. "Give him a break, Mouse. Not tonight."

"If he ain't playin', he ain't sittin'."

Elric

Elric nodded, gladly getting up and standing behind Thali, enthralled to see such a different side of her. Thali played cards for hours, losing some and winning more. Elric was surprised to see how easily she fit in among the rough men. Eventually, Elric melted away from the group and returned to his room. He would leave her to her family. For the first time, he wondered if she'd miss this life. He was fighting tooth and nail to ensure her freedom as long as he could, but there would only be so much he could do once they were married. She'd have responsibilities just as he would.

Thali

Thali noticed Elric slip out but was enjoying her time too much to follow. Some of the guards even took part after Elric had left, making Thali happy that they were fitting in. Besides, she hadn't seen the crew for so long, and it felt good to spend time with them again. It felt even better to win their money.

CHAPTER FORTY-NINE

T HE NEXT MORNING, THALI woke to Crab pounding on her door as daylight was just finding its way above the edge of the ocean.

As Thali rolled out of bed, Indi groaned and flipped over while Ana got up, stretched, and curled up the other way. "Fine," Thali muttered as she pulled on leggings and a loose shirt before stumbling out into the corridor and onto the deck.

She had dreaded this morning. She knew she'd be soft, at least according to her mother, and was not excited to hear about the extra drills she'd have to do. Once on deck though, she was surprised to see Elric already there and sparring with one of his guards.

"Ahh. There you are, daughter. Come along. Your mother's been waiting." Thali's father was as chipper as ever. He had drills of his own to do later, but he manned the helm while Crab and his wife supervised combat training.

Crab poked Thali forward with his staff as she joined her mother on the upper deck at the bow.

Everyone who was able participated in combat drills or sparred with someone else. Some of the royal guards had to pick their jaws up off the floor when they watched Lady Jinhua move with swords.

"Do your warm-ups before you start. I want to see you at your best, see what Aloysius has taught you," her mother shouted as she took on Crab, who was easily twice her size, if not three times.

"Maybe you should have gone to bed earlier," Crab whispered under his breath so Lady Jinhua couldn't hear when his bout with her mother was over.

Thali rolled her eyes. She'd played cards late into the night and was now paying for it. She couldn't wait to arrive in Bulstan, where she'd have coffee in the mornings. She was excited to see Tariq, but she was worried about how Elric would fit in. He'd never really left Adanek before and customs were quite different in Bulstan.

Rolling her shoulders, Thali started to warm up, waking up as the blood began flowing in her body more readily. Crab finally tossed her a staff, and she faced her mother.

"You look tired, sweetheart. Did you sleep well?" Lady Jinhua grinned as if she knew what her daughter had been doing all night with the crew. She normally would have chastised her but didn't say anything else this morning.

Thali answered by making the first move and flicking her staff down toward her mother before changing directions suddenly and moving to sweep up and to the side with the other side of the staff. Her mother blocked easily but seemed surprised. Pretty soon, Thali and her mother were a flurry of *clack, clack, clacking* as they danced around each other, back and forth. Thali fell flat on her butt numerous times, but she could have sworn it was a little less than usual. Perhaps having Alexius as a training partner had its benefits.

Finally, Lady Jinhua stopped, and they bowed to each other before hugging. "Alexius must be teaching you well," her mother whispered as the crew cheered at the performance they'd just witnessed.

Thali practiced another round with Crab, then a third with Alexius, before she was allowed to go eat. Finding Elric in the galley, she plunked down next to him, already exhausted.

"Do you think your mother would teach me?" Elric turned and asked, fumbling with the two sticks again.

"Be careful what you ask for." Thali couldn't spare any more words as she grabbed two sticks of her own and dug into her morning porridge. Elric stared openly at her, watching her use the two sticks like a shovel to scoop the porridge into her mouth with one hand and bringing the bowl closer to her face with the other hand. Then, he put his hand on her knee under the table, patting her leg until Mouse sat down next to him, giving him a questioning look as he glanced at Elric's wayward hand.

Elric snapped his hand back and Thali offered him a sympathetic look. He grabbed Thali's cup and went to refill it with hot tea for her before coming back to the table and attempting to eat with the sticks again.

Every day thereafter played out in similar fashion. Thali even took her turn at the helm, surprised but grateful at her father's offer. Elric often sat with her on deck and at dinner. Everyone on the ship could see he was smitten with her, and despite the extra nudges and many eyes that watched him, Elric eventually relaxed and soon his trademark confidence returned.

Thali was soaking up the routine. Combat practice in the morning had become even more mingled with Crab trading drills with the royal guards. But Thali's partners were never different; she always sparred with her mother, Crab, and Alexius, though sometimes she'd have a fourth round with Elric. He was a good warrior, though only trained in one method, and he stood his ground against her. After lunch, she either stood at the helm or took to Elric's rooms for training with Alexius. Elric often would sit in the windowsill and read a book while Alexius taught Thali. She was getting better at controlling the tendrils of her magic, especially at being aware of magic in general.

Her evenings were spent in raucous games with the crew until late at night. Elric eventually tried his hand at dice, but after a few terrible rounds, no one would play him since he was so terrible.

"Don't want ya to lose yer kingdom to cards, Yer Highness," Mouse had said.

It was the early hours of the morning when Thali and Elric found a quiet moment to themselves.

"Are you enjoying the voyage at all?" Thali asked.

Elric grinned. "I'm enjoying watching you here. Playing these games, you're quicker to laugh, quicker to express yourself, and quicker to exclaim. You're unguarded here among your family, and it's a privilege to witness it."

Thali smiled at that, and Elric wrapped his hand around hers as they sat huddled together, foreheads pressed together.

"It's so different from when I first met you. You've always been confident, but meek, as if you prefer to stand aside instead of claiming your space. Here, you're open. Charismatic and pulling attention. You'll make a great queen."

Thali didn't quite believe his words yet, but his expression and the look in his eyes was honest when the words had spilled out on a whisper.

It took them ten days to get to Bulstan. The morning of their imminent arrival, drills were confined to a single round before everyone ate quickly and it was all hands on deck. Elric had never been this far away from his own kingdom, and Thali thought he looked awfully vulnerable being in such a strange place. She knew what that was like, so she kept her eye on him.

As they neared, colorful buildings dotting the shoreline came into view. They sailed up along the coast before turning sharply inwards to follow another coastline mostly populated by forests and the odd tower.

"You should go stand at the bow. That's the best spot." Thali gave Elric's hand a squeeze. "But I have to go. I'll be back!"

At Elric's nod, Thali ran to the helm. She had been recruited to help steer the ship, and she was a little nervous at the prospect of directing the ship to their destination. Tariq would never let her live it down if she so much as rubbed anything.

Elric

Elric stood at the bow, looking at the coast, when someone tapped him on the shoulder. Mouse was there, handling the ropes for the sails. He pointed off to the opposite side and Elric realized that this wasn't a coastline they were following but a wide channel between two strips of land. As Elric watched, the armada of ships fell into line, with theirs leading the way as the channel gradually narrowed. When Elric glanced straight ahead, his jaw dropped. Directly before them was a massive wall. He watched, awed, as the ship slowed to a stop in front of it. The wall was easily three times the size of the ship itself. He was even more amazed when the bottom half of the wall opened, and Thali sailed the ship right through the opening to face a second wall. Two more ships had squeezed in with them. Elric felt panicky as the first wall closed. He glanced back at Thali, who had her tongue stuck out as she concentrated on the crew around her. They were acting as her eyes and ears around the ship's edges. Elric noticed the ship was starting to rise. Looking over the front rail, he realized water was filling the space between the two walls, truly raising the ship.

Just as Elric could see the top of the first wall, the second wall opened and they sailed through to face a third wall, again easily three times the height of the ship itself.

They continued through more walls, water rising at each point to raise them to the next level another four times. At the last wall, the channel had become too narrow for more than one ship. As the last wall opened, Elric's jaw dropped again. The sight before him couldn't compare to anything else he'd ever seen. Though they were still quite a distance from land, an enormous building that could be nothing other than the royal palace loomed, taking up the entire landscape. From here, it looked like a rounded mountain, but as they approached, Elric realized the palace looked like many domes had been lumped together. The middle dome, the largest, was gilded in gold and sat atop all the other buildings. The first dome at ground level was a bright white, the middle dome was dove-gray, and the topmost dome was a shiny bronze, its gilded edges radiating down the sides. Four tall towers delineated the corners of the building, the only clue as to the boundaries of this expansive building. It looked nothing like the palace he had grown up in, but there was no doubt in his mind this was a palace.

As they sailed closer, Elric saw a dock at the tip of the channel. The shore was beautifully landscaped, with a line of manicured trees fencing in a wide path of sand. A multitude of bright, rectangular gardens led all the way to a set of colossal bronze doors.

Along the sand pathway—brightly-dressed palace guards in bright pink puffy pants that ballooned at the bottoms, pointed hook shoes, and tight, tropical-green leather cuirasses—lined the way to the palace. And just beyond the dock, on an almost flat, rounded sandbar, more royal guards in colorful uniforms surrounded what Elric assumed was the royal family.

A black horse caught Elric's eye as it streaked across the sand from the right. A familiar form leaped off the horse, slapping it on the hindquarters to send it off as he straightened his clothing and joined the royal family as they lined up, waiting to greet their guests.

Thali

As Thali directed the crew, she needed to say very little as they'd docked here many times before. Once she'd maneuvered the ship into position and some of the crew had jumped onto the dock to secure the ship, Thali went to join Elric. Except instead of stopping at his side, she grabbed his hand and leaped off the side of the ship, landing on the dock lithely as a cat before running up to the family that had assembled. Elric barely had any time to catch up to his hand as he ran behind her.

Tariq had also broken formation and was running up to Thali. They met at the halfway point, Elric finally winning his hand back as Thali and Tariq crashed into each other. Tariq lifted Thali clear off the ground and spun her around a few times to dissipate the momentum of their collision.

"I can't believe you're going to get married!" Tariq finally stopped, placing Thali back on the ground. Thali's family finally caught up then, along with Thali's royal guards, as Elric stood awkwardly beside them.

Tariq shook hands with Elric as Thali straightened her clothes.

"Routhalia, Tariq, a little decorum. It's a formal occasion," Lady Jinhua hissed at the two, who were still holding each other by the shoulder and waist.

"I'm sorry, Auntie." Tariq blushed and looked at his shoes. "Your Highness, it is an honor to have the opportunity to host you at my home." Tariq bowed but he didn't let Thali go, so she bowed with him. Then, she reached over and took Elric's arm. Thali walked with Tariq on one arm and Elric on the other. She led the group to the waiting family ahead. She couldn't help but smile as she took in her surroundings and the two men at her sides. If the sea was her first happy place after her home, this would be a close second.

As they approached the rest of the royal family, Thali watched Bree brush down her skirts with her hand. That one small action made Thali smile as the small loss of decorum was Bree's own way of showing how excited she was to see them.

"Father, Esteemed and Mighty King Shikji, please allow me to introduce to you His Royal Highness, Prince Elric of Adanek." Tariq bowed his head.

Elric bowed low to the king, showing as much respect as he could. The king looked stern and was unsmiling as he examined Elric closely and nodded.

Thali wasn't sure if she should bow or if she should greet them as she normally did, so she dipped her head in respect. Tariq was still holding her arm and didn't let her bow as deeply as she would have liked to.

"Your Highness, it is an honor to host you here in our lands, and we hope you will find many pleasures here. Let me introduce you to my eldest daughter, Princess Rania. You've already met my son, Tariq, and this is his betrothed, the Lady Ambrene."

Thali noticed that Rania looked like a shadow of her former self. She was much thinner, almost a wispy shadow. As the king introduced her, she just stood there, her previous bubbly, smiling self absent. When Rania met Thali's gaze, Thali only saw hollowness there. Thali wondered whether she might have a private conversation with Rania.

Thali watched Elric closely as he bowed to Bree. People often suspected Thali and Tariq were together, but once people met Bree, there was no doubt as to who the better choice was, if you could pull yourself away from her long enough to even think straight that is.

Thali sighed as she looked upon her friend. Bree was the epitome of what a lady should be. She had flawless olive skin; long, dark ringlet curls that cascaded down her back, deep-brown eyes; and dark, luscious lashes that were impossible not to stare at and admire. She even had the perfect hourglass figure that Thali had thought only possible in drawings. Thali watched Elric, holding in a laugh as even he stumbled on his words as he looked upon her friend. Every person to meet Bree reacted the same way. Bree's full lips curled into a smile, and she politely nodded and gave Elric the opportunity to gather himself.

"Thali. Why are you bowing? Come, come, it has been too long since I have seen you for myself. Come here child." The king beckoned to Thali, and she ran up to embrace him. Her family followed suit, while Elric stood to the side. Thali hugged her way down the line, her mouth becoming a frown as she hugged Rania and felt each vertebrae in her spine sticking out. Finally, when she got to Bree, they both let out a squeal as they embraced each other excitedly, swaying from side to side.

As the king led Thali's parents to the great palace, Bree kept hold of Thali and they whispered among themselves while the others walked ahead. Thali glanced up at Elric every once in a while, aware that he was the fish out of water here. Thankfully, Elric was holding his own, and Thali was close enough to catch snippets of his conversation with Tariq.

"Don't worry," Tariq said, glancing over his shoulder at the girls. "They'll resurface eventually."

As Tariq led Elric to the grand palace, the prince admired the gardens around them.

"It's very different from your palace. Color brings us happiness and wards away evil," Tariq explained as they walked. "My sister is a great lover of flowers and plants, so this entire lane was my father's gift to her."

Elric nodded and glanced back at Thali as Tariq described some of the foreign gardens and flowers that lined their path. Thali smiled and winked at Elric in return.

Bree didn't let go of Thali all the way to the palace as the two bent their heads together, whispering fervently.

Chapter Fifty

"**T**HALI! YOUR PRINCE IS so handsome!" Bree exclaimed.

Thali smiled. Thali and Bree were sequestered in Bree's rooms, drinking tea and catching up after all the formal greetings had been concluded and Thali's parents and Elric had been shown to their rooms.

"I think he returns the sentiment. Bree, how did you get even more beautiful since the last time I saw you?"

Bree turned to her as she pulled a dress from the closet, smirking. "You are too kind, Thali. Honestly. Now, try this on. I'm hoping you can wear it tonight so we can match."

"It's going to make me look like a child."

"Nonsense."

"Bree, standing next to you, I will always look like a child ... or a boy ..." Thali let the words trail off as she glanced at her reflection in the mirror for a moment, unable to not compare herself to Bree behind her in the reflection.

"Thali, you're being ridiculous. You've always been blind to your own beauty. It's charming I suppose, but honestly, you connect with people in a way I'm incapable of."

Thali snorted as she let Bree strip her down and help her put the dress on.

"But truly, Thali, how are you? You've suffered so many ups and downs since I last saw you," Bree said. She looked at Thali through the mirror and paused, watching her friend's reaction.

As Thali squared her shoulders so Bree's seamstresses could adjust the dress to fit Thali better, she glanced in the mirror and saw Bree still examining her face closely. Thali was almost as close to Bree as she was to Tariq, and Bree, Tariq, and Mia were the only ones who knew about Garen.

"I'm ... I'm happy now," Thali said haltingly. She was very much aware of the small crowd around her.

Bree nodded, clearly taking the hint that her friend didn't want to discuss the mysterious prince of thieves. She changed the subject to lighter topics.

"See these sleeves? These are my new favorite." Bree paused to direct a seamstress. "Shorter right here." Then, playing with Thali's sheer red sleeve, she turned back to Thali. "Less fabric, easier to move around in."

The dress was unlike anything she'd ever worn before, but nowadays, most of her clothes were new and different. She would forever be Mia's clothing pet. But while Mia ordered her to put this or that on, Bree always explained how clothes worked and why they looked the way they did. Bree was also gentler in persuading Thali to try something on.

Seemingly reading her mind, Bree asked, "How is my dearest Mia?"

Knowing Mia would love Bree, Thali realized she wasn't quite sure why they hadn't met yet. She loved them both so dearly; she knew they would love each other.

Thali and Bree had been locked up in Bree's rooms for the entire afternoon, leaving Tariq to show Elric around the palace grounds before parting at Elric's rooms so they could freshen up before dinner.

At dinner, they were all seated at a round table only a couple feet off the ground, and Elric looked confused. Thali smiled as she showed him how to cross his legs under the table as they sat on cushions on the floor. Thereafter, he watched what Thali did before he did it as he learned the proper etiquette, so Thali ensured she took each movement slower than she ordinarily would have.

"You look beautiful tonight," Elric whispered in Thali's ear.

"Thank you, Elric. How was your afternoon? I'm sorry if you felt abandoned."

Elric waved her off. "Tariq showed me around. Did you have a good time with Lady Ambrene?"

Thali nodded. She looked over at Bree quietly sitting with Tariq, demure and beautiful. Maybe she'd have to ask Bree about how to apply some of her pastes and paints to her face. While Mia was known to apply berry juice to her lips and pinch her cheeks, face paints weren't as popular in Adanek. But Thali loved how the paints highlighted her features when she did wear it.

As the food arrived, Elric looked around the table, "Utensils?"

"Like this." Thali demonstrated how to scoop up food with her fingers bunched together. She knew most people had never eaten without utensils and that eating with your fingertips was unusual, so she made sure to point out that everyone was using their left hands to eat as if their right was tied behind their back.

Elric gave it a try and smiled. "This is a lot easier than using the sticks."

After supper, Bree rose and asked Elric if she could have the honor of showing him the gifts His Majesty would like to send to Elric's father. He nodded graciously and followed Bree out of the room. From the tilt of his head, Thali knew he was a little suspicious about why he was being separated from the group.

Rania, Tariq's sister, had barely eaten anything at dinner, and Thali got the sense that she did not often dine with her family. Once again, Thali worried and vowed to talk with her one-to-one at the first opportunity.

Once Elric and Bree had left, King Shikji turned to Thali, who was seated next to her mother and father.

"Thali, Jin, Ranulf. Again, I'm so very sorry for the loss of Rommy. But there is more to the story, and I feel in part responsible for what happened in the end. I couldn't speak of it last time you were here, and now, well I've wanted to write, but I decided I better share it with all of you in person." The king looked down at his hands. Thali had never seen him this somber.

She clasped her hands together at the pain of hearing her brother's name. Tariq moved to sit closer to her, and she leaned into his side as he put an arm around her shoulders.

Lady Jinhua and Lord Ranulf grasped each other's hands and looked to the king, one of their dearest friends, for answers.

"Two years ago, Rommy came to visit Rania and asked for her hand in marriage. While I'd always known they were close, I wasn't prepared for that. Perhaps if my own dear Yani were still alive, she'd have dealt with it much better than I did. But unfortunately, I told him I needed to think it over."

Thali's father sat up a little straighter.

"You understand, Ranulf, I love your family dearly, but I expected Rommy to take over your work, and I knew Rania did not enjoy traveling. I was thinking only of her future happiness. Normally, Rania would marry a foreign prince to strengthen relationships between our kingdom and another, but I was willing to forgo that if her happiness would be assured." King Shikji's eyes filled with tears as he looked pleadingly at Thali's parents. Thali had never seen her uncle cry. His shoulders sank and he looked like an old man instead of the vibrant king she knew him to be.

"Rommy misunderstood and thought that I had refused him. He took off in anger and left here the next morning."

It was quiet for a whole minute. The king couldn't look his dearest friends in the eyes as he tried to gather his composure.

"Mupto, you've done nothing we wouldn't have. Rommy knew what he was doing when he left here, and he had a good crew and a good ship. You did not create the storm that overwhelmed his ship. You're not at all to blame." Lady Jinhua reached across the table to grasp both the king's hand and Rania's.

"Your family has been so good to me—to us. I'd hoped that Rania and Rommy would join us in our union, and I regret not answering him more quickly and positively," the king said. He put an arm around a wavering Rania. She bit her lip, visibly trying to hold in tears.

Thali's parents nodded. Thali was surprised at the confession, but the letter she'd received from Rania the year before had explained the same, and she'd not been brave enough to broach the subject with her parents.

"But I will not miss the opportunity again." Mupto turned to Thali. "So, Routhalia, with your parents' permission, I would like to adopt you, bring you into my family."

Thali blinked, unsure of what that would mean. She turned to Tariq. He shrugged his shoulders. "It was his idea. I already see you as my sister," Tariq said.

"What exactly are the terms you're proposing here, Mupto?" Thali's father asked.

"I mean no disrespect toward either of you, Ranulf, Jinhua. I just mean I'd like to officially become her uncle. She would receive an allowance, as well as diplomatic papers. She would always be welcome here no matter what. She would have her own permanent rooms in the palace and lands in the kingdom if she'd like. And most importantly, you and your family would have the protection of my army should you wish it."

"And what do you request in turn?" Thali's father, even though he considered Mupto his best friend, was always suspicious of generous offers.

"That she visit every two to three years if she is able. Ranulf, I only look to make official what our families already enjoy. There is little I would not do for Routhalia. And if there was something I wouldn't do, Tariq would do it without my knowing. So, I would just like to make our family ties official."

"What would that mean for my betrothal?" Thali was honored, but the ring on her finger reminded her of her other responsibilities. She also thought about her gift with animals. What would Tariq's father think of that?

"It would give you the power to make your own decisions." The king looked at her directly. "Routhalia, I do not want anything from you. But I have known you your entire life, and I've always thought you would sail around the world as a merchant. Now that you've chosen a different path, I thought this would afford you some protection. Some freedom to sail here too, whenever you desire."

Thali wondered if the king thought she was being pressured into marriage with Elric, and she said as much. "Uncle, I'm not being pressured into marrying Elric, if that's what you think."

"I'm glad to hear that. I know your parents wouldn't allow it, but nonetheless, I'm glad to hear it from your own lips. I did wonder when Tariq told me. It doesn't seem like something you would do," Mupto said.

"What do you mean?" Thali asked.

"I only mean to say that we enjoy quite a bit of freedom as royalty here. But this is an island. Royal life on the mainland is quite restricting. You will have many responsibilities and duties and very few of the freedoms you enjoy now."

Tariq squeezed her shoulder reassuringly.

Her mother spoke for the first time since the king had voiced his proposal. "Thali, he's also giving you some freedom. If you're required to visit here every few years, then no matter what your duties are in Adanek, you must leave to come here. You will have the opportunity to take to the sea and come here for a month or two."

The king nodded. Tariq held his breath.

When Thali still didn't answer, the king added, "If you accept, I'd like to make this retroactive, Routhalia. I'd like to present it as old news so no one thinks it's some political maneuver—because it's not. It's really just a gift to you and your family."

Thali thought of Elric. And his parents. Tariq's father was trying to shield her from a lot of the things Adanek's royal family wanted from her, yet she hadn't given any real thought to what her palace life would be like in the future. Not for the first time, she felt guilty for not having had that conversation with Elric yet. Being part of this court, having some weight in her corner, would be beneficial for her. And she already considered Tariq a brother and Mupto her uncle.

She looked at her parents. They both nodded, though her father's brow furrowed.

"Uncle, I accept. Thank you," Thali said.

Tariq let out a breath and squeezed Thali's shoulder.

Even Rania smiled a little.

"Now, should we have some fun with our dear prince?" The king's glint of mischief reminded her a lot of Tariq.

As if it had been planned, a guard stuck his head in the door. "Your Majesty?"

The king nodded and the table was cleared as Elric and Bree walked in.

With his most serious face, Mupto turned to Elric. "Your Highness, a great slight has been committed, and the details of my retribution must be decided."

Elric's face paled visibly as he looked from Thali to Mupto, then around the table.

Thali sucked her lips in and looked down to stop herself from laughing.

"Your Majesty, I am deeply sorry for ..." Elric began, but Mupto himself broke into laughter as he interrupted him.

"I'm sorry, my dear boy, I couldn't help it. You look so serious all the time." Mupto slapped his knees as he ushered Elric back to his seat. Tariq's shoulders shook as he nodded, and Bree's smile filled her face as she approached the table again.

"We will chat about your challenges tomorrow, but for now, let us celebrate your betrothal!" Mupto smiled and gestured for the servers to bring dessert. Elric blushed but smiled as he looked at Thali.

As they all drank cool mint tea and indulged in the decadent sweets passed around, they chatted and laughed late into the evening.

CHAPTER FIFTY-ONE

THE NEXT MORNING, THALI got up extra early to visit her parents before they were all to meet for combat drills. She knocked on their door, and her father answered before she could even push the door open. She hugged her father and flopped down on their couch.

"Our official relationships will help you too, won't it?" Thali asked.

"Yes. We've always had a good relationship. But now it's official, so it'll be good for our business."

As usual, her mother cut right to the chase. "What's wrong, Thali?"

"I'm just trying to figure out why he'd offer this now."

"He feels guilty about Rommy. It also probably helps him solidify his relationship with Adanek."

"Am I being used?" Thali asked bluntly.

Her mother finished braiding her own hair, pinned it up, and came to sit down next to Thali. "Thali, you are about to become a princess. Everyone is going to want favors or relationships. Mupto adopting you is his way of offering you protection. I'm glad of it. We might carry weight in commerce, but now you have foreign nobility and a title. Elric was probably supposed to marry a foreign princess anyway, so now he gets two for one."

Thali nodded. Politics made her head hurt. If her parents trusted Mupto, she had no reason to doubt it.

"Thali, did you know about Rommy coming here to propose to Rania?" Her father looked at her, examining her face, ready to detect a lie.

"No. I didn't know. He asked if I had anything to bring Tariq and Bree, but he didn't say he was going to propose."

Thali thought about all that had happened since her brother had died. A tug on her heart reminded her how much she wished Rommy was here to give her advice, to offer his own thoughts on all that had happened to her. And she wondered what he would think of Elric, what he would have thought of Garen, and of how he would have scolded her about Garen.

"He'd like him." Thali's mother guessed at her thoughts.

"Hmm?" Thali shook her head to clear it.

"Rommy would have liked Elric. They met you know. Once, at the palace when they were little. We went there on business, and I left Rommy in the practice yards to play. When I came back, he was there with Elric, sparring."

Thali imagined what Rommy would have said about Elric. Would they have gotten along? Would Rommy have sparred with Elric now? Would they have been friends? Thali felt hollow as she realized her brother would never see the next chapters of her life.

"I know. I miss him too. I think he would have been proud of you." Her father placed a hand on Thali's shoulder, giving it a supportive squeeze.

"Ready?" In typical Jinhua form, Thali's mother had shaken off the sadness and was now holding her favorite staff.

Thali sighed and pulled herself up off the plush couch. Together they walked to the training room at the top of one of the highest domes. Thali always thought the many stairs acted as a warm-up before practice. Stepping into the vast space, she looked out onto the expansive field of guards and soldiers training. Her family made their way over to join Tariq on an elevated platform at the end of the room. Elric was already there, too, and was working hard with some of Tariq's guards. Thali enjoyed the silent stares they received as Thali's mother walked past. She was a legend here.

"Auntie." Tariq bowed to her before they started to spar. Knowing her mother, Thali suspected she'd already warmed up that morning and done several drills before Thali had walked into their room.

"Wow." Elric joined her and her father as they watched Tariq and Lady Jinhua face off.

"I know. You thought I was good? Well, Tariq is the only person I've ever seen land a hit on my mother."

Her father snorted. "Her brothers. They're even better than she is."

The trio stood silently watching the two become a blur of flying legs and feet and arms and staffs.

Bree walked up then, dressed in leggings and a loose shirt, her long, dark curls twisted into an intricate bun.

"Ready, Thali?" Bree threw Thali a staff, and they broke off to the side. "Let's see what you've learned these last two years." Bree smiled before charging her. They sparred back and forth for a while, Thali feeling like she was finally matching Bree, like Bree wasn't holding back anymore.

"You've gotten better," Bree said as she moved to disarm Thali. Thali saw it coming and stepped into her staff, bracing her arm to take the force of Bree's staff so that she could keep hers.

"I've got a new training partner," Thali said.

"Oh? You'll have to tell me about him," Bree said.

"How do you know it's a him?"

Bree smiled.

"Well, you can test him for yourself, if you like. He's here," Thali said.

"Really? I'd love to," Bree said.

She hadn't seen Alexius in a couple days but felt his presence in the training room this morning.

I shouldn't. Not here. Take a closer look at your friend, he said in her mind.

Bree knocked Thali to the ground when she opened the door in her mind and looked at the threads beyond the door. A faint golden thread emanated from Bree.

She's not very magical. But she has sight. She'd be able to see me for what I am if she looked closely, Alexius said.

I've never seen a thread from Bree before. Thali stayed on the ground a second as she focused on the conversation with Alexius.

You're getting stronger, so you're going to start seeing more, Alexius said. Thali stood, brushed herself off, and tried to focus on sparring. Part of her wanted to be upset that Bree hadn't told her, but she herself hadn't told Bree or Tariq about her own ability. She wondered if Tariq knew. And who else had magical abilities?

Do you want to keep your true self a secret? Thali asked. She felt guilty for having outed him twice already.

I do prefer it, for now, but people will probably know in time—oh, human emotions are intriguing. Please don't feel guilty. It was easier that they know about me, Alexius said.

Does Bree know about my abilities? Thali asked.

I doubt it. She doesn't seem to have much magic. Enough to tell who's human and who isn't. She might see that you have some magic, but that's it.

Tariq called them over and they switched partners. She'd have to finish her conversation with Alexius later. For now, Tariq and Thali squared off as Lady Jinhua and Bree sparred.

Despite everyone saying she had improved in her time away, Thali was continually knocked over or pelted with the wooden staff the rest of the morning. She was going to be covered in bruises.

CHAPTER FIFTY-TWO

THALI WAS IN HER room, rubbing salve into the many bruises that had popped up after this morning's training. She was glad that she liked the smell of the minty lavender salve as it covered more of her body than not. It had been a while since she'd had a quiet moment to herself, and she reflected on how different her life had become in the two short years since her brother's death. She wondered how different her life would have been if her brother had lived. Would she be captaining her own ship within her brother's fleet? Would she ever have met Garen? Elric? Daylor and Tilton? She realized she missed her friends at school and was excited to return to school for her final year. That alone was one of the biggest ways she had changed since Rommy's death. When she'd been sent away to school after he'd been lost to the sea, she'd dreaded being with other people, dreaded interacting with people her own age. She'd had no idea how to make friends and had been really rather terrified to go to school. Now, she had a close group of friends and missed the camaraderie of people her own age.

A gong rang somewhere in the distance, and Thali quickly donned the latest outfit Bree had given her. She left her rooms—her guards joining her the moment she stepped into the hall—and joined her family and Elric in the royal dining room for lunch.

Tariq winked at her as they sat down, the food arriving as soon as the last person had crossed their legs.

"Your Highness, we have something of great importance to discuss," the king began.

Elric visibly swallowed before pasting on his best smile, "Please, continue."

"As mentioned in the letter we sent, you've requested Lady Routhalia's hand. And as I mentioned, Lady Routhalia is a lady of this court. In fact, she is my adopted daughter with her own title."

Elric threw a quick glance at Thali before taking a deep breath and smiling politely as he turned back to Mupto.

"At the time, I was not aware of Lady Routhalia's official standing with this kingdom and court, so I'd like to apologize for any offense I've caused," Elric said with a bow of his head.

Thali bit her lip to keep quiet, recognizing the mischievous glint in her uncle's eyes as he continued. "Normally, it takes years for us to determine the eligibility of a suitor for one of my daughters." Mupto gulped and Thali knew he thought of Rommy. "But I realize that time is of the essence, so I'm willing to challenge you to a series of tests instead. Upon completion of these tests, I will make my recommendation to Lady Routhalia. Your performance will also determine how much I will favor our kingdom's relationship in the future." Her uncle had somehow maintained his sternest expression as he spoke.

"I accept and promise to perform with as much humility and skill as I have to show my worthiness for one of your kingdom's daughters." Elric bowed his head.

Tariq covered his mouth to hide his snicker, and even Thali looked down to hide a smile.

"Indeed, then come to my study this afternoon, and we shall see about these challenges," Mupto said.

Thali was surprised at the king's seriousness and the concern on Elric's face. She squeezed Elric's hand, hoping he wasn't about to abandon her now. She wasn't sure whether she would ever understand why he had chosen her.

The mood lightened considerably over lunch, and when they had finished, Thali and Elric went for a walk in the garden before Elric had to report to the king.

"I'm sorry, Elric. I thought he was joking when he said he had challenges for you," Thali said.

"I can't believe you didn't tell me," Elric said. His fists were clenched.

"What do you mean?" Thali asked. She was surprised at his anger.

"If I'd known you were a princess, there would have been months of different protocols to follow. My parents are going to have so much apologizing to do. I'd thought—we'd all thought—you were just a well-to-do merchant from an elite merchant family." Elric increased his pace.

Thali hadn't realized her decision to become Mupto's adopted daughter would upset him so much. She felt like he'd just slapped her in the face. "I'm sorry," Thali said. It was all she could think to say. She was afraid his anger would worsen if she told him that she herself didn't know until yesterday.

Elric ran his hands through his hair as he walked ahead, then turned back to her. "I love you, but this isn't how I thought this would go."

"What do you mean?" Thali asked. She felt fault lines form in her heart, ready to crack.

They stood under the cool shade of grand trees, hidden from public view. Even their guards had melted away.

Elric looked at Thali and must have seen her expression because his own softened. He took her hands in his. "Thali, I've known from the first time we met that you're unlike any other girl, no, any other person, I've ever met. I'm not at all surprised that you have an army of people vowing to protect you. I've been told my whole life exactly what's going to happen next. If 'A' happens, then you do 'B,' if 'C,' then 'D,' etcetera. There's a protocol and a procedure for everything. But ever since I met you, most of what I've expected to happen has gone out the window. It's exciting, but sometimes, it's overwhelming. Does that make sense?"

Thali nodded. She wasn't sure what to do. He'd never confessed so much of himself, and she was realizing that was as startling as her inability to help.

"I'm glad. I'm glad all these people care about you as much as I do. And I'm honored to prove to them that I deserve you," Elric said. "But it would be nice if it weren't constantly a surprise."

Thali smiled a little then. "My whole life has been mostly unpredictable and surprising."

Elric closed the distance between them. His arms encircled her waist, and he buried his head in her shoulder. "I'm sorry for exploding at you. It's been a little stressful meeting your extended family," he mumbled.

Thali's heart lightened. "So, we're … all right?"

He raised his head and stood back a step. "Of course. That was just my bad temper showing. I'm sorry. It changes nothing of my love for you, or our plans for marriage."

Elric had spoken so matter-factly that Thali laughed, though her heart clenched at the thought of how Garen had left and how her brother had disappeared from her life so suddenly. "And here I've been thinking that any moment now, you're going to turn to me and say, 'You're not worth this much trouble.'"

Elric grasped her arms, looked her in the eye, and said, "You're worth every bit of trouble."

Thali looked down but didn't mind that he closed the distance between them. She reveled in the warmth that blossomed in her as Elric slipped one hand up behind her head, his other raising her chin as he leaned in. A guard in a bright pink-and-green uniform coughed as he appeared suddenly from behind a tree.

Thali laughed as Elric hung his head. He kissed her hand, and they continued their walk, hand in hand.

Chapter Fifty-Three

T HALI WALKED ELRIC TO the king's study after their walk in the garden.

"Good luck," Thali said as they lingered in front of the doors.

"Any ideas what the challenges might be?" Elric asked, taking both of her hands.

"I don't think you'll be in any real danger. Uncle Mupto likes his pranks, so I'd bet it's more humiliating than physically difficult." Thali squeezed his hands.

Elric nodded. "I would happily stand naked in the busiest markets for you." Thali looked down as heat touched the tips of her ear. "I'll come find you after."

Thali nodded and Elric's fingers drew her chin up as he leaned forward. Another guard coughed before opening the door to the king's study. Elric stopped just before their lips touched. "Have a good afternoon, Thali." Elric straightened his coat and faced the open door.

Thali reached up and kissed his cheek before turning away and returning to her rooms.

The moment she entered, she saw a folded note on her desk and went over to open it. There was a smudge of dirt on the back of the folded paper, and one of the edges was a little burned. After she opened it, she had to reread the familiar handwriting a few times before she registered the words, the air leaving her lungs. Then she looked around the room; nothing was out of place. There was no sign of anyone having entered through a window or one of the hidden passageways.

Thali stormed off to Tariq's room, note in hand. Indi and Ana chased after her. She burst into his room, not caring if she were interrupting him. It was just like Tariq to pull a prank like this. Ana and Indi excitedly greeted Tariq, who was momentarily caught up in dog and tiger before he noticed Thali's expression.

"Tariq, how could you!" Thali seethed. Tariq had been sitting on a cushioned chair, reading a book. She was so angry, she grabbed the closest thing—a book—and threw it at his head. He caught it in a single motion and closed the book he was reading, putting both aside before rising and striding over to her. His brows furrowed as he looked at the note she held in her shaking hand.

"What? I didn't send you a note."

"I'm not joking this time, Tari. Did you really not send this?"

Tariq stayed calm as he gently took the note from her shaking hand. His eyes went wide as he read it.

Then, he looked at Thali and said, "Thali, I swear to you, I didn't do this. Who's Alexius?"

"What? It doesn't ..." Thali snatched the note back again, realizing that a second line had appeared where there had only been one single line before. She stared down at the unmistakable loop of her brother's handwritten "R."

Ten Years Earlier

"Rommy, why do you write your 'R's' like that?" Thali asked her big brother, charcoal clutched in her hand, trying desperately to copy her big brother's writing.

Rommy lifted Thali up from the barrel she had been kneeling on to practice writing her letters. He carried her over to the makeshift table the crew had put together for her and steadied it. Taking a seat, he placed her on his lap, gently holding the hand with the charcoal in it with his own. Putting it to paper, he guided her as they swooped up to the right, around, and straight down. Then, their hands flew back up to trace the first loop of the 'R,' touching the line in the middle before swooping down and out.

Thali giggled. "It looks more like a 'B' than an 'R.'"

"But I bet you don't know anyone else who writes their 'Rs' like that," Rommy said.

Thali shook her head.

"See this line here? It makes it look like a 'T.' Maybe that 'T' is for Thali ..." Rommy raised his eyebrows comically high.

Thali giggled some more, trying out the fancy 'R' on her own under her big brother's supervision.

Thali had copied that 'R' a thousand times thereafter, even using it herself for a few years before simplifying the 'R' back to its original form.

Present Day

Thali stared in shock at the note in her hands. She sunk to the floor, and Tariq went to lock his door before sitting down across from her.

Come find me, Rou.

Alexius knows.

"Lili, are you sure it's real? Are you sure it's from him?" Tariq asked.

There was only one person in the whole world who called Thali "Rou." Only her family and Tariq's knew that. Tariq sat across from her, and they stared at the note together. She saw the wheels turning in his mind as quickly as her own.

"Tari, look, the 'R.' No one else ever writes their 'R's' like that. I'd know my brother's handwriting anywhere." She couldn't explain it, but she felt in her heart that her brother really had written this. Maybe she'd never fully grieved for him because a small part of her had always felt he was still alive.

"There aren't a lot of people who can get into your rooms. But what ... how ...?" Tariq leaned back against a low table. "Who's Alexius?"

"He's ... my training partner but also a ... oh, Tari, there's so much I haven't told you," Thali said.

"Then start now. We'll figure this out together." Indi pushed her head under Tariq's hand, demanding to be petted even now.

Ana pushed her way into Thali's lap. She'd told so many people her secret in the last few years, it was almost easy now. But first, she reached into her mind to find Alexius.

Alexius. I need to talk to you. Now.

I'll be there as soon as I can. Are you all right?

Just get here.

Make a bubble, like we practiced, Alexius said.

Thali crossed her legs, having enough presence of mind at least to use her magic to weave a bubble around her and Tariq so no one would hear all her secrets. He glanced to his right and left, furrowing his brows, almost like he felt the walls closing in around him.

"Tariq, you've always known I have a way with animals. I suspect you've figured out that it's more than just a knack."

Tariq nodded. He looked uncomfortable.

"Well, it turns out I have magic. Magic that lets me communicate with animals. I see their thoughts as threads that connect me to them and them to me, and I can influence their thoughts by sending them images or ideas. And two years ago, when I went on my first final exam, remember how I went missing for a few days?"

Tariq nodded, his brows furrowing deeper still.

"Well, my ship was mistakenly sent to Star Island, and we unwittingly performed a ritual of some sort. I still don't know what we really did, but I'm scared that I opened something, some sort of portal," Thali said.

Tariq listened without interrupting, regardless of what he was thinking.

"Well, Alexius is a dragon. A powerful one from what I can tell. He's been sent to protect me. He's been protecting me this whole year at school. That's why he came with us on this trip. He's also teaching me about magic. Plus, he's helped me learn about my abilities and how to control them."

Tariq nodded. "I suspected as much about your way with animals. But thank you for telling me. Now it's my turn."

Thali's eyes widened. "What?"

"Thali, you're not the only one with magic. It's more common here on this island than in your kingdom, but I have some magic with the weather. Haven't you ever noticed it's always sunny and warm when you visit us?"

"But ... how ... Alexius didn't say ... I've never even ..." Thali stumbled over her words.

"I learned to control it at a very young age. And I'm also not as powerful as you. Bree, she's a seer. I'm surprised she didn't spot Alexius." Tariq's lips tightened into a thin line for a moment.

Thali nodded. "He knew about her—and stayed out of her way."

Tariq coughed and cleared his throat. "Thali, are you doing something right now with your magic? The air, there's no movement to it."

"Oh. Sorry." Thali unraveled her thread, spinning it back into her spools.

Thali was relieved that Tariq knew her secret, and despite the shock, she felt even closer to him now that she knew he had magic, too.

"Tari, did Bree see my magic?"

"Kind of. She knows you have powerful magic. But her sight is limited. If she left our island, she'd be as normal as anyone else."

"What's so special about this island?"

Tari grinned. "It's said there are gateways to a land much more magical than ours. There are four in total and our family guards one on the island."

"Wait, Alexius said his family guards a gateway. You're not ... you're not a dragon, are you?"

Tari laughed. "No. Alexius's family probably guards one from the magical side. Why do you think my family are such good fighters?"

"I always assumed it was maybe some special effect from the gems your kingdom mines and exports," Thali said.

Tariq smirked. Then the smirk fell away and he paled. "Lili, I think you're right. When you went to Star Island, you opened a magical gate."

Thali leaned back. During her first year in school, no one had known about her ability except her parents, Rommy, Crab, and Mia. But after her experience on Star Island, she had come to the conclusion that someone had guessed at her ability and used her.

A knock at the door made them both jump.

"Is that Alexius?" Tariq asked.

Thali could feel Alexius's presence—on the other side of the door—so she nodded.

"Watch." Tari grinned as he waved his hand and the door unlocked and opened.

"Interesting." Alexius stepped through the door, closed it, and locked it.

"Pleased to meet you, Alexius the dragon." Tari rose and bowed his head.

"And you, Prince of Weather." Alexius grinned and revealed his pointy canines.

The two turned their attention back to Thali, who was back to staring at the note on her open palm.

"Alexius, this is from my brother. He said you know about him, about how to find him?"

Alexius frowned. "Yes, I know how to find him."

"All this time, I thought he was dead. And he's not. And you've known all this time that he's alive. AND you know where he is?" Thali growled in frustration and anger. "I thought my parents found you to teach me? What more do I not know?" Was this the secret he'd been keeping from her?

Alexius sighed. He walked over to Thali and rested on the edge of a low table. He outstretched his arms, then brought them back to his body. Thali noticed it was a movement much more fitting of a dragon than a human.

"Thali. I haven't been completely honest with you. Your brother sent me. I knew your parents were looking for a teacher, so I made myself, well, 'findable.' Your brother forbade me to tell you he was alive and where he was. He said he'd let me know when I could tell you. And when to bring you to him." Doubt flickered in his emerald-green eyes.

She could see Rommy. Alexius could take her to see her brother. Those were the only words Thali heard. "Let's go. Take me to him, now. Please." Thali was still sitting on the floor, the note carefully tucked between her hands. How many times had she wished to speak to her brother, to ask his advice, to hug him one more time? She would do anything.

Alexius turned his attention to Tariq. "You can't go."

Tariq turned to Thali. A look of incredulity quickly turned into anger. "Do you really think I'm going to let you go to some unknown place alone? To face who knows what? What if that's not your brother's handwriting? What if he was forced to write it?"

"Tari, Alexius will be with me. As angry as I am with Alexius right now, this is my brother we're talking about. It's Rommy," Thali said. "He would never let anything happen to me. You know that. I have to go see him. This note doesn't sound forced."

"Lili, you're not going without me," Tariq said.

"Tariq, who's going to cover for me here? You're going to have to keep this a secret from everyone until I find out more," Thali pleaded.

"Let them wonder, Lili! I'm coming with you."

"No. You're not." Alexius chimed in. "I can only bring one person. The orders were to only bring Thali."

Tariq clenched his teeth, narrowed his eyes, and stared at an invisible spot on Alexius's forehead. Thali could feel the fire in that gaze.

Thali took a deep breath. "Tari, if it were Bree or Rania that went missing and only you were allowed to go bring them back, wouldn't you go? Please. Let me go alone. I'm not incapable. You've seen to that."

Thali watched as the tension in Tariq's jaw relaxed and he stared a little less intensely at Alexius.

"Fine."

Tariq finally sighed, crossing his arms. "But you have to be back in three days, or I'll tell Elric, and he and I will send our entire armies to track you down."

"Fine," Alexius agreed.

Thali looked from Alexius to Tariq, not enjoying the feeling that her own fate was out of her hands.

"One more thing." Tariq was still staring Alexius down. "I've heard dragons are honorable. So, Alexius, I want you to swear on your family's honor that you will protect Thali and transport her safely there and back. She will be your first priority."

Thali started to roll her eyes. She didn't feel it was necessary to make her feel like an invalid.

Alexius and Tariq both rose as they faced each other. Alexius said, "We take oaths very seriously, Princeling. And I can tell you that I do swear upon my family's honor that no harm will come to her. I will take that upon myself, though I can guarantee you that her brother loves her dearly now, just as he has his entire life."

Alexius and Tariq stood toe to toe, staring at each other for a long moment before Tariq finally broke eye contact first.

A knock on the door startled them. "Tariq, is Thali here?" Elric yelled through the door.

"We don't have time to waste." Alexius turned to Thali. "Are you ready?"

Thali felt immensely guilty to be abandoning Elric without an explanation, but the pull she felt to see her brother was far greater.

"I'll handle it." Tariq nodded at them as he walked to the door. Then, he turned back and took the dagger off his hip, strapping it on Thali before going back to the door.

Alexius walked over to the mirror in Tariq's dressing room and focused on it for a moment. The reflective surface became hazy and unfocused, rippling like liquid within its frame.

"Three days," Tariq said.

Thali and Alexius nodded before Alexius took Thali's hand and stepped through the mirror and into the fog.

EPILOGUE

T ARIQ WATCHED THEM LEAVE, then without saying a word to Elric still knocking on the door, turned and headed for a man-sized painting of a landscape of a forest in autumn. He swung it aside to reveal a door. Tariq patted his leg and Indi and Ana came to him. He pushed the door open, stepped through, and held it for the tiger and dog. Bardo always abandoned Thali for Bree when they were in Bulstan, and now he wished the snake had stuck with Thali. He carefully closed the door, knowing the painting would swing back into place. It was pitch black, but Tariq knew this hallway well and the animals had better night vision than he did. He strode forward a few steps, then turned left. He'd made this trek many times and knew exactly where he was going without looking. He stopped at an alcove and placed his hand along the wall at chest height. There he found a box, slid out a match, struck it, and lit a candle on the shelf in the wall. From beneath the shelf, he took a piece of parchment and the coal stick tucked in next to it.

My dear beloved,
As usual, I am in need of your bravery in the face of
my cowardice. I cannot explain it all, but I promise I
will. Please tell my father that Thali and I have left for
a spiritual retreat in the forest for three days. I will meet
you in the place with the good smells later tonight and
tell you everything.

-T

Tariq folded the note and tucked it under the candle before blowing it out.

He then continued along the secret passageway for some time, taking all the twists and turns in the dark as he'd done thousands of times. He heard the soft pads of paws behind him and it made him feel less alone. Finally, he came to the door he'd been anticipating and grinned. Raising the hatch, he crawled out into the sun, holding it open for Indi and Ana.

A prince didn't often have a lot of time to himself, so Tariq always enjoyed being here. He hiked through the forest until he reached a field of white flowers, of which each had five petals. Making his way to the edge of the field, he climbed a low tree and lay on the platform he had long since installed there. He lay in the shade of the leaves on this sunny day, letting the smell of jasmine surround him. Indi and Ana ran around amongst the flowers before finally joining him for a nap. Tariq had long wondered if Rommy had actually died. Their parents had believed it so, and Thali had initially believed it. But Rommy was wickedly more intelligent than he let on, and he let on plenty.

The only reason Tariq had let Thali leave was because he knew there were two people Rommy loved and cherished above anything and anyone: Thali and Rania. He wondered if Rania knew. He let his thoughts drift until he woke suddenly and discovered it was dark. He reached into a hole in the tree and pulled out a blanket as the night air was a little chilly. He wondered if Indi would let him snuggle her for warmth. Ana was already curled between Indi's legs. Then a bread roll hit him in the forehead before being swallowed by Ana.

Tariq blinked and looked down to see his beautiful beloved reaching a hand up. He leaned over the platform and pulled her up easily. She had a basket on her other arm.

"Supplies, you coward," Bree said.

"I'm sorry." Tariq batted his eyelashes at her.

Bree rolled her eyes. She opened the top cloth and pulled out a handful of dates, shoving one in her mouth.

"Where's Thali?" Bree asked as she looked around and up. Bardo was around her neck and his head waved around in the air scenting it.

Tariq swallowed. Then he recounted everything to Bree. Bree's mouth hung open as he finished. "I always thought he was too smart to die on the ocean. That boy could sail a toothpick through the canals."

"How did Elric take Thali leaving?" Tariq asked.

"He didn't. Your father has him cleaning the armory with a toothbrush. He won't be free for two days," Bree said.

Tariq nodded.

"I should get back though. That new guard rotation is tougher to get through when they switch to the twilight schedule," Bree said.

"Wait." Tariq slid his hand to her shoulder. He kissed her deeply, tasting the sweet dates that still coated her mouth.

"You owe me." Bree pushed away. But she was smiling, so Tariq knew he was forgiven. "You both do."

Tariq bowed over her hands, kissing each precious knuckle. "You brought Akila?"

A cough below answered his question.

"And I brought Salman and Nasir," Bree said.

Tariq's shoulders slumped.

"You had Nasir guarding Thali, so now Elric can't be too mad that you left without guards." Bree raised her eyebrows. Tariq knew she'd also brought more guards to keep him safe.

He bowed his head. "My brilliant goddess strikes again." He showered her arms with kisses and Bree giggled. Bardo wrapped himself more securely around Bree's arm.

"Now get going. Be safe," Bree said as she started to climb over the platform. Tariq took hold of her arms and lowered her, while Akila grasped her legs and brought her down the rest of the way. Tariq blew her kisses until she drew the hood of her cloak up and was out of sight.

Tariq looked at the basket Bree had brought him. He was wondering what goodies she'd brought when he saw the cloth move. He slowly peeled it back to find Lari, his hawk, snuggled up next to a wrapped bread-loaf shaped package.

"Well, I guess you might as well come along," Tariq said. Lari shrugged her feathers and settled back against the loaf. Tariq hopped carefully off the platform, basket on one arm, and climbed down. Indi and Ana followed closely. He handed the basket to Salman before leaping the last bit to the ground. If he was going to sell his cover story, they better disappear into the forest for a few days.

For a bonus scene where Thali meets a fellow animal lover, visit: https://geni.us/TheAnimalCaretaker

Buy book three – Of Blood and Tides, by clicking here or visit: https ://geni.us/OfBloodandTides

Acknowledgements

If one thing has blown me away, it's the support, encouragement, and excitement of my friends and community when I launched the first book. Thank you for your support; for reading, for making memes, for asking me questions, for sharing your thoughts. I love it and am grateful for all of it.

There are so many incredible people I have to thank in making this book a reality.

From the first eyes that see my words and help me decide on a title, my dearest friends and family. Your support, kind words, encouraging words, bolstering words make this author sit down at her desk and get it done.

To the fellow artists that take a deeper look – my fellow grapes, Charity, Natalya, Jennifer, and Sadie.

To the professionals – Bobbi Beatty of Silver Scrolls Editing has gently held my story – and helped me craft it to make it better.

And Lorna Stuber, who continues to entertain my many random questions about all manner of things, but who I especially appreciate to examine those details that make my eyes cross.

And to the team at MiblArt, I truly appreciate your patience and dedication to making beautiful art.

Indie publishing is a vast adventure, and I couldn't have done it without the help of Sarra Cannon's Publish and Thrive. Thank you Sarra, for sharing your knowledge so generously and openly.

The adventure continues in...Of Blood and Tides

Click here to purchase the 3rd book in the Threads of Magic Series: Of Blood and Tides or visit: https://geni.us/OfBloodandTides

About the Author

C AMILLA IS A LOVER of many mediums of storytelling. She loves to write strong heroines who can kick butt and find the love of their life. She always has projects on the go and loves to consume stories of all kinds—books, shows, movies, plays, amongst many others.

When she is not writing, Camilla is often found exploring animal behavior, crafting, drinking a hot beverage, and clicker training her animals.

Come visit her at CamillaTracy.com Or on instagram @camilla_tracy Or sign up for her newsletter by visiting: https://geni.us/CamillaTracynewsletter

FROM OF BLOOD AND TIDES

Tariq

Three days.

Alexius the dragon had whispered those three words in Tariq's head just as Thali had disappeared with her new dragon friend and protector through a mirror. Ever since his boyhood, Tariq had wished to live among dragons, Pegasi, and the creatures in the tapestries and books in his father's library. Never had he thought his childhood fantasies would come true. But there he'd been the other day, conversing with a dragon telepathically.

Now Tariq was on his way back home after hiding in the forest of his home kingdom for a few days. He'd needed to give Thali an excuse to disappear without suspicion, so he'd disappeared into his childhood treehouse in the forest. His family and staff knew he wasn't to be disturbed there. Bree had taken the brunt of whatever fallout had resulted from his disappearance, supposedly, with Thali. His darling Bree was too good for him. She had probably smoothed things over with Thali's betrothed, her golden prince, with a single cup of tea.

Tariq paused at the crest of the hill where the trees started to thin out. "Home," he said with a sigh as he gazed upon the shimmering shapes that were the outline of his palace. Even though he'd only been gone three days, he felt a shift in the world. Maybe it was because of his magic that he could sense it. He'd wanted so badly to show Thali his magic ever since he'd used his mind to make a leaf move when they were kids, but his father had forbidden it. He had instructed Tariq to only reveal his weather magic if Thali revealed her own magic first—but to be careful. Magic hadn't existed in Adanek for centuries, and the people would be frightened. Tariq had always suspected Thali's magic was with animals, but when she'd explained it to him initially, she'd described it as threads of magic connecting her to animals. That made sense to him. His magic was like wind to him; hers was like threads.

He'd started vibrating when Thali had finally told him about her magic. He'd sensed its strength when she'd visited this last time. She'd developed her magic much farther and faster than he had. It had taken him years to learn to control wind currents, and there was still a limit to his abilities.

Tariq swallowed as he strode back into the palace. He nodded to a guard as he snuck back in through a quieter, less-used entrance, one Thali could also have snuck through without much notice or fanfare. He hoped she would show up today; he couldn't justify staying in the woods any longer. Alexius had said three days, and three days it had been.

Tariq silently made his way across the cool stone floors, moving from gem-encrusted statue to gem-encrusted alcove on his way to his rooms, careful to stay on the plush gold rugs. Finally reaching his destination unseen, he slipped inside and closed the heavy stone door, hoping Thali would come back before anyone could notice he'd come back alone.

To continue reading, buy Of Blood and Tides by clicking here, or visiting: https://geni.us/OfBloodandTides

Manufactured by Amazon.ca
Bolton, ON